D0065095

THE WOMAN TRAPPED
IN THE DARK

THE WOMAN TRAPPED IN THE DARK

J. D. MASON

THORNDIKE PRESS
A part of Gale, a Cengage Company

Farmington Hills, Mich • San Francisco • New York • Waterville, Maine
Meriden, Conn • Mason, Ohio • Chicago

Copyright © 2018 by J. D. Mason.
Thorndike Press, a part of Gale, a Cengage Company.

ALL RIGHTS RESERVED

This is a work of fiction. All of the characters, organizations, and events portrayed in this novel are either products of the author's imagination or are used fictitiously.
Thorndike Press® Large Print African-American.
The text of this Large Print edition is unabridged.
Other aspects of the book may vary from the original edition.
Set in 16 pt. Plantin.

LIBRARY OF CONGRESS CIP DATA ON FILE.
CATALOGUING IN PUBLICATION FOR THIS BOOK
IS AVAILABLE FROM THE LIBRARY OF CONGRESS

ISBN-13: 978-1-4328-6237-4 (hardcover)

Published in 2019 by arrangement with Macmillan Publishing Group, LLC/St. Martin's Press

Printed in the United States of America
1 2 3 4 5 6 7 23 22 21 20 19

To Storytellers —
Keep telling, no matter what.

ACKNOWLEDGMENTS

It's hard to say good-bye to characters you've fallen in love with. This is the second time I've said good-bye to Gatewood, and the last, but regrettably so. I will miss him, because I know that there's so much more to him than I've been able to tell, but sometimes, a writer has to know when to say when. And now is that time, for real.

Thank you to some amazing folks who've helped me, inspired me, and supported me. The funny thing is, I've never met most of these people, but we've become good friends online, and they are my friends.

Naleighna Kai, I don't think I've ever met anyone as exciting, energetic, creative, insightful, and as Superwomanish as you. You're an incredibly talented author, and one hell of a businesswoman. You have been so very gracious with sharing insight, feedback, time, and space, schooling me on how it "should" be done. You are a superstar in

7

every sense of the word, and thank you for being my friend.

To the lovely Miss Ella Curry, you are absolutely brilliant, elegant, and one of the most generous people I have ever known. Your efforts are nothing short of amazing, and I am both humbled and thankful for every kindness you have ever shown me.

Lisa DeNeal, if you aren't a book doctor, you certainly should be. Your insight, vision, and attention to detail definitely helped me to craft the story I'd hoped this would be, and I am truly grateful for the sacrifice of your time. Thank you so very much and I wish you nothing but the best on your own writing journey.

Johnathan Royal, maybe you know how you bless me, and maybe you don't. But let me tell you, your uplifting spirit and endless passion for books is inspiring, and we authors owe so much to you for championing our books the way you do. Thank you for all of your hard work, attention, and love for the stories we tell. And I wish you well, my friend.

U. M. Hiram, thank you for helping me to pull together this story, and more important, thank you for allowing me to be a part of your journey as a new author. You are so talented and I am absolutely looking forward to reading much, much more from you. Keep doing what you're doing and I have no doubt that all of your dreams will come true.

Jessica Rickerson, my friend, my breakfast buddy. I can always count on you to meet me someplace pretty damn early on a Saturday or Sunday morning for coffee and good food. I love you so much. Thank you for taking the time out of your busy life to support me while I chase this little dream. I admire you so much more than you know, but if I told you just how much, you'd make a joke out of it and we'd just laugh.

As always, I've got to give a shout-out to my friend and agent, Sara Camilli. You have no idea how much your patience has meant to me all these years. Thank you for supporting every wacky idea I've come up with and pretending that they aren't wacky at all.

Finally, to my editor, Monique Patterson, it has been my honor working with you, and I will sing your praises to anyone who'll listen. You gave me a chance when no one else would. I hope to see you on the road somewhere in the coming years, but even if I don't, I can always stalk you online. Be well, my friend. I wouldn't trade one single moment of this incredible journey with you. Thank you! Thank you! Thank you!

■ ■ ■ ■

THE WOMAN
TRAPPED IN
THE DARK

■ ■ ■ ■

WAVE MY OWN PRIDE

"Back then, he was as dumb as a rock." Lars Degan laughed. "Young and pretty as a peacock, but stupid. I did like him, though. Truly, I did."

His son, Brandon Degan, stared quizzically at his seventy-nine-year-old father, watching fascinated as the man's expression melted from one of amusement into a genuine fondness at the memory of a young Jordan Gatewood. Once again Brandon was reminded of just how passionately his father's obsession with Gatewood merged seamlessly from loathing to admiration, and it was that obsession that had tortured Brandon for as long as he could remember.

"I told you what happened. Didn't I?" Brandon's father asked, staring at him as if he suddenly realized that Brandon was still sitting next to him on the deck of Lars's massive Fort Worth house overlooking the lake.

13

Brandon sighed. "You've told me several times, Dad."

Not that it mattered. Blame it on old age, or just the desperate need to repeat the damn story again, adding fuel to his hatred of Gatewood before that flame burned out, Brandon knew that he was about to sit through the tale again. Sometimes, names would change in the retelling, dates or places, but the heart of the story was always solid.

"His father, Julian Gatewood, was as sly as a snake," his father began. "Slippery and aloof. Acted like he was better than the rest of us," he explained with disdain. "He looked white, you know. Could've passed and we wouldn't have known that he wasn't until he opened his mouth to say something. That's when you'd know you were talking to a black man, through and through."

Once again, Brandon sarcastically marveled at his father's mystical abilities. That this man could tell a white man from a black man simply by the sound of his voice when he spoke was nothing short of extraordinary. It took every ounce of Brandon's restraint not to roll his eyes.

"We threw a party when we got the news that the sonofabitch was dead." He chuckled. "Got drunk on whiskey and pussy for two whole days in celebration."

Julian Gatewood died thirty years ago. Brandon was only thirteen at the time and was too much into skateboards and soccer to remember much about his passing.

That forlorn look returned to his father's light-blue eyes. "I almost felt sorry for that boy when that pretty momma of his planted his narrow behind in his father's chair. It was much too big for him," he said sadly. "In more ways than one."

That was about the only thing Brandon and Gatewood had in common besides both being in the oil business. Brandon knew all too well that same fear that Gatewood had probably felt that day. The trepidation of being expected to fill your father's shoes, and to be forced to put aside your own dreams to live those of another man.

"I knew he'd fail." Brandon's father's face lit up. "Hell, we all did, and we wanted him to. It was imperative that he did."

His father stared back at Brandon, waiting for him to ask the same question he always asked at this most poignant point in the story.

"Why?"

The gleam in Lars Degan's eyes expressed his approval that Brandon egged him on. "Because there were egos at stake. An old doctrine in place that didn't include his kind. We couldn't do much about the father," he said, remembering the force that had been Julian Gatewood, "except smile and nod and mutter under our breath when his back was turned. To his credit, he was a keen and astute businessman. We didn't like him or approve, but there was no denying his prowess. However, Gatewood Industries was an insult to every oilman in Texas."

Brandon wanted to say, *But Dad. You worked for the man for fifteen years.* But he knew better.

In his father's mind and in the minds of relics like him, oil was a white man's business. They'd built empires on the shit, and damn anybody who didn't fit the mold and who dared to trespass on those empires. It should've been easier being the son of a racist, considering the environment that he'd grown up in, but Brandon hated his father's attitude toward anybody who didn't look exactly like him. Of course, he knew to keep his mouth shut.

"Gullible is what he was," his father continued thoughtfully, describing Jordan. "He was so eager to learn, and who else did he have to rely on but us?" He stared earnestly at his son. "He trusted us. He had no choice. Hung on every word we said as

16

if we'd dipped them in gold, committing what we told him to memory, taking our advice to heart. He respected us."

It was cruel what Brandon's father and others in the company had done to twenty-year-old Jordan Gatewood. Brandon listened as his father recounted the brutal ways that they conspired against him, setting him up for failure, only to stand him up again long enough to catch his breath, pat him on the back, tell him how good a job he was doing, then pressed down on him again, driving him into catastrophe after catastrophe, subtly blaming him for destroying his father's business, his legacy.

"It was a slow but steady dismantling of this boy's psyche, his spirit. That's how you do it." He nodded his affirmation as if Brandon needed or even wanted to know the process for destroying a man from the inside out.

"A young man's mind is the easiest to break. It's fragile and uncertain of itself. He was so afraid of failing, and yet that's all he ever did. We made sure of it," he said proudly. "We were patient, Brandon. You see, we didn't want to crush the business completely, but we were like sharks, taking chunks out of it as we watched it die a slow and agonizing death. We all wanted a piece of it, the choicest pieces, of course. So we had to be careful how we took it from him. We had to be careful to feed that boy just enough advice and encouragement to keep the corporation from going under too quickly, but only barely. And we had to be careful not to tear him down too much. He needed some fight. Not a lot, but enough."

It was morbid. Heartless and selfish what they did to him. Physically, of course, they never laid a finger on Jordan Gatewood, but they didn't need to. They poisoned his mind, his soul. They tortured his self-esteem, devoured his faith, crushed his sense of duty and obligation to the man who had built this unlikely empire, reminding young Jordan day in and day out of how he had failed his father.

Lars slowly dropped his gaze. "We made him suffer for over a decade. Some might call it abuse, but, no" — he shook his head — "it was a lesson. We were putting him in his place." His father looked back to Brandon. "All that ego he'd gotten from being touted for his exceptional skills as a college football player, and swooned over for his good looks, born into money, that boy had never known what it was like not to think so highly of himself. But all that arrogance seeped through his pores like sweat as, year

18

after year, he lost millions of his father's hard-earned money. More than half of his employees had been let go, and Jordan had resorted to liquidating company assets just to keep the lights on. We'd done what we'd set out to do, and we were so damned proud of ourselves for it."

Lars's respect for his son was a private point of contention, balancing precariously on a line as thin as a strand of hair. Brandon had always been a simple boy, too eager to please but with no conviction, no spine or balls worth swinging even when he and Lars didn't see eye to eye. Lars had always resented that about his son. He held Brandon's gaze with his own, daring that boy to look away or to protest, his disapproval of how Lars had treated young Gatewood. Brandon had his mother's eyes, expressive and telling. They gave away his secrets.

"You think I'm silly," Lars said unexpectedly, catching his son off guard. "A silly old racist? Is that it?"

Brandon shifted and cleared his throat. "Of course not, Dad."

Brandon was a coward. There aren't too many things that can break a man's heart more than realizing that his son lacks courage. Jordan Gatewood had always had plenty of it, which, admittedly, was the one thing that Lars had always admired about him.

"I don't hate him because he's black, Brandon, although it doesn't help," he said with a smirk.

Lars thought back to that place in time, ten years after they'd begun the systematic destruction of Jordan Gatewood, when he suddenly realized that instead of breaking him, they'd actually created a monster.

"We almost had him," he said, recalling the excitement of victory and satisfaction he'd reveled in back then. But Lars was tired. Tired of plotting and of having to overthink every move, every word, every action and counteraction. Jordan proved to be smarter, more diligent and determined than any of them had expected. His resolve had kept him motivated longer than they had hoped. That pretty boy of Julian Gatewood's had had more of his father in him than any of them could've imagined. Finally, though, it was nearly over and all that was left was to drive the wooden stake into that boy's fragile heart.

"He'd made the biggest mistake of his short career," Lars recalled. "Bought the rights to drill in this section of the Gulf near Louisiana." Lars frowned. "It was a tricky site. Everyone else who'd tried to drill there had failed, lost millions in equipment and even lives. Jordan had been researching how to dig in a place like that and found a young engineer to build him a special drill bit, and rigged it some kind of crazy way." He waved his hand dismissively. "I don't know. But it was expensive. He drained the company's reserves dry to pay for it."

Jordan had taken on this venture all on his own without the advice of Lars and the others. He'd been doing that a lot lately, going off on his own with some harebrained scheme of how to hurry up and recoup millions in losses, failing time and time again.

"There's nothing there, son." Lars sat behind his desk, rubbing frustration and exhaustion from his eyes over yet another disaster this boy had walked this corporation into.

Lars tossed a binder across his desk to Jordan. "Bone-dry, Jordan," he said irritably. "Read it. Since you didn't have the money to pay for it, I paid for the geologist to come out and survey the site my damn self. Ain't nothing down there, and even if you get lucky and hit pay dirt, it won't be enough to cover the cost of that fancy equipment you wasted company funds on."

"I don't need your report," Jordan said indignantly, staring at Lars. "My gut tells me

I'm right."

Lars sighed irritably. "Your gut's full of shit, boy. Literally. Face it. You fucked up, Jordan, again. This is it." He threw his hands up in disgust. "You wanted to bankrupt your father's corporation, well, pat yourself on the back, son. You've certainly done that."

There was a time when Jordan would've hung his head in shame, but Lars hadn't seen him do that in years.

"Mark Waters has made a generous offer," Lars said calmly. "One you need to consider taking because, frankly, you're all out of options. He'll buy that equipment of yours, all your deeds, and anything else you're willing to sell him at ten percent above value, Jordan. It's a good deal, son."

All Jordan had to do was agree and this long, arduous ordeal would've finally been over. "Use your head, Jordan," he encouraged him. "Take the offer, walk away, and get on with your life."

Without saying another word, Jordan stood up and walked out of Lars's office.

Lars always got quiet at this point in the story. He'd never been the kind who believed in miracles, until one day Jordan Gatewood showed up and pulled one right out of his ass.

"Two months later, that bastard found it,"

he said dismally. "He found every gotdamned drop."

Of course Lars knew. He'd known all along how much oil was there. It was just a matter of getting to it. That's all. A picture of Jordan, standing tall and proud on that rig, graced the covers of *Money, Inc., The New York Times,* and *World Money* magazines. He'd not only found one of the most expansive oil pockets that this country had seen in decades; he'd patented that new drill and rigging system, and all of a sudden, Gatewood Industries had a heartbeat again.

"He came back into my office a month later and handed me a file."

"I took the liberty of hiring my own geologist," he said smugly. "And I expect your resignation by morning," Jordan said, looming over Lars still sitting behind his desk.

Lars stood up. That impertinent bastard needed to be put in his place again. "Remember who you're talking to, boy."

Jordan planted his fists on Lars's desk and leaned close to him. "No, Lars. You remember who you're talking to," he said threateningly. "I'm your Frankenstein monster, motha fucka. You got sloppy. Weak. Maybe sentimental," Jordan said with a wry smile. "Eight million, wouldn't you say?" Jordan shrugged. "Ballpark? Is that how much you've stolen from me over the years?"

"I haven't stolen a gotdamned thing," Lars shot back.

"No. You've stolen eight million gotdamned things. I've been keeping track. I'll admit it, man" — Jordan straightened his stance and stuffed his hands in his pockets — "you had me going in the beginning. It was rough and your ass put me through it." Jordan nodded introspectively. "But you taught me lessons I could've never learned in college. Fuck an MBA." He smiled. "Right? The school of hard knocks taught to me by my enemies. Pure gold."

Gradually, Lars began to understand what they'd done to young Gatewood.

"You get the fuck out of my building," Jordan said calmly. "On your way out, I want every gotdamned stock option you ever put your fuckin' hands on."

Lars was livid. How dare this black bastard threaten him and threaten to take any damn thing he'd worked all these years for.

"Who the hell's going to believe you, boy," he growled. "You dumb fucker. You think because you hit pay dirt it makes you more than what you are? You're a nigger, Jordan. An ignorant nigger who's got no business —"

"I'm a niggah who's got you dangling by your balls over a fire, Lars. I'm a niggah with no fear. I'm a niggah with money. And I want you out of my sight. I don't want you on my board or owning my stocks. I don't want your fucking name on none of my business cards, and if you take so much as a pencil, I'll spend my last dime personally pile driving your ass into the ground. I will ruin you. I will humiliate you and your family. I will tear down the walls of your reputation until there's nothing left but ash and shit."

"You've got nothing on me, son."

Jordan glared at him. "That you know of," he said coldly.

He was bullshitting.

"Call it, Lars," he threatened. "Call my bluff. Force me to show my hand. Please."

"I was tempted, but that look in his eyes —" Lars shook his head. "I was almost proud of him," Lars continued somberly. "I was certainly afraid of what he'd become. Jordan's successes began to pile up one on top of the other. Even his failures had a way of working out in the best interest of Gatewood Industries." Lars looked at his son. "You see, it's not his skin color that I hate so much. This kind of loathing doesn't just happen overnight. It grows. Festers. It's like a cancer, spreading and gnawing at a man. Maybe it's because I know I'm running out of time, Brandon," he said, his voice tinged with melancholy. "There's a sense of urgency to finish what I started, to see him ruined."

A long silence hovered between the two of them before his son finally said something that caught Lars by surprise.

"If you hate him so much," Brandon began cautiously, "why not just have him killed?"

Lars shook his head in dismay at such a question. "Killed? No." He sighed. "No, Son. It's not his life I want. It's something much more valuable and lasting. It's his legacy. There's no real gratification in taking your enemy's life. If there is, it's short-lived. But to see him suffer, to watch him suffocate in regret and sink into the muddy despair of his failures and losses. To humiliate him." Lars smiled. "Dignity. It's the one thing a real man values more than his own life." He nodded, sighed, and closed his eyes. "You take that from him, that thing he loves most, that he'd die for, and leave him stripped of respect, honor, and hope." Lars smiled. "That's the sweetest kind of victory. That's the kind that lasts forever."

Love does not begin and end the way we seem to think it does. Love is a battle, love is a war; love is a growing up.
— James Baldwin

Go My Severed Way

A creaking floor.

Subtle vibrations shifting air, filling space.

Hushed voices and soft sounds of shoes shuffling along the corridor outside her bedroom.

Who's to say for sure what combination of these things caused her to stir awake suddenly from a deep sleep? Abby blinked her eyes open in time to see a shadow fill the doorway to her room.

Panic, fear, ballooned in her chest. Was she awake or still asleep — dreaming?

As the shadowed person crept into her room horror gripped her.

"Who? W . . . what — ?"

She pushed up on the bed, still half asleep — still desperately trying to will herself awake. The soles of her feet touched the floor as Abby started to run, but not before seeing another shadowed figure appear behind the first, both reaching for her.

She screamed! She fought! *Wake up, Abby!* Jesus! Jesus, this was real!

"Cover her mouth!" one of them yelled. "Cover her fuckin' mouth before I smash her in it!"

She couldn't breathe — or see. Abby clawed at the hand covering her face until he was forced to let go. She kicked the other one, twisting in their grasp, fighting for her life, using every ounce of strength she had to get away until she broke free and landed on the floor. Abby crawled on all fours, struggling to get on her feet to run to the front door. Just as she crossed the threshold between her bedroom and the hallway, Abby was lifted off the floor by her waist from behind and spun around to the bedroom.

Jarring pain shot through her jaw. Her body went limp. All of a sudden she felt as if she were floating. Struggling to force her eyes open, she managed to get a glimpse of the dark figure at her feet. They were carrying her.

"We ain't supposed to hurt her, man! What the fuck?"

"What else was I supposed to do? This bitch wouldn't be still. How the hell else were we supposed to get her . . . ?"

Voices faded. The space around her went completely black.

Abby sat around the dinner table with her daddy and brothers, laughing so hard she nearly cried. She laughed at — What was so funny? It was — hilarious and ridiculous. Without thinking she raised her hand to her mouth and cringed when she felt it. She had a toothache? Was that why it hurt to laugh? Blood.

Someone moaned. As her senses began to awaken Abby gradually became aware of the sound of the tires meeting the road. Someone moaned again. Was it her? Vinyl or leather pressed against her skin. Abby tried to move her hands but couldn't because they were tied at the wrists. Her fear deepened when she realized that her legs were bound too, at her ankles. She couldn't see anything and the sensation of something in her mouth, cloth, stretching around her jaw, caused it to ache even more.

No. No. No. This couldn't be happening. Things like this didn't happen in real life. A garbled sob escaped and the taste of blood on the material in her mouth, her blood, caused her to gag. Someone touched her leg and she jerked and cried out.

"Keep your gotdamned hands off her!" a man shouted.

"Shut the hell up!" another blurted out.

She let loose with muffled and panicked

screams.

"Shut up before I knock yo' ass out again!"

A hand gripped her by the throat, digging fingers into the sides of her neck. The car swerved. He let her go.

"The fuck is wrong with you?"

"Keep your hands off of her or we don't get paid, motha fucka! That's what's wrong with me."

"She needs to shut the fuck up. If we get pulled over and she's doing all that scream-ing, bruh, it's our asses."

She had to get out of this car. Abby started kicking at the door. If she could kick it open and manage to get out before they could stop that car, maybe someone in another car would see her. She kicked and yelled at the top of her lungs until one of the men grabbed hold of the binding on her ankles.

"I'll bust you in your fuckin' jaw again, bitch! I swear to God!"

"We're almost there," the other man said. "Here. Get the picture."

"Got it."

Pay attention, Abby! Some small part of her challenged her to calm down, to pay at-tention, to be smart. She was smart. Two — two of them. There were two. Abby could feel the car turning. How long had they been driving? She didn't know. She had been knocked out — she didn't know. Straight. They'd mostly driven straight. The highway? Abby ran through a mental list of all the cities surrounding Blink. Maybe they hadn't left Blink at all. But if they did . . . if they did then where could they be taking her? Clark City? Norvo? Tyler? No. Too far.

"This is it?"

"Yeah."

Her heart pounded. A lump began to choke the breath from her. The car slowed, turned again onto what sounded like a gravel road, and then finally stopped. Thoughts raced through her mind. They were going to have to open the door to get her out. Not both doors, but one. Which one? The one at her head or at her feet? She wouldn't be able to run, but she had to do something.

She heard the sound of keys being taken out of the ignition. The front car doors opened and a rush of cool air washed over her. The door at her feet swung open. Good. Good. Abby had strong legs. She could do this. A pair of hands grabbed hold of her calves and started to pull her out of the seat. Instinct and desperation took over and Abby started to kick as hard as she could, to scream at the top of her lungs. She thrashed around in the backseat like a wild animal trying to free herself from a trap.

The man pulling on her laughed. "Can't nobody hear you out here, baby. Scream all you want. In fact, I'ma scream, too."

He started yelling and Abby was pulled from the backseat and carried away with one man holding her legs, the other holding her underneath her shoulders. The men stopped walking and it sounded like someone kicked a door.

"Open up!" the one at her head shouted.

"Pretty thighs," the one at her feet muttered.

"That's her?" a woman asked as they carried Abby inside.

"Nah. This is just some random chick we found laying on the side of the road like this," the man holding her legs said sarcastically.

"Is the room ready?" the one at her head asked.

Abby still fought. She didn't want to think about what they would do to her once they got her in that room. But hope was fading.

What are they going to do? She cried. *What are they going to do to me?*

They carried her a bit farther. Details! If by some chance she survived this ordeal, then she would need to remember details.

Wooden floors? Definitely not carpeted. Their shoes made too much noise. Shoes? Boots? Voices and sounds echoed. Tall ceilings or just an empty space? Maybe both. Another door opened. It sounded heavy.

"She ain't going to stop," the man at her feet said.

"Stop fighting!" the other man said. "We're not going to hurt you."

"She ain't trying ta hear that, D. I'm telling you."

"We'll untie you if you stop fighting."

Why should she believe him? They'd broken into her home and abducted her in the middle of the night. Why would they have taken her if they hadn't intended on hurting her? This was her life, and as far as she was concerned, Abby was facing her death, but she would fight until she couldn't.

The one at her feet let her go. "Move!"

"No, J!" the one at her head shouted as the other one lowered her feet to the floor.

Concrete!

She struggled to keep her balance as the one who'd been holding her feet grabbed her around the shoulders as he pushed the other man out of the way, wrapped his other arm around her neck, and . . .

■ ■ ■ ■

THE WOMAN
TRAPPED IN
THE DARK

■ ■ ■ ■

MY WORLD CRUMBLES

Jordan couldn't take his eyes off the photo sent to him on his phone. It was a picture of Abby. How was it possible for a man to fall in love thousands of times with the same woman? He had no idea, but it had happened to him every time he laid eyes on her, every time he thought of her or heard her voice. She had this effect on him — call it supernatural, magical, or unnatural. Perplexing. That's what it was and it had changed him, drilled down to his center and tapped into a part of him that he never knew was there. Jordan had just turned fifty, and for the first time in his life he was keenly connected to another human being in a way that was so addictive that even the thought of losing that connection terrified him.

"You know better than anyone just how unfair and cruel the world can be, Mr. Gatewood."

The woman on the other end of the phone had a sultry, raspy voice.

"Who the fuck is this?"

Sitting here now, an hour after hanging up from that conversation, Jordan recalled the unfamiliar tinge of panic rising in his own voice, a kind of fear and desperation that he could always identify in others, but coming from him, it sounded odd.

"What have you done?" he demanded to know, his voice cracking as it pushed past the lump in his throat. "Where is she?"

"I need for you to calm down," she demanded. "I need for you to listen."

"I don't give a damn about what you need! You tell me where she is."

If he could've reached his hand through that phone and wrapped it around that woman's throat, he'd have crushed it.

"You tell me where she is, or I swear to God —"

"God abandons men like you, Mr. Gatewood. But I'm sure you already know that. How does the saying go? It's easier for a camel to pass through the eye of a needle than for a rich man to get into heaven? I'm paraphrasing, of course."

"Choke on your philosophic bullshit and you tell me where she is!"

"Safe," she said, and paused. "She's as safe

40

as a kitten in a box for now. Safe as long as you listen to me and do what I say."

Jordan's chest heaved with rage. He gripped the phone so tightly that it was a wonder the damn thing didn't shatter in his palm.

"If you put your gotdamned hands on her," he threatened through clenched jaws, "if you hurt her, I'll find your ass. That's a promise, not a threat. I'll find you and shred you with my bare hands."

"Of course you will," she responded unemotionally. "So we will keep ourselves hidden. But if I were you, I'd stop wasting precious time threatening me, time which she has very little of. The clock's ticking, Mr. Gatewood."

This wasn't happening. Was this what helplessness felt like? For the first time in a very, very long time, he was at a loss for what he could do. Jordan couldn't bellow out a command and suddenly have his wishes turned into reality. He couldn't go after this woman because he had no idea who or where she was. The weight of this situation as it settled in suddenly made it difficult to stand.

"Time is of the essence, Mr. Gatewood," she told him as he sank into the sofa on his deck.

"Time. Time? Time for what?" he eventually managed to say.

"Time to pay your dues. To reassess your position on the Dakota Pipeline endeavor."

How in the hell did she know what his position was?

"I don't know what it is you're getting at, but I don't need to reassess a damn thing."

Jordan had been in on talks about the pipeline along with other oil and gas corporate leaders, but he'd decided against it once he discovered that the land was sacred to the Sioux. He was no saint, but he respected the passion that those people had for their lands and the passion they held to the promise made to them by the government.

"Your recent successes are legendary, Mr. Gatewood. First, you manage to achieve the impossible, winning a multibillion-dollar research and development bid from the Department of Defense, and most recently an acquisition with one of the most promising alternative fuel producers in Tanzania, Batenga Enterprises."

"Get to the fucking point."

"You've got so many people fooled," she said condescendingly. "People who believe in the halo you've worn so well lately. You, Jordan Gatewood, the golden boy. The one they're starting to believe might actually be able to walk on water, perhaps? There are those of us, Mr. Gatewood, who, though we might not know where the bodies are buried, are very much aware that you have buried many on your rise to success."

"You tell me what the hell you want."

"On Friday an e-mail will be sent to you. A contract that you will sign, agreeing to invest one hundred million dollars into the pipeline endeavor."

"You've got to be kidding me. You take her so that I'll sign a gotdamn contract?"

"Yes," she said simply. "You sign it. Invest the funds. And by Friday night, pretty little Abby Rhodes will curl up next to you in bed purring like a pretty kitten. Don't sign it, and you'll never see her again."

Jordan's whole life had been filled with absurdities and moments that would seem impossible if it weren't for the fact that he'd lived them. Meeting and falling in love with Abby Rhodes was one of the most unexpectedly peculiar things to ever happen to him.

Jordan had unwittingly stumbled into that small town on a whim, because he was bloated with some overblown need for a sense of purpose and searching for the meaning to his life. He was chasing a ghost, his father's, in the hopes of finding answers to a deeper question of who and why Jordan had become the man that he had become. He found her instead, and maybe she was all he was ever supposed to find.

The photograph was disturbing. Abby sat

in what looked like the backseat of a car, her wrists bound, her knees drawn to her chest with a zip tie securing her ankles. Blood splattered the front of her T-shirt. A dark bandana was tied around her head, covering her eyes, and another around her mouth. The blood on her lips, on the front of her shirt, were both alarming signs to him that that bitch on the phone had lied already and that they had actually hurt her.

Time. She had said it was against Abby. According to the woman, the contract would be arriving in six days, soon to be five, and Jordan was wasting precious seconds sitting here, paralyzed by a sense of helplessness. Abby needed him. He closed his eyes and tried to imagine her confusion and fear. Did she blame him? He blamed himself.

" 'All dreamers and sleepwalkers must pay the price, and even the invisible victim is responsible for the fate of all.' " Half an hour after hanging up from the call with that woman, Jordan recited the line from Ralph Ellison's *Invisible Man* to the man on the other end of the phone.

It was a silly ritual that this dude insisted on his potential employers following if they wanted to get in touch with him. A cloak-

and-dagger and pomp-and-circumstance tryst that Jordan found tedious and ridiculous.

"What can I do for you?" the man responded, sounding as if he had been asleep.

What could he do for Jordan? Jordan felt absolutely at a loss for words to answer that question. So much was at stake — his world, his sanity. How do you sum something like that up in a simple answer? You don't.

"I need to see you," Jordan said without thinking.

He needed a face, not just a voice, not just a concept.

"I don't do face-to-face, man," the man on the phone responded coolly. "You should know that."

Jordan looked at his phone, pushed a few buttons, and waited. "I just sent you a picture," he said gravely. "Look at it. Study it. Commit it to memory."

After a lengthy pause, the man finally responded. "Yeah," he said. "I got it."

She was Abigail Rhodes. An engineer. A country girl. She was funny and beautiful and had changed him in ways he'd never thought possible. "You're looking at my heart and my soul, man," he desperately explained.

There was another long pause between the two.

"And you want her found," the man stated.

"I need you to come to me. I need to know who you are, and yes, I need for you to find her."

"You don't need to see my face for me to do that."

Was this motha fucka really trying to be coy? "Gatewood," Jordan abruptly said.

"I don't want your name, man," he snapped.

"Jordan Gatewood," he continued unabated. "That's who you're dealing with."

"Rule number one, no names. Number two, no face-to-face. You just blew it, asshole."

Jordan sensed that he was about to hang up.

"Who do you have?" Jordan blurted out.

"What?"

Jordan slowly rose to his feet. "Who do you have? Your woman. A kid? Your mother? Father? Anybody? Somebody you'd kill for or die for? Who the hell is it?"

Silence.

"Who would you do anything for? Who is the one that saved you? Maybe you lost her. Maybe she's still in the picture. I don't

46

know. But she sparked something inside you that no one else ever did. Would you trust some nameless, faceless sonofabitch to save her and to bring her home to you? Or would you want to look him in his eyes and let him see just what she means to you when he looks back into yours?"

"The clock's ticking." That woman's words washed over him.

"Don't make me ruin you, man," Jordan said gravely.

This dude was the ace in the hole for the rich and powerful. His number wasn't exactly published on a Web site or readily searched for on the Internet under "Killer for Hire." Affiliation with this dude was exclusive and could be deadly if you weren't careful with his privacy. As far as Jordan knew, no one had ever met him in person. Jordan would be the first.

"You don't want to make me your enemy, man," he responded to Jordan.

Jordan was numb to his threats. "If anything happens to her, I won't give a shit about you or what you *think* you can do to me."

It was a sober revelation but a true one. His life was forfeit without Abby.

"You get your ass here or take your chances with the next motha fucka who calls this number."

Jordan had no idea what the man looked like or where to find him. But he could always find a way to contact him, even if it wasn't as Jordan Gatewood. It wouldn't be the first time he'd rewritten a script to suit his needs.

After a moment of silence, the man on the other end of the phone finally responded. "I can be there in a few hours."

Jordan nodded. "Pull up to the parking garage at Gatewood Towers and ring the buzzer," he said wearily. "Security will let you in."

Jordan hung up. By sunrise, he'd have five days to find her. Only five.

■ ■ ■ ■

Day 1

■ ■ ■ ■

Ashes in Your Ashtray

Plato drove up to Gatewood Industries headquarters, marveling at the nearly thirty-story tower in the heart of downtown Dallas. Plato's cardinal rule was to never meet his clients in person. His anonymity was his power. The man had threatened that anonymity. Plato wasn't convinced that Gatewood could really do him any harm, but it was probably in his best interest not to put that cat to the test. After all, he was hurting and he was desperate, and when a man was put in that position, he was liable to do anything.

And then there was Abby Rhodes. More than even Gatewood's threats, it was the fact that it was Abby in that picture making the world suddenly as petite as she was. Plato knew the woman, a friend-of-a-friend sort of thing. More specifically, Ms. Rhodes was a friend of the woman who had stolen Plato's heart, Marlowe Brown. So, yeah. He understood where Gatewood was coming from when he insisted on having this up-close-and-personal meeting. Both women lived in a no-place little town called Blink, Texas. Plato had stumbled upon the place and left his heart in it, and apparently Gatewood had done the same, which left Plato speculating. What the hell kind of magic was hovering over Blink, Texas?

Love made ya crazy. Love made you desperate. Love made you call up a man like Plato and dare him not to stand in front of you and look you in the eyes to see that he really did mean it when he said, "I'll do everything in my power to help you find her."

Shit. Gatewood's penthouse must've been next door to God's, because when those elevator doors opened, Plato felt like he'd stepped into another dimension, with sky-high ceilings, wooden floors polished to look like glass, chandeliers that were probably as long as he was, and floor-to-ceiling windows overlooking the whole state of Texas. Coming here went against everything in his nature. Plato made it a point never to get to "know" the people he worked for, not even their names, if he could help it. But this couldn't be helped. He apprehensively walked into the expensive decor of the living room and stopped behind Gatewood standing, facing the window with his hands in his pockets.

Plato had taken a few minutes to do his homework before coming here. He'd done an Internet search on Jordan Gatewood. As soon as he saw his picture, he recognized him. A few years back, Jordan had been one of Plato's marks. Plato had been asked to keep an eye on the man by a friend to send a warning to Gatewood if he decided not to play fair in that particular game. The fact that he was standing in the same room as Plato, alive and well, pretty much summed up how that whole situation had played out.

Gatewood turned around and stared quizzically back at Plato. Yeah. Gatewood recognized him, too. Would he mention their brief encounter from back then? And could he possibly know that Plato had become a casual acquaintance of the man's lady love?

"We're down to five days," Gatewood said stoically, glancing at his watch. It was just after two in the morning. "Five days to find her and bring her home." He took a deep breath. "The first mistake they made was putting their hands on her," he continued, angrily. "The second was to let me know it."

"How much are they asking?" Plato asked.

"It's not just money they want, exactly."

Plato looked at him. Gatewood was a tall dude. Almost as tall as Plato, who stood six four. He didn't have the bulk of Plato, but he had to have weighed in at a good 220. His profile on the Internet said that he was forty-nine.

"Then what are they asking exactly?"

"For my investment in a business venture that I have no interest in," Gatewood explained. "A substantial financial investment." He shrugged. "The details aren't important. They've demanded that I sign the contract by Friday."

In a world where unicorns pranced in flowered meadows, where random people broke out in song and dance, and where fairy godmothers flew around granting wishes, Gatewood would do whatever they wanted him to do just so his lady would be dropped off at his doorstep all nice and shiny, looking better than ever. But in this world . . . There was an unspoken understanding between them. If Abby Rhodes wasn't dead already, she soon would be regardless of whether or not he signed his name and handed over a dime.

"I did not get to where I am in this world by being naïve," Gatewood continued, as if reading Plato's mind. "They don't plan on letting her go and I need her home."

The expression in Gatewood's eyes said it all. From everything Plato had read and seen about the businessman, Gatewood had had his choice of a bevy of beauties. He'd chosen this one. It was a heart and soul thing. Country and cute, Abby was no supermodel or Dallas socialite. She could wield a hammer like a sword and was a monster with power tools. The two were as different and unexpected as . . . well, Plato and the love of his life, Marlowe.

"She was living here with me," he explained. "Had been for about a month. I met her in a town called Blink, Texas." He shook his head as if he couldn't even believe that he'd actually been to the place. "Ever heard of it?"

"Maybe," Plato lied.

It was instinct that made him do it. Plato had figured out a long time ago that it was best never to stick a pushpin on a map that actually placed him anywhere in particular.

"She went back there yesterday morning," he continued. "We're planning a trip and she went back to get her passport."

Irritation shadowed his expression.

"She was supposed to wait," he muttered, lowering his head. Gatewood became sullen and contemplative. "Stubborn." He looked up at Plato. "Hardheaded."

Plato knew the type.

Gatewood visibly swallowed. "She was at her house in Blink when they took her. It was late when I got the call."

"A man?"

"Woman."

It was odd for a woman to make the ransom call in an abduction.

"The clock's ticking," Gatewood said, unmoved. "She — the woman on the phone — kept telling me that, and now I'm telling you. My world will be a much darker place without her in it. I've lived in that abyss my whole life and I won't go back to it."

His passion for her was real. That might've been the only thing about him that Plato was convinced was real. Dudes like Gatewood were hard to read. They spent most of their lives caught up in corporate and political games of cat and mouse, so Plato never could tell where the authenticity began and bullshit ended. Still, it was the passion that he obviously had for the woman that Plato could readily relate to, and the more he realized that, the more it pissed him off. Loving Marlowe had done something to him, something that left an uneasy feeling deep in his gut. Most of the time he tried to ignore it, but standing here now, empathizing and shit, it set off a silent alarm in him.

"What's my payment?"

Gatewood paused as if the thought hadn't occurred to him that he couldn't just snap his fingers and make Plato jump like he was probably used to other people doing when he made his demands known. "What do you want?"

Odd. His clients never offered him a blank check. But that's exactly what this dude was putting on the table. Money? Plato had money. He had plenty of it. He didn't have Gatewood money, though, but did he need it? This man sat perched on top of the world. A black emperor ruling a big-ass empire. In Plato's line of work, sometimes money wasn't the prize. A debt owed and paid at the most crucial time could mean the difference between his life and death. To have Gatewood indebted to him, something like that could be worth a fortune.

"I want a get-out-of-jail-free card," Plato told him. "I want a guarantee that should I ever need something, anything, you will come through for me like we're homies," he said, finding it difficult to hide his amusement at the analogy.

"No matter what it is?"

"No matter what or when or why."

Gatewood nodded and gave it a momentary thought. "All right. But only if you get her back home to me alive." Gatewood fought back his emotions. "If anything happens to her, though" — he visibly swallowed — "if she dies, then you don't get shit."

Plato shrugged. "Fair enough," he said, turning and leaving.

"Hey," Gatewood called after him.

Plato stopped and turned.

"What's your name?"

Plato thought against telling him because it was against his rules, but hell, those damn rules had all been broken in a matter of hours. So, why not break one more?

"Wells," he said before turning and leaving.

Coincidence freaked him the hell out, and this one was huge. He'd never sat and held a real conversation with Ms. Rhodes, but she'd come by Marlowe's a few times when he was there. Abby always made it a point to speak when she saw him, but she never pressed. He doubted that Gatewood knew of the connection between Plato and Abby. It was important to keep the secret. And somehow, he'd have to find Abby in time to be sure that she kept it, too. The last thing a man like Plato needed in his line of work was too many lines connecting him to too many dots. Of course, he'd have to keep all of this from Marlowe. Complications. Love was riddled with them.

Working Too Hard

DJ Washington drove a truck for a living, which kept him on the road for days at a time.

"Hey, baby," his girl Nia said, giving him a quick peck on the lips as he was coming inside and she was leaving.

"Hi, Daddy," his five-year-old son, Darius, said, giving him a hug.

"Hey, lil man."

DJ leaned in and kissed his one-year-old daughter, Tamia, perched on Nia's hip, on the cheek. "Hey, baby girl."

She managed to smile without letting that pacifier fall out of her mouth.

"Momma asked if you could pick them up by five?" Nia asked. "She's got choir practice tonight."

He looked at his woman and smiled. "Yeah. I'll get 'em before that. I just need a few hours of sleep."

Nia had been his high school sweetheart

and not once had the thought ever crossed his mind that he should be with anybody else. Pretty sandy brown hair hung down to her shoulders, redbone, with freckles, and pretty lips. Their daughter looked just like her, and Darius was the spitting image of DJ.

"Okay, we gotta go before I'm late again. You know my boss throws a fit when I walk in thirty seconds after nine."

"Yeah, you get outta here," he said warmly. "I'll see y'all later," he said to the kids. "Love y'all."

Nia and Darius said that they loved him, too. Tamia waved.

The night had been too damn long, and DJ was exhausted. He was thirty-two but felt more like eighty-two right now. Trucking was good in the beginning, before Darius was born, but more and more it was beginning to keep him away from home too long, away from his kids and his queen.

They were saving up to buy a house, their own house, because he'd promised her one before Tamia was born, but even in Clark City, the housing market had gotten tough for folks who didn't have a lot. But DJ was determined to get his family into a home of their own. It was a promise he reminded himself of each and every day.

He made some bacon and eggs, ate, and then jumped into the shower. His eyes burned from exhaustion. That bed felt so damn good when he stretched out in it that he moaned, turned over to Nia's side, pulled her pillow to his face, and inhaled. Yes. The scent of his baby was all over that thing. DJ hugged it to his chest, and gradually dozed off.

The abrupt sound of his phone ringing startled him from the heavy restlessness he'd had the nerve to call sleep.

"Yeah," DJ answered, feeling disoriented and weighted down.

"Let me in, man."

It was his brother, James, on the phone and pounding on the front door.

"Hold on, J," DJ said irritably.

James came in carrying a take-out box and large soda from the Yellow Dragon Chinese restaurant a block from DJ's place.

"You 'sleep?" he asked sarcastically.

"I *was* 'sleep," he snapped. "Like you give a damn," DJ said, closing the door.

The two ended up in his living room. James made himself at home, spreading his meal out on the coffee table and damn near swallowing that shit whole.

"Ever heard of chewing?"

"Ever heard of kiss my ass?"

DJ was the younger of the two, but he'd always been the responsible brother, the one who stayed out of trouble and always tried to do the right thing. James was James. There wasn't anything else to say about him.

"What the fuck you doing here, man?"

DJ's eyes were still burning and he felt like shit.

James finished swallowing a piece of orange chicken the size of a man's fist and then looked at him. "Where'd you find that white woman?" he asked abruptly.

"What does it matter?" DJ responded reservedly.

He loved his brother, but he was never comfortable bringing him in on this. DJ needed help, though. If nothing else, James knew how to keep his mouth shut, and he needed money as much as DJ did.

"She looked too nervous, D. Too damn nervous. We can't afford no weak link."

"I told you she was cool."

James, the biggest fuckup in the history of fuckups, always had the nerve to question DJ's choices on everything, and it pissed him off. But he was too tired to argue.

"So, she's gonna be watching her?" James asked for clarification.

"I told you that. She's gonna check on

her during the day, take her food."

"She's keeping the key."

DJ nodded. "Yeah. Ain't no reason for either one of us to have to go to that place until it's time to cut her loose."

James smirked, grunted, stuffed his mouth, and shook his head.

"What?"

"Nothing, man."

DJ didn't really want to press James for what that look on his face meant. See, doubt was DJ's biggest enemy right now. He'd been straight-arming it since he'd agreed to do this. All they had to do was take her. That was it. Hide her and keep her safe until the call came to let her go. DJ and James had been careful. They'd worn knitted face caps when they took her so she couldn't identify either of them. And she was kept in a safe place. They'd keep her fed and watered, and she'd be cool until the end of the week.

"What'd you do with her truck?"

They couldn't have left the woman's truck parked in front of her house. People who knew her might believe she was home and go snooping around.

"I parked it behind an old abandoned barn off Lee Road on the edge of town," he said indifferently. "Can't even see it from

64

the street. Ain't nobody gonna notice nothing."

James had gotten out of hand with her.
And DJ was pissed about it at first, but
James had actually done what needed to be
done. She was small but tough, tough
enough to nearly fight off the two of them
and get away. He'd hit her, though. DJ
could never reconcile with hitting a woman.
James, obviously, had no problem with it.

"We need to stop talking about it," DJ said
curtly.

James wiped his mouth, leaned back, and
draped his arm across the back of the sofa.
"Stop talking about kidnapping a woman?"
He laughed. "We could go to prison, D. I
know you don't want to think about it, but
what we did could get us life."

DJ's stomach turned, but he breathed in
deep to keep what was left of his breakfast
down. They'd scared the hell out of the
woman taking her like they did. DJ had
been assured that all they had to do was
keep her hidden until the end of the week.
That's all. He knew that she'd be all right
when this was over. He just wished that she
could know that, but the best thing for all
of them was to keep their distance as much
as possible. Nay would take her some food,
but she wouldn't talk to her and she'd never

let the woman see her face. If they played it smart, then no one would ever know that they were involved in any of this.

"We're not going to prison. This will be over in less than a week. We'll take that woman back to her house —"

"You believe that?"

"That's what we're doing, James," he said defiantly. "That's the only way this is going to end. Then we'll get paid and get on with our lives. That's it. It's what I agreed to."

James's dark eyes bore into DJ's, threatening to derail his faith in the promise he'd been given. What they'd done was wrong. It was illegal and yes, if they were caught, then they could go to prison. He hated having to scare that woman like that. DJ didn't want to think about what it'd be like if Nia had been in her place, but he couldn't dwell on that. This woman was worth a lot of damn money. More than any of them had seen in their lives. When it was all said and done, James would walk away with five hundred thousand dollars.

DJ challenged his brother. "As long as we don't do nothing stupid, James, we'll be cool. We'll be rich. I can take care of my family and you can do whatever the hell you wanna do. But we cannot fuck this up."

DJ knew when he brought James into this

that he was going to have to keep reminding him of that. James was a hothead, impulsive.

"Oh, I'm cool, man," James said casually. "I want my money, so I'll do what it takes to get it. You just make sure that white woman does her part. You know how women talk."

"She won't."

Naomi Simpson was her name. Her role was simple. Make sure to provide food and water to the other woman. Check on her twice a day, once in the morning and once at night. She wasn't supposed to talk to her or even look at her. It wasn't hard.

"We'll get together in a few days, the three of us," DJ said calmly. "Just to be sure that we're all cool."

James shrugged and started to get up to leave. "That'll work," he said leaving his mess on the table. "Put this in the trash for me," he said, grinning.

I TRY TO HIDE

Abby jolted awake, disoriented, terrified. Poised to fight. After several moments she realized that she was alone and on a yoga mat on the floor of a small room. What had they done to her? The thought struck fear in her so strong that it was nearly paralyzing, and without warning she started to cry as she intensely focused on her body. Abby ran her hand down the front of her T-shirt and shuddered at the thought that came to mind. *Rape!* Had they —

She collected herself enough to assess her body. Abby still had on the clothes she'd gone to bed in the night they took her, a pair of cotton shorts and her T-shirt seemed to be intact, and nothing seemed . . . She took several deep breaths. Abby reached inside her shorts to discover that she was still wearing panties. If they had assaulted her, she couldn't be sure, but it didn't seem like they had.

Her stiff jaw ached from where she'd been hit, and there was a cut on the inside, tender and raised. She noticed it when she raked the tip of her tongue across it. Abby surveyed her surroundings, and when she saw the door, she shakily struggled to get to her feet and made her way across the room. It was a hollow steel door with a latch plate shielding the locking mechanism in the seam between the door and frame, screwed in next to the knob. Abby pounded her palm against it.

"Hey!" She waited for a response. "Let me out! Let me . . . Help me! Somebody, please! Help!"

She pounded until her hand ached and she was almost hoarse before finally giving up.

Sunlight filtered through one small window near the top of a nine-foot-high ceiling. A window too high for her to reach and too small for her to fit through. A small air vent was at the opposite end of the ceiling. The walls were painted white but were concrete like the floor. Abby sat on the mat on the floor with her back pressed into one corner of the room, her knees drawn up to her chest, sobbing uncontrollably. This whole ordeal was like something out of a nightmare that she couldn't shake herself awake from. What did they want with her? Why had they done this? Were they going to kill her? Why?

Was she still in Blink? She didn't know. Abby had been unconscious part of the time when they had her in the back of that car. She had no idea how long they'd driven before she'd finally come to. Suddenly it dawned on her that nobody even knew she'd been back in town. Abby had only planned on packing up a few more of her things to take back with her to Dallas, and spending the night had been a spur-of-the-moment decision. She hadn't called anybody, not her father, or her best friend, Skye. The only person she'd spoken to about even being in Blink was Jordan.

"You were supposed to wait," he'd said over the phone, doing his best impersonation of being the boss of her.

But Abby wasn't accustomed to being told what to do. "I suppose I could've waited," she said calmly, "but I didn't want to. Besides, I needed to pick up a few other things and figured that today was as good a day as any to do it."

Jordan sighed deeply and took his time responding. "Things are different now, Abby. People know about us and precautions need to be taken where your comings and goings are concerned."

"So, what you're trying to tell me is that I need a bodyguard?"

"I mean like a bodyguard or two."

She found the whole notion ridiculous.

"That's just silly, Jordan," she quipped. "Not to mention embarrassing. What would I look like coming back to Blink, Texas, with armed guards surrounding me? People would think I was acting like Beyoncé or somebody."

"I don't care what people would think. You'd be safe."

"I'm a big girl. I can take care of myself."

Abby got it. He wasn't happy about her leaving alone. But Blink, Texas, was her home. Of course she felt safe there, safer than she ever did in Dallas. She appreciated his concern, but it felt like overkill. Obviously, it wasn't.

Abby had promised to call him before she'd left the house the following morning to head back to Dallas. She'd promised to be back at the penthouse first thing, but what if she wasn't? Abby put herself in his shoes. Jordan would call her, and when she didn't answer, when she didn't show up like she'd promised, he'd worry. A small light of hope sparked inside her. Jordan would come looking for her. He'd call the police and her father. It wouldn't be long before the whole town knew that she was missing. The police would go to her house and they'd see that there'd been a struggle.

"He'll look for me," she whispered. "He will." She swallowed and fought to compose herself.

Suddenly, it was all starting to come together. Since the Governor's Ball a month ago, Abby had become the new phenomenon. She was the mystery woman on Jordan Gatewood's arm that night, and the public had become more and more curious about her. Those men had found out about her too, and they'd probably been waiting for her to show up at the house or something. Ransom. This was about money. Abby had been abducted because of Jordan and who he was and what he had. The more she thought about it, the more it made sense. Jordan already knew. He had to know. They had to have called him and told him what they'd done and what they wanted.

Instead of sitting here and falling apart, she needed to pull herself together. Abby took a deep breath and released it slowly, then dried her tears. Yeah, she was scared. And she had no idea what these people were planning on doing to her, but she wasn't dead yet, and Jordan or no Jordan, she needed to find a way out of here.

"Think, Abby," she murmured, scanning the room for even the smallest details. The blue mat was basic. There was no zipper or buttons on it that she could possibly remove and use to try to pry open that door and escape. Other than that, there was nothing else in that room.

"Shit," she said in frustration and pushing back panic.

Abby had to pause to calm herself. What the hell was she even looking for? She looked up at the door. She'd picked the lock to her front door once with a credit card when she'd lost her keys. They'd made sure that she wouldn't be able to pick this one.

Just then, Abby heard noises on the outside of the door, the sound of another door opening and closing. Fear washed over her as she thought about those two men who'd abducted her last night. Her heart racing, she pushed back against that wall, bracing herself, recoiling and preparing to fight them again. Hot tears pooled in her eyes. Abby strained to try to hear voices, but there were none, just the sounds of heels clicking against the floor, getting closer to the door leading to this room.

A key turned in the door and it was slowly pushed open. Abby was trembling but didn't realize it. It was a woman, tall, lean with an almost boyish build, wearing black jeans, a long-sleeve gray V-neck shirt, and low-heeled black leather boots. Like the two men, she wore a black ski mask to hide her face, but long waves of blond hair hung down her back and shoulders. She cautiously entered the room, wearing dark sunglasses, carrying a clear plastic bag with a sandwich in it and a small bottled water. She set both items on the floor. Then stood next to the door and waited.

"Eat," the woman said.

Abby glanced down at the sandwich and almost threw up just looking at it. She swallowed bile rising in her throat and then looked back at the woman.

"Please let me go," she begged. "Please. I won't say anything. You don't have to do this."

"Eat," she repeated, sounding like a robot.

"I don't want this."

The woman seemed uncertain as to what to do next.

"Please let me go," Abby said, detecting what seemed to be a sign of weakness in this woman. "You're a woman," she continued.

"Eat."

"Whatever you want," Abby promised shakily. "I can get you whatever you want.

74

Money? Do you want money?" Abby nodded. "I have money, and if it's not enough, I can get more." She sniffed. "Those other two don't have to know and I won't tell. I swear to God, I won't tell."

"Eat."

Abby shook her head. "I don't want to eat. Let me fuckin' go!"

Without uttering another word, the woman bent down to pick up the sandwich and the bottle. Abby sprang up from the floor and bolted, pushing the woman so hard that she fell as Abby raced past her, through the door, out into what looked like a dishwashing area of an old restaurant. She ran past rusted sinks and through a doorway that led to an open eating area filled with old wooden tables stacked with broken chairs toward another door next to a big window.

Adrenaline drove her to run as fast as she could, as far as she could. Abby was getting away! She'd escaped! Sunlight flooded in, momentarily blinding her as she finally made her way outside. That woman was behind her. Abby could feel her closing in. She glanced at the car parked out front, and started to head out onto the road when she spotted another car barreling toward her. Abby pivoted and ran toward the wooded area behind the building.

Twigs and thorns dug into Abby's bare feet, but she didn't dare slow down. Her chest burned.

"What the fuck?" she heard a man say. "Dammit, Nay!"

"Sh . . . she won't get far!"

Don't stop! she commanded over and over again in her mind. *Don't fall.* She had to go faster. Abby could almost feel the pounding of his steps behind her reverberating up through the ground, closing in — getting closer as she wound her way through the maze of trees with agonizing pain shooting through the soles of her feet from splinters embedded in them. She felt herself starting to slow down . . . or maybe he was speeding up — she wasn't sure.

"Just go, Abby," she sobbed desperately. "Keep going. Keep —"

She was grabbed by her shirt from behind and pulled down to the ground. Abby kicked and screamed as he lifted her off the ground by her waist. She clawed into his arms with one hand and reached over her head for his face with the other.

He never said a word to Abby or to the woman.

"Look at him!" she told herself, trying to

turn to see his face, but he pushed her head down.

"Get my mask from the car," he told the woman as they made it back to the building. "Hurry up!"

He stood there, holding Abby still fighting to free herself.

"Stop it!" he demanded, shaking her like a toy. "I mean it!"

The woman came back, and moments later, Abby was back inside that room and dropped on the floor. By the time she looked up, both were gone and the man was closing the door behind him. The sound of the key turning in the lock sent a chill up her spine, and Abby collapsed, exhausted, and afraid, and pissed at herself for getting caught.

Abby crawled over to the mat. God! She'd almost gotten away. If he hadn't showed up, she would've. This wasn't happening. It was all too surreal and ridiculous. She was still waiting for the sound of the alarm on her phone to go off and to finally wake her up. *Please let it go off.*

She had no idea how long she lay there, staring up at that small window before a thought came to her and reminded her of a time in the very beginning of their relationship when Jordan had asked her to be brave.

He'd said that the kind of love that the two of them shared would take courage. It was a strange thought to have at a time like this, but somehow she knew that it had come to her for a reason. Abby had to be brave if she was going to make it through this. And if it did have something to do with Jordan, then she had to believe in him, believe that he'd find a way to get to her. She had to believe in the two of them. It soothed her, calmed her — thinking of him. And maybe it'd even keep her from going crazy.

"If I don't get out of here first, Jordan," she murmured, "you find me, Jordan." She sobbed softly, closed her eyes, and focused on a single thought: *Please, find me.*

I LOVE YOU NOW AND EVER

Would that woman come back? She was a whole lot taller than Abby, but that didn't mean she was any stronger. Abby imagined herself lowering her head and barreling into the woman's midsection with her shoulder, knocking her long ass down onto the floor, then running past her. She was more determined than ever to escape the next time. Abby promised herself that she would.

As she lay staring up at the ceiling, exhausted, Abby drifted in and out of memories until she came to one that made her forget where she was, just for a little while.

Abby was anxious and she sensed that he was, too. It took everything inside her not to let instinct take over and send their lovemaking into a heated frenzy.

"Look at me," he told her, placing his hand beneath her chin and raising her face to look into her eyes.

She nervously pursed her lips together and blinked, and then shyly averted her gaze. She had never felt more vulnerable or emotionally exposed.

"No, Abby," he gently demanded, insisting that she not turn away. "You look at me. You belong to me, sugah," he whispered. "You belong *with* me."

Her breath quickened, and Jordan guided her breathing back to the same cadence as his. Slow, even, and steady. Abby lost herself in the soul of his eyes. She wondered if he was lost in hers. God! She hoped so. The tips of his fingers lighted a trail down her back, stopping at the curve above her behind. Abby pushed into him. Waves inside her caressed him, threatening to make her lose control and —

Tantric. Jordan had been telling her about this. It wasn't about fucking, bucking, and pounding into each other, chasing orgasms — his or hers. It was about her. Him. The two of them together, meeting in the middle and erasing the world outside of this room. It was about a single moment and making it last for as long as it possibly could.

She loved him. She trusted him. Still, he seemed to need even more from her. No other man had ever held her hostage the way that

Jordan Gatewood had done. He had no idea of the depths of her obsession for him. It'd scare him if he knew. Hell. It scared her. So Abby worked overtime meting out manageable doses of herself to him, being careful not to come on appearing too needy or to cling to him the way she knew that she could if she wasn't careful.

Jordan braced his back against the headboard of the bed, bending one leg at the knee, pressing his thigh against her bottom to hold her in place. His other leg stretched long and relaxed in front of him. He was buried deep inside her. Abby pressed her chest against his, her lips less than an inch from his, but he wouldn't kiss her. She'd lose her mind if he kissed her, and this would be over with entirely too soon.

He steadied her and stopped her from speeding to the end too quickly. Abby tucked her lower lip between her teeth but held his gaze. Again, he guided her breathing until they breathed as one. Tears pooled in her eyes.

"You feel so good," she whispered, bracing her hand against his chest. "Oh, Jordan."

"I love you," he promised her.

She lost track of how long the two of them made love barely moving. Just when she thought she couldn't take it anymore, he hardened and expanded inside of her. Abby perched precariously between pleasure and pain. The ache low in her gut signaled that she wouldn't be able to hold out much longer.

She hesitantly raised her mouth to his and grazed her lips lightly across his. "I love you so much," she said, with an unexpected tremble in her voice.

His breath deepened as Jordan willed himself to stay still. And then Abby let her eyes close.

"I'm coming, Jordan." Her voice trailed off as she rested her chin on his shoulder.

He held her and watched as she arched her back, clamped her thighs around his waist, and shuddered. Abby held him, and then pushed away, and pulled herself close to him again, as she cried out at her release. Jordan exploded without warning, without meaning to; his cock thickened and throbbed inside her. Powerful convulsions gripped his body as he wrapped both arms around her and pinned her to him.

"Oh, shiiiii— ! Fffffuck! Abby!"

She tried to push herself away from him, but he wouldn't let go. Jordan buried his face between her shoulder and neck, palmed her head, and held on as if his life depended on it — on her.

Less than an hour later, while Jordan slept

soundly next to her, Abby stared out through the open doors across the pool and out at the moon hovering over the ocean. She could hardly keep her eyes open, but Abby was worried that if she closed them, she'd wake up to find herself back in her own bed in Blink, Texas, pissed that she had to wake up from the best dream she'd ever had in her life. Jordan had mentioned that he'd wanted to get away for a little while. He'd been working fifteen-hour days, starting up a new division at Gatewood Industries, and he was exhausted.

Abby had had a bucket list of places she wanted to visit when she finally found the time and courage. Bali hadn't been on the list, and now that she was here, she decided that it belonged at the top. They'd flown here on his private plane. It was her first passport stamp. And there was nothing about this place that she didn't like.

Jordan had rented a villa at the Bulgari Resort in a town called Banjar Dinas Kangin Uluwatu. It was absolutely beautiful, built on the side of a cliff and overlooking the ocean, and every night they slept with the doors open. Abby was worried at first about bugs getting into the place, but they must've known that they weren't welcome, because she hadn't seen one since she got here.

He stirred a bit and pulled her closer to him.

She sighed and melted against him as if it were actually possible that she could somehow blend her body into his until they were one person. Jordan's strong heart beat steadily against her back. She loved the feel of it, the sound of it, the rhythm. Something about it made her feel settled.

Jordan loved having her close, almost as much as she loved being close to him, which wasn't nearly as much as she'd have liked. During the weeks back home, Abby spent most of her time in Blink, while Jordan stayed and worked in Dallas. He didn't like the two-hour distance between the two of them any more than she did, and had asked her, on more than one occasion, to pack up her life and move into his penthouse with him in Dallas. Deep down, she wanted nothing more than to spend every waking second with this man. But Abby fought hard to keep a level head about all of this — them. She had a business to run and responsibilities and if she wasn't careful he could make her forget that there was the real world, and then there was Jordan.

Somehow she managed to ease out from underneath the weight of Jordan's arm without waking him. Abby walked naked out onto the massive lanai and looked out at the ocean, listening to the waves ebb and flow gently against the beach below. It was okay to be naked in a dream, because that's all it was. Just a dream.

The responsible Abby Rhodes stirred inside her.

"C'mon, Abby," she murmured softly. "You know that alarm clock on your phone is going to chime at any moment." She sighed. Of course it would. Abby went through an agenda cataloged in her mind.

"Wade and PacMan should be showing up at Mr. Bergman's first thing in the morning to get started on replacing that roof. I'll have to swing by before lunch to see how they're coming along."

She resisted the temptation to concede that she was actually sleeping anyplace but in her own bed.

"I need to have Patty reconcile those invoices I got the other day for the new floors we installed at Pritchard's Fish Boil over in Clark City."

That's it, girl, she mentally coaxed herself. Get back in touch with reality and leave all this dreaming nonsense where it belongs — on your pillow.

Abby glanced over her shoulder at the beautiful man sleeping in that gigantic bed. Jordan Gatewood was larger than life and it wasn't his fault. He ran a multibillion-dollar corporation. All he ever had to do was snap his fingers and every request he made was immediately answered. He was king and Gatewood Industries was his kingdom and the people working for him worshipped him. So he couldn't possibly be real in her life. Right? And that ocean wasn't real, either. Neither was Bali.

Abby closed her eyes and waited, anticipating the sound of her alarm. She still had some leftover pizza in the fridge. She licked her lips at the thought of warming up a slice for breakfast and making herself a cup of hot, steaming coffee to go along with it.

"Abby."

That wasn't her alarm. Abby opened one eye, expecting that ocean to have disappeared. But it was still there.

"Come back to bed, sugah."

She opened her other eye and turned slowly. Jordan had pushed himself up on one elbow, waiting for her. His dark gaze tugged at her, drawing her over to the bed like she was a puppet. Abby couldn't have resisted if even if she'd wanted to. And without protest, she crawled back into the bed next to him. Jordan pulled the sheet up to cover the two of them to their waists, lay back down, and kissed the top of her head before eventually drifting back off to sleep.

The sun was starting to come up. Abby's eyelids were so heavy that it took all of her strength to try to keep them open. Maybe she wasn't dreaming. Maybe she'd fallen off a ladder or something, died, and this was heaven. It was a rather morbid thought but one that she could reconcile with, at least making more sense than the idea that this was her life now, that she was in Bali, and that Jordan Gatewood was her man.

THIEVES IN THE TEMPLE

Plato stood outside of Abigail Rhodes's brick bungalow thinking about how much it looked like Marlowe's house, which looked like nearly every other brick house in this town. The truth was, Plato hated Blink, Texas, but he loved a woman in it, and considering that he was never one to put down roots or to call any one place home for too long, lately this town was where he'd felt he belonged. In less than twenty minutes, Plato could be at the place he shared with Marlowe on the other side of town. The coincidence of Gatewood's woman and Plato's woman knowing each other still blew his mind. The shit was just eerie.

Plato's phone rang and Marlowe's picture showed up. He grinned. "Hey, baby. You must've read my mind, because I was just thinking about you."

She laughed. "I did, which is why I called."

"You know I was kidding. Right?" he said,

trying not to sound as uneasy as he felt. Marlowe really was psychic or something, which still freaked him the hell out.

"Oh, really?" she casually responded.

"What do you need today?" Plato asked, to hurry up and gloss over the exchange.

"You," she said seductively.

"Aw, yeah." He nodded.

"And eggs. Can you stop at the store on the way home and get a dozen eggs, unbleached flour, and vanilla flavoring?"

He frowned. "Vanilla what?"

"It's in the seasonings sections of the store, where you find salt and pepper, and in a little brown bottle that says 'vanilla extract' on the label." She explained it to him like he was six.

"Send me a text, 'cause you know I ain't gonna remember all that."

"I'm sending it now. Where are you?"

"Working." He waited for her to ask for more detail, but Marlowe was finally learning the ropes of being in a relationship with a man like him. It was in her best interest not to ask and it was also in her best interest not to try to read his mind, or tarot cards, or bones, or . . .

"Okay," she said with reservation. "But you'll be home tonight?"

"I'll be home soon," he promised before

declaring his undying devotion for her and hanging up.

The domesticated life was entirely too out of character for him, but despite some uncomfortable moments, he actually dug it. Or rather, he dug her, which made everything else bearable. Plato made his living doing some unsavory things, and the last thing he wanted to do was taint her world with any of the details of what he did to earn his money. Marlowe was his light force. She was his breath of fresh air, a love song with a pretty melody, and any other corny shit that came to mind. She saved him from the abyss of himself just by being, and he'd grown addicted to her, obsessed by her. It was downright unnatural but felt so damn good.

He started his inspection of this place on the perimeter. Plato made his way down a path along the side of the house leading to the gate of a six-foot-tall privacy fence. It was latched from the inside but had a lever that he could pull on the outside to open it. Plato noted that the gate was closed. A minor detail, but every last one of them mattered.

The yard was nicely manicured with a Zen type of quality, a swinging bed hung from an old elm tree, exotic grasses, succulents, and shrubbery. He made a couple of mental notes of some things he liked so that he could do them in his own yard. *His yard.* His house. His woman. No. Nothing about how he lived his life now made any sense, and yet he was living it. He carefully examined areas around the windows and doors, stopping and squatting underneath one particular window located in the back of the house. Plato spotted footprints, dried in the mud directly beneath that window. He stood up and looked inside. It was a bedroom.

Making his way back to the front of the house, he noticed that the front door was closed. He played out a scenario in his mind. If he were abducting someone from inside a house in the middle of the night, would he have the presence of mind to close the door behind him? Plato tried the knob and pushed open the unlocked door. Once inside, he leaned down to examine the lock, noticing small scratches around it, and he concluded that it had been picked, not broken. Plato closed the door behind him, stood in the middle of the small living room, and without moving assessed the area.

The living room seemed mostly intact, except for the small drops of blood on the floor. On one of the end tables was a framed black-and-white picture of a pretty young black woman and an older man. They looked too much alike to not be related. Abby and a relative.

On the breakfast bar was a cup and a saucer with a half-eaten sandwich still left on it. Plato walked slowly down the narrow hallway and noticed more blood splattered on one wall and smeared on the opposite one. Every discovery was always open to interpretation, and he couldn't afford to take anything for granted. Through the years, he'd come to understand that. Plato passed a small office and bathroom and finally stopped in the bedroom he'd looked into from outside. The struggle had started here.

She'd been in the bedroom when she'd been taken. Pillows, a blanket, and a lamp were strewn on the floor. She was a fighter. An image flashed of her at the house talking to Marlowe. Abby in her work boots and jeans, with a utility belt strapped around her petite frame. Abby was a little superhero and he wasn't surprised that she put up a fight. Her abductor would've had to incapacitate her, subdue her, to control her. He'd have had to hit her. Hence the blood.

Plato turned in a slow circle, seeing in his mind how the scene might've played out.

Abby sleeping. Kidnapper creeping. Covers her mouth with his hand. Abby scratching and kicking and swinging.

Plato left the bedroom and slowly headed back down the hallway, where he saw a wooden matchstick on the floor. He picked it up and examined it. One end of it looked as if it had been crushed. Plato looked around the house for candles. He looked through kitchen drawers for a matchbox and came up with nothing. It was just a matchstick and probably meant nothing. But he tucked it into his pocket and left the house, making sure to close the door behind him.

"Hey, baby," Marlowe said to him as he was coming up the steps to the house, carrying a bag of groceries.

Her cousin Belle was leaving, leading their blind and mean old aunt Shou Shou from the house.

"She knew you wouldn't be able to find it," the old woman said gruffly.

Find what? He wanted to ask but then thought better of it. Shou Shou didn't like him. Not that he gave a damn, but she was dangerous and spooky and knew how to cast spells and shit like that.

"It's good to see you too, Shou," he said sarcastically. "How're you doing?"

"Don't give me no lip," she warned as Belle escorted her down the steps of the porch to the car. "I'll sic the ancestors on you."

He shook his head and turned to go inside. "What the hell's that mean?" he muttered under his breath.

"Try me and find out," she shot back over her shoulder.

"Hey, Plato," Belle finally said, greeting him with a sweet smile.

Thankfully, the two of them left, and he followed Marlowe into the house to the kitchen to the scent of something that smelled so good it made his knees weak.

"I asked Shou to bring me the vanilla extract," she said as he set the bags on the counter. "I knew you wouldn't be able to find it."

Marlowe wore a colorful cloth wrapped on her head, knotted in front, a fitted yellow T-shirt with a peace sign across her inviting and ample chest, and black leggings, clinging for dear life to those hips and that lovely ass of hers. She had a lovely golden-brown complexion, hypnotic eyes, and big lips that he sucked on like a babe every chance he got.

"What?" she asked, looking over at him. She'd caught him staring.

"What's for dinner?" he asked.

"Smothered pork chops for you and baked lemon-pepper salmon for me." She smiled.

And she loved to cook? He'd kill for this woman. In fact, he had. He'd die for her with a smile on his face.

"What's the vanilla for?" he asked, hoping that she wouldn't put no shit like that on his pork chops.

Marlowe smiled, bent over, opened the oven, and pulled out a golden pie. She held it under her face and inhaled. "Coconut pie," she said luxuriously.

His favorite.

DUG MY OWN GRAVE

Jordan hadn't slept all night, but he arrived promptly in his office at eight, logged on to his computer, and held his customary morning meeting with his executive assistant, Jennifer, over coffee the way he did every morning to review his schedule for the day.

Routine was everything. Jordan did not have the luxury of allowing himself to become undone. He couldn't give in to the unraveling threatening to take him apart inside. Abby needed him to be focused and strong. For her sake and for his own sanity, he needed to keep up appearances. The thought was never far from his mind that he was being observed, that whoever was behind this was waiting, watching, and expecting him to crumble under the weight of her abduction. Jordan was unraveling internally, but on the outside, he believed that he needed to appear steady and sane, to be the force he was expected to be.

Is Abby still alive?

He'd made a promise to himself not to give that question any credence and certainly not to let it settle in, but it flashed in his mind all of a sudden and immediately made him uneasy.

"Jordan?" Jennifer asked, staring at him. "Do you want me to accept the meeting notice from Mr. Miller for this afternoon?"

Had she asked him about that already?

"No," he responded. "See what's available for tomorrow."

She nodded. "That's it, then. Anything else?"

"No, Jennifer, that's all."

"It probably doesn't need to be said, but no police, Mr. Gatewood," the woman on the phone had told him. "They make things unnecessarily complicated and messy. I'm sure I don't need to go into detail."

Jordan clenched his jaw. "You just make sure that she isn't hurt," he warned. "Not a scratch. I fucking mean it."

"I can hear it in your voice that you do," she said calmly. "We'll handle her with kid gloves."

But they hadn't. Jordan found himself staring at Abby's picture again that the woman had sent to him. She was bleeding and he was keeping score.

97

Jordan's personal assistant, Phyl Mays, came into his office half an hour after his meeting with Jennifer had ended.

"You feeling all right, boss?" she asked, sitting on the other side of his desk. "You look a little tired."

If candid wasn't Phyl's middle name, it should've been.

"I am tired," he admitted.

Phyl smiled. "How's Abby?" She winked.

The expression on his face must've sent a warning, because Phyl quickly wiped that grin off her face.

"Sorry," she muttered sheepishly, clearing her throat. "Are you going to need a driver tonight?"

"Driver?"

"For the McCall cocktail party at the Eidleman Country Club?"

"Am I RSVP'd for that?" he asked, having forgotten all about it.

"You are."

The last thing he wanted was to go to a cocktail party.

"Do you want me to cancel?" Phyl asked reservedly.

"No," he said quickly.

Don't bend. Don't break. Don't stop. The sonsofbitches, whoever was behind this, were watching, waiting for him to flinch. Don't.

"I'll drive myself," he added.

"Oh, and I managed to get a few résumés together for Abby to take a look at," Phyl casually explained. "I called and left her a message, but she hasn't gotten back to me yet."

Jordan had asked Abby to consider hiring her own personal assistant. Of course, she found the whole idea silly, but he'd asked Phyl to reach out to a few agencies for résumés for Abby to review anyway. In time, he had hoped that she'd see the value in having her own "Phyl" to help manage things for her.

"Is she out of town?" Phyl inquired.

"Send them to me," he said casually. "I'll see that she gets them."

"She doesn't seem too keen on the idea, boss."

"She's not, but that doesn't mean it's not a good one."

"Well, when you talk to her please have her call me. Until she gets her own PA, I'm sort of helping her navigate her way around D-town. She wanted me to find her a good mani-pedi shop and I've got a couple in mind that she might like."

Jordan's expression must've begged the question for him.

"Manicure-pedicure," she clarified.

In lieu of everything that was happening, it took everything in him not to scoff at something as inconsequential as a pedicure. But Phyl couldn't know that anything was wrong. Jordan's instinct warned him that no one could know that Abby had been abducted.

"I need you to gather some information for me," he continued, preparing to wrap up their meeting.

"Sure."

"Find out everything you can on who the investors are on the Dakota Pipeline project. Names of corporations, individuals, investment amounts if possible."

She stared blankly at him. "Anything in particular you're looking for?"

"No."

Phyl paused for a moment, but when he didn't elaborate, she finally stood up to leave. "I'll get you that information as soon as possible."

"Thank you," he said curtly.

Jordan stared at his computer screen, forcing himself to read and respond to e-mails. Without realizing it, he glanced constantly between that screen and the cell phone on his desk, waiting for it to vibrate with news about Abby. None came.

He had to go through the motions. Jordan

trudged through meetings during the course of the day like a fish swimming through mud. He held conversations with people, pretending that he was listening, that he gave a shit about whatever it was they were talking to him about. Push through. That's what he did. Minutes ticked by like hours. Was she still alive? How badly had they hurt her? Were they still hurting her? Why the fuck hadn't Wells contacted him yet? Jordan remembered that passivity was not in his nature and he decided to be the one to make the first call.

The phone rang several times before going to voice mail. "Where are you?" he demanded to know.

Maybe it was too soon for him to be calling, too soon for the man to have discovered anything, but still, Jordan couldn't sit here waiting and doing nothing.

"Have you been by the house? Let me know what you found," he said before hanging up.

This was his fault. Jordan should've known better than to make their relationship public. He'd dated more than his share of women, but Abby was different. He made it a point when they were in public together to kiss her, hold her hand, showing the world that he was truly in love with this woman, and that was where he'd fucked up. Even with Claire, things had been different. He wasn't as well known back then. His face wasn't on the covers of national and international magazines. He wasn't who he was now, but he had been careful with Claire, providing security for her whether she knew it or not, whether she wanted it or not, because Jordan had enemies. He always did and always would.

"Jordan," Jennifer said over the intercom, "you're late for your two o'clock. They want to know if you're still planning on joining?"

Jordan glanced at his watch. The meeting had started ten minutes ago.

"Yes. Let them know that I'll be there momentarily."

This was just the first day. Jordan needed to keep his sanity in check and not panic. He had to pace himself, to not give in to his darkest fears, but to brace himself for whatever happened. It was the first day of what would undoubtedly be the longest week of his life, and if he was going to get through it, then he had to know that he would get her back. Abby had to believe it, too. Jordan momentarily closed his eyes and willed her his determination, his promise that he would find her. Abby had to know that he was coming for her. God! Please let her know that.

GAMES, CHANGES, AND FEARS

Brandon's half sister, Bianca, had finally managed to get him to visit one of her coffee shops. Drugstore Cowboy, on the surface, was everything you'd expect from a modern-day Texas saloon, with its rustic wood bar, tables and chairs, cement floors, and exposed ductwork. His opinion was sarcastic, of course. Located in downtown Deep Ellum, on the outside it was nothing fancy, but inside it was a millennial's dream. With things on the menu like Honey Greek Yogurt and Maple Bourbon Coffee, he doubted that many real cowboys actually frequented the place. But surprisingly, he liked it.

"You saw him today?" he asked, staring across the table at her.

She nodded slightly. "Only briefly, on the elevator."

"How'd he look?"

"Tense," she said simply. "And handsome."

The twinge of jealousy sparked by her last comment caught Brandon by surprise. She was his sister, after all. And Brandon shouldn't care that she found Gatewood handsome, but again — it was the admiration, near cultlike worship, of the man by Brandon's family that had been a thorn in Brandon's side for too many years.

He sighed heavily, wondering if it were possible to pass down hatred through DNA. Or was it really something that was taught? Either way, Brandon and Bianca had come from a highly potent gene pool, or their father was one hell of a teacher.

"It seems silly," she said introspectively. "Don't you think? Carrying on with this elaborate scheme for something as insignificant as a thirty-year-old grudge."

He returned a seesaw nod. "Perhaps if you look at it that way, then, yes, I suppose it does."

She smiled. "What other way is there to look at it?"

"As more than a grudge. A disease, perhaps," he offered. "Like cancer, spreading and festering, changing you, even defining you."

"You let it go before it gets to that point,

Brandon. Our father should've let it go."

"Our father should have," he responded thoughtfully. "Had it been anyone else but Gatewood, he likely would have."

"His hatred of that man has poisoned him."

"Only because he underestimated Jordan and it cost him."

She lingered on that thought.

"Jordan turned the rules of the game, our father's game, against him, and played it better than he ever could," Brandon explained. "I don't know if it's that Dad hates Jordan Gatewood as much as he hates himself for losing to him."

"It's a shame."

Brandon was thoughtful for a moment before responding. "You have to look at the bigger picture."

"How so?"

"In a perfect world, a man like, say, David can take down Goliath with a slingshot and a stone." He chuckled, amused, but then he stopped laughing. "But the world's not perfect and it takes more than slingshots to bring a giant to his knees. Gatewood wasn't created overnight. It has taken decades of fire and pressure to build him up into the Goliath he has become."

She pondered his analogy.

"Defeating him requires a more systematic approach to his unraveling."

"Taking him apart at the seams?"

He offered a curt smile. And then his thoughts drifted to her. "I met her," he said, suddenly lighting up at the memory. "And until I did, I didn't believe that the man had any weaknesses. His staunch and dignified demeanor, worn like armor, had always made him seem absolutely infallible."

"Is this hero worship I'm seeing in you?"

He was caught off guard by her observation. "Yes," he said, making the surprising admission.

"Where is this coming from?" she probed.

Again, he thought long and hard before answering. "He is truly self-made," he explained. "Oh, sure. He inherited the business from his father, but he was ill equipped to run it, nearly destroyed it, and yet, despite all of the obstacles — being a person of color, his youth, having those he trusted most sabotaging his every move — he still succeeded. He found a way to overcome and to not only keep the business from going under but to turn it into something his own father would never imagined it could be." He leaned back and sighed. "And who knows, left to his own devices, how much farther he could take it?"

She nodded affirmatively. "You're right."

Brandon chuckled again. "Me against him was like Daffy Duck going head-to-head against Superman until I saw her. No. Until I saw the way that he looked at her."

He hovered over his cup of coffee and recalled the memory. No man is ever prepared for the kind of effect that she had on Brandon that night. He looked up at the landing in the governor's mansion, right on cue, as she emerged through the entrance and stood on the landing above the crowd, looking out across the room searching for Gatewood.

"She appeared like something out of a dream," he said, staring into his sister's eyes. "A dark beauty with sensuous curves poured into a sky-blue sequined gown. Her hair worn short, and you know me, I hate short hair on a woman, but on her it was perfect, highlighting beautiful cheekbones, full lips, and bright dramatic eyes; oh, she was lovely."

He shook his head slowly in dismay.

"And I watched him make his way up the staircase to her, locking on to her the whole time, unable to take his eyes off her. She met him halfway, placed her hand on his shoulder, smiled, and whispered something to him." He smiled, too. "He kissed her cheek, held out his arm for her to take, and escorted her down the staircase. The whole room watched the two of them as if they were royalty."

He'd never seen anything like it, and Brandon had been to a dozen Governor's Balls in his lifetime. He'd even been to a royal wedding once in Denmark, and seeing the two of them together had at least that same effect. He was sure of it.

"All of a sudden, Jordan Gatewood was just a man." He looked amused again. "Or rather, he was still Superman, but she was his kryptonite."

And just like that, his hero had fallen. What he thought of Gatewood defied logic. Yes, he loathed him because he'd been taught to believe it was the thing to do, and he understood his father's reasons behind why he felt the way he did, although he didn't necessarily agree. But above all else, blood was loyal. Jordan Gatewood was also his hero, for all the reasons that he'd just explained to his sister, but he was also something else. He was everything that Brandon could never be.

"You made them promise not to hurt her," his sister reminded him. "But no matter what, it doesn't make sense to let her go, Brandon," she regrettably explained.

"I spoke to her," he said, forcing a smile. "She surprised me, because she wasn't the type of woman you'd expect a man like him to be with."

"What you mean? You said she was beautiful?"

"Oh, she was — is. But he's used to having beautiful women on his arm. She stood next to me at the bar, waiting while he stood across the room holding a conversation with someone." He waved his hand dismissively in the air. "She leaned over to me and she admitted to feeling out of place. She joked about how awkward she was and how worried she was about offending someone by being blunt and too damned honest." He laughed. "She asked me who I was and shook my hand. It wasn't long before he, of course, came looking for her," he said, disappointed. "Before she left, she placed her hand on my arm and told me how nice it was to speak to me, and she thanked me for my patience."

A dreadful feeling washed over him.

"I told them not to hurt her," he said, collecting himself.

"But when this is over?"

Abby Rhodes was never far from his thoughts. It mattered to him that she was safe, as safe as she could be under these circumstances. She was a sweet beauty who didn't belong in their world, caught up in their deceitful webs and ugly games. Gatewood kept her close to him for the rest of that night, hovering over her like some protective guardian, being selective about whom he let into their small circle. Shame on him for falling in love with that woman and for letting her fall in love with him. Shame on all of them for what he knew to be their only recourse.

"She won't feel a thing," he said sadly.

HE LOVES ME WRONG

Flowers always did the trick. Thomas believed that and she'd let him. Naomi stood over the kitchen sink, staring out the window into the swing set in the backyard. The kids never even played on that thing anymore. It was just in the way now, an eyesore, really.

"Hey, baby," he said, coming up behind her, tenderly wrapping his arms around her waist, kissing her on the side of her neck.

It was best not to cringe. So she pressed her lips together to keep her protests to herself.

"What's for dinner?"

Mercifully, he didn't hold on to her for too long.

"Your favorite," she said, mustering up as much sweetness as she had left inside her. "Steak, potatoes, and a salad."

"Sounds good, sweetheart," he said, making his way through the kitchen, out into the living room, and up the stairs to shower.

The kids were well trained. They knew to be quiet and sit and do their homework by the time he came home from work.

"Hey, Daddy," she heard them call out in unison when they saw him.

"Y'all 'bout done with that homework?" he asked, pounding up the stairs.

"Yessir."

This house was full of eggshells that Naomi and the kids were careful to try not to break. And he was full of appreciation and apologies and compliments and guilt. This was the cycle of abuse. Everyone knew the rules and how to play. Of course, he loved the meal, and she looked so pretty tonight. He was proud of the kids. Everyone smiled and paid special attention to every word said at the dinner table, politely waiting until it was their turn to speak, especially if he was talking. You had to make sure that he saw you hanging on every word, that he had your undivided attention, admiration, and forgiveness. And you'd better be convincing.

Making love with a cracked rib was excruciating. Naomi had to pretend that she wasn't in as much pain as she was. She had to pretend to get lost in the throes of his lovemaking and to cum with such abandon

113

that he believed he was a god. He had to believe that the tears she shed were a result of being so overcome with her release that it made him stick out his chest a little more tomorrow when he went to work.

While Thomas slept, she stared up at the ceiling, recalling the fear she felt when that woman escaped. It had happened so fast, and Naomi had been left scrambling, frantic and confused. Even if she'd chased her and caught her, what then? DJ had promised her that this would be simple. All three of them had had their roles. Naomi's was to keep the woman fed, but the situation had turned crazy in a matter of seconds.

"What the fuck happened, Nay?" he yelled after shoving the woman back into the room and slamming the door shut behind him. "How the hell did she get out?"

Naomi yanked off the hot ski mask. "It . . . it just happened," she tried explaining. "I don't know —"

He grabbed her by the elbow and ushered her outside. Naomi winced from the injury Thomas had caused a day ago to her side.

"We can't fuck this up, Nay," he said, forcing himself to calm down. "You have to be more careful."

"I know. I know. I'm sorry."

She didn't want to do this. But Naomi

needed this. It was her last chance, her only chance, to get away from Thomas.

She swallowed. "I was careless," she said apologetically. "It won't happen again."

DJ had promised her more money than she'd ever dreamed she'd get her hands on, and she'd nearly blown it. Naomi could not afford to blow this.

Naomi was a dispatcher at the trucking company where DJ drove. She'd been there the day he'd applied for the job and she'd liked his smile. Not in a sexual way, but he reminded her of a younger brother. DJ was always quick with a joke. When he was in, he made it a point to see if she wanted anything back from any one of his trips. He was easy to like, and observant.

"What's going on, Nay?" he asked one day when she'd failed to adequately cover up a bruised cheek.

She'd gone out of her way to avoid people as much as she could, but he found her sitting in the back of the cafeteria. He sat down and immediately noticed her piss-poor makeup job.

"You okay?" he asked, half smiling at her.

"I'm good," she lied. "Ran into a door," she said, embarrassed.

"Right," he said doubtfully.

She could see it in his eyes that he didn't

115

believe her. Eventually, she stopped lying. And she started telling him her dreams, about taking her boys and getting away from Thomas. When DJ came to her with this plan, at first she thought he was joking. And if he was, it was cruel and she had made up her mind not to be his friend anymore. But when she realized that it wasn't a joke, and that he had a way to help her get some money together to follow that harebrained dream of hers, it was as if God had finally heard her prayers.

"It's crazy," he said at a restaurant they'd agreed to meet at outside of town. "I know."

If word had gotten back to her husband that she was meeting another man in a restaurant, Thomas would've killed her.

"It's not crazy, DJ," she retorted. "It's criminal. You could get life in prison for something like this."

"Or I can make a whole hell of a lot of money. We could make a lot of money."

"For kidnapping?" she said, being careful to keep her voice down, but still glancing around the room to make sure no one heard her. "Do you even know these people? These people who want you to do this? Who are they?"

"I don't know and I don't want to know. Look, they found me. All right?"

"How'd they find you?"

He turned his gaze from hers. "I can't say,

Naomi. Look, the less you know, the better. I'm just —"

DJ was a young man, with a young family, and it wasn't surprising that money, or the lack of it, was an issue.

"They promised that it'd be easy. Nobody gets hurt. Some rich dude has to part with some money. That's it."

"Yeah, and some woman is abducted and afraid for her life."

"But she won't get hurt. They made me promise, Nay. They made me promise to keep her safe, and it's for less than a week. Five days. Tops."

She couldn't believe what she was hearing from him, and she wanted no part of it.

"It's stupid, DJ, and just ridiculous. Why would you even tell me some mess like this, and why you'd even consider doing it is beyond me. If you get caught, then who's going to take care of your family?"

Her words hit home, because all of a sudden he looked sheepish and like his head was full of second thoughts.

"I'd love to have the money, but not like this. The risk is too high."

She left him there, meaning every word she said. Until she walked into her house and Thomas met her at the door with a slap across the face.

Five hundred thousand dollars could put a lot of miles between Naomi and her husband, Thomas. It wasn't enough money to last a lifetime, but it was plenty to leave him and to build a new life for herself and her kids. She would change her name and her boys' names. She'd go someplace where no one knew them, and they'd start over from scratch. Brand-new.

Twice a day, Naomi was tasked with going to that old restaurant and taking her a sandwich and a bottle of water. The woman hadn't eaten today, but Naomi would see to it that she ate tomorrow. They needed to keep her alive if they were going to get paid. Naomi's and her sons' lives were at stake; her freedom was at stake. And that was worth everything.

No More Dawn

Abby bolted upright, panicked and blanketed in darkness. Disoriented. Confused. Abby had no idea where she was. Had she fallen asleep? Was she dreaming? Not a dream, but a nightmare. She took several deep breaths before tentatively stretching out her arms and spreading her fingers, widening her eyes, straining to see. Gradually, she began to adjust to the darkness.

"Oh, God," she gasped over and over, repositioning herself to kneeling. Abby cried out, "Help!" She sobbed, her throat constricting with fear. "Help me!" she cried out again. "Somebody, please! Please." Her voice trailed off into sobs.

In time, Abby managed to calm herself, to get her bearings as she bought her focus back to her surroundings. She wiped the tears from her eyes and cheeks with the heels of her hands and shifted into a cross-legged position and finally noticed the tenderness on the soles of her feet. Abby grazed her fingers over raised cuts and punctures on them from that daring escape of hers. If that man hadn't shown up, she might've gotten away. She swallowed and drew her knees to her chest, suddenly realizing how cold it was in this room.

Teeth chattering, trembling, and thinking back to the foolishness that put her in this position, Abby shook her head in disgust. "Don't go by yourself, Abby," she scolded herself, repeating Jordan's warning, sobbing, pissed that she hadn't listened. Resolve set in. "Dumb. Dumb move, Abby."

Pushing herself up, Abby limped over to the door and tested it to see if maybe she'd gotten lucky and those people had forgotten to lock it. Of course they hadn't. Resting her forehead against it, she accepted the fact that, barring some miracle, there was no way that she was getting out of here tonight. So she turned and hobbled back over to the mat, carefully lowering herself down onto it, grimacing as she took the weight off of her feet.

Why the hell hadn't she listened to him? She leaned back against the wall behind her and fought back tears. Crying wasn't going to help, but dammit if she didn't feel like bawling her eyes out.

"Things are different now, Abby. We have to take precautions now that people know about you."

To her, Jordan was overthinking the situation and making a big deal out of nothing because she wasn't the rich and famous one in the relationship. He was. So what would anybody want with her?

Each moment was a constant struggle to push away thoughts of not getting out of this room alive — or worse. Would it really go that far, though? Would they kill her? She couldn't allow her mind to give in to that kind of thinking. So Abby forced herself to focus on something else — on him.

She'd agreed to move in with Jordan, temporarily, just to see what it would be like, because she was being silly thinking that she wasn't already living with him when she really was. For the last two months she'd set up camp in his place, leaving her house in Blink to drive the two hours to Dallas to stay with him every couple of days because she couldn't stand to be away from him. Jordan's trips to Blink had lessened as he became more involved with a new division he was setting up to support a contract with the federal government that he'd won, not only to develop a new fuel source for space vehicles but also to come up with a new long-range engine for rockets.

He worked long hours, but she liked being there when he came home at the end of the day, or when he found time between meetings and stole time with her in his penthouse above his office. Abby was at his place three or four days a week on average, but as long as she took her toothbrush with her when she left and headed back home to Blink, it was like she was still holding on to her own life, or sense of separation. Deep down, Abby didn't want to be separated from him, though.

You couldn't be around Jordan and not get lost in his shadow. That's what scared her about being with him. In Blink, she was Abby, and she owned properties, and people knew her, she had her family and her business. In Dallas, with Jordan, she was a woman waiting for him to come home at the end of the day. Abby wrestled with herself to hold on to her own separate and viable identity and not to be swallowed up by the whale-size persona of the man she loved. He loved her, too. And knowing him the way she did, Abby knew that Jordan had to be going crazy right about now worrying over where she might be. It wouldn't surprise her if he was at her house now with the police.

They'd see that she'd fought, and hard, too. Maybe one of those fools who'd taken her had left behind evidence, something that would immediately identify him, and they'd find him, arrest him, and make him tell them everything. She refused to give in to crying again, but fear filled her chest. They had to be caught. If they weren't found, and if they disappeared, then she'd be here, locked in this room, alone, and nobody would ever know where to even look for her.

So many things could go wrong. Abby had to try to get out of here. If she could somehow escape and make her way out to a road or something . . . She'd done it once, already. She'd gotten out of this room, and she could do it again. She had to do it again, and this time, she had to run faster, be smarter.

"They can't keep me here," she said, realizing that she was crying again. "That ain't happening."

She took deep breaths to calm herself. Abby couldn't think rationally if she wasn't calm. Her hands and feet were so cold. The only thing she had was a mat to lie on. She crossed her legs, tucking her feet underneath her thighs as much as she could to try to keep them warm. Abby pulled her arms from the sleeves of her T-shirt and folded them around herself against her skin underneath it.

She closed her eyes and thought back to the conversation she'd heard after being caught.

"Nay," she murmured.

"We can't fuck this up, Nay."

The man had said that. The woman's name was Nay.

"It won't happen again," the woman said.

"She's going to be more careful," Abby surmised in deep contemplation. "Know your enemy."

Abby was going to have to be smarter because she'd nearly gotten away and they were going to be much more careful now.

Her guess was that they wanted to keep her alive at least for the time being. If they'd wanted her dead, they'd have killed her by now. Maybe they'd called Jordan asking for money. They'd have probably told him not to contact the police. She'd seen enough movies to know that that's how it usually worked. She was being held for ransom.

"Good grief," she muttered, shaking her head in disbelief. How silly it all seemed on the surface. Abby felt like a character in a bad movie script. The more she thought about it, the more ridiculous, insane, all this was, and the more she realized that she should've stayed her ass in Dallas.

Love Come in a Hurry

Guests at Ted McCall's cocktail party sounded to a highly preoccupied Jordan like birds chirping. Somehow, he managed to find a way to interact and at least look as if he gave a damn about this event or these people. Jordan made his way out to the massive deck overlooking a large lake to escape the claustrophobia of that crowd, their questions about him and his business endeavors, and the weight of Abby's abduction pressing down on him. He'd been here an hour and decided that that was long enough.

"The insatiable need of the wealthy to get dressed up in fancy suits, dresses, and pretense to talk a lot of nothing and stupid shit never ceases to amaze me."

Jordan turned to see Lars Degan coming out onto the deck.

"Maybe we do it to remind ourselves of who we still are and what we still have," the old man concluded.

126

"How've you been, Lars?" Jordan asked unemotionally.

"Getting older by the second, son."

Jordan made a lame attempt at a smile. "Why should you be any different from the rest of us?"

Lars Degan and Jordan went way back to the beginning, to when Jordan, at twenty, suddenly inherited his father's kingdom and damn near drove it into the ground.

Lars sighed. "Oh, I think you've likely found a way to escape the perils of old age, young man," he said with a chuckle. "Clean and righteous living certainly does have its benefits."

"Sarcasm has always been your strong suit, Lars. Fortunately, I've become immune to it."

"That's because you're smarter than most," he said unemotionally. "Always have been. Congratulations on that new federal contract," he quickly added. "You're in the space business now. Oil and gas weren't enough for you?"

"Oil and gas have their limits. Space does not."

For a moment, the two men made eye contact and locked on to each other in silence.

Lars turned his attention back to the view

in front of him. "And we both know, you have no limits," he said introspectively. "Isn't that right?"

Thirty years ago, Jordan had looked to Lars Degan almost as a father figure. After Julian Gatewood died, Jordan depended on Lars to help teach him how to run a corporation. The old man nearly destroyed him, but time and invaluable lessons Jordan had learned from Degan had dulled any animosity he'd once held against the man.

Jordan finished the last of his drink, turned, and patted Lars on the shoulder. "Good night, Lars," he said, turning to leave.

"Leaving so soon?" Lars tilted his head to one side. "Was it something I said?"

Jordan shook his head. "Early meetings in the morning. That's all." He smiled and left.

On the drive home, the empty seat next to him resonated with Abby's absence. She wasn't just back at home in Blink, Texas. She wasn't even a phone call away and he couldn't just reach out to her the way he'd become so accustomed to doing. For some strange reason, his mind locked on to a memory and he allowed it the space it needed to play out while he continued his journey home.

"Hey, boss," Phyl said over the phone.

Jordan had arrived at the governor's mansion nearly an hour ago, and Abby still hadn't arrived.

"Where are you?" he asked, stepping away from the crowd to a more secluded corner of the room.

"We're about five minutes out."

"Tell him it was my fault that we're late," he heard Abby say in the background.

"She'll be there soon." Phyl sighed.

"Well, if it isn't the country's newest billionaire," a black man, maybe slightly older than Jordan, said, approaching Jordan with a handshake as he ended the call.

Jordan's expression must've begged the question.

"Senator Sam Addison," he said proudly. "We met at the launch ceremony for Variant's new Synthetic Fuels division back in October," he reminded Jordan.

Jordan couldn't remember meeting Addison, but he'd heard the name. "Nice to see you again, Senator," he said cordially.

"Oh, the pleasure's mine, sir." He rested a firm hand on Jordan's shoulder. "And congratulations are certainly in order. Gatewood Industries was already impressive, but this new government contract really takes it to new heights."

The man talked too loud on purpose, making sure that he was seen and heard, wearing thin on Jordan's patience.

"Well, thank you, Senator," he said humbly. "But winning the contract was the easy part. The real challenge will be living up to my end of this very difficult challenge."

Addison's head reared back as he laughed.

"It's a tall order, for sure," Addison finally composed himself and said.

Jordan might have missed it had he blinked, that all too familiar glimmer of something warning Jordan not to let his guard down around men like Addison. He'd seen it too many times to ignore or to miss.

"Well, the taxpaying citizens of this country are counting on you to make it happen. Now's not the time to start second-guessing your-self."

"I wouldn't have bid on it if I wasn't confident that I could make it happen."

Maybe it was what Jordan had said or how he'd said it, but all of a sudden that cocky at-titude of the senator slithered down his spine like a snake.

"You've got the attention of a lot of people, son," he said, sounding dangerously conde-scending.

"I've had it for as long as I can remember, Senator," Jordan retorted.

Just then his cell phone vibrated in his

pocket. It was a text from Phyl.

"We just pulled up in front. Abby's on her way in. Look up."

"Excuse me," Jordan said abruptly, leaving the man standing there with his mouth open, and heading over to the massive double-sided staircase.

He looked up at the landing. Moments later Abby appeared and Jordan froze where he was.

"Damn," he murmured to himself.

He was hardly a poet, but she looked like something otherworldly stepping out from the crowd and onto that landing. The sky-blue dress layered with stones that sparkled like stars looked magical against the contrast of her smooth, dark skin. There wasn't much to it. It was simple, with a dramatic V neckline highlighting Abby's full and lovely breasts, thin straps left her soft shoulders exposed, and the dress fit like it was painted on to her. She'd cut her hair months ago, but it was perfect, revealing the delicate slope of her pretty neck and curve of her cheekbones. Without hair to hide behind, Abby's big brown eyes were even more dramatic, her lips more pronounced.

Jordan was so captivated by her appearance that it took him a few minutes to realize she'd spotted him in the crowd and was looking to him for some indication of which staircase she should use. It wasn't until then that he realized he wasn't the only man in the room captivated by her. Her lips curved into an appreciative but hesitant smile when she realized that she had his attention. Jordan began moving to the left staircase. Abby followed, and as she started to make her way down the steps toward him, he subtly raised his hand to stop her. She wasn't supposed to come to him. It was his role to go to her.

The two of them stood on the staircase for several moments before either of them said a word. Jordan couldn't take his eyes off of her.

She looked uncomfortable by his staring. "I don't think I've ever been this dressed up in my life," she said nervously.

Jordan absently raised his hand to her waist.

"You look so handsome," she murmured appreciatively.

And she took his breath away. Jordan compulsively leaned close to her and planted a soft kiss on her cheek and shoulder. Abby sighed and pressed against him, sending shock waves up his spine.

"You stay close to me," he said softly. "And hold on to me."

He straightened up and stared into her eyes.

Abby smiled. "You know I've got no problem staying close to you."

He wished she were close to him now.

More than anything he wished that. Five months ago, his corporation, Gatewood Industries, had been awarded one of the largest defense contracts in years to help develop not only a new fuel alternative for rocket engines but also a new engine, one more cost-effective than what was currently being used and more powerful. The contract was worth billions; so, consequently, was Jordan's net worth. Before the ink had even dried on those contracts, Jordan's face was plastered on magazines and the Internet, touting him as the wealthiest black man in the country.

He found it odd that Buffett and Gates were never referred to as the richest white men in the country, but ultimately, none of it mattered. Jordan was the same man he'd been before that government deal, and right now, he was up to his eyebrows in starting up a brand-new division and knocking heads with a ton of engineers, physicists, and scientists, looking for a starting point on this project.

He had a "very big life," according to Abby, and she was terrified of it. But he had no intention of letting it swallow her up, despite her misgivings. Jordan was quickly mastering the art of tightening the wide-reaching net that had anything to do with him, and shrinking it to a size she was comfortable with.

He thought he'd been careful. Jordan had made a promise more to himself than to her that he'd keep her from being overwhelmed by the residuals of being with a man like him. And he'd failed. Jordan tried to swallow the lump in his throat as he turned into the parking garage of Gatewood Industries. If anything happened to her, if they — she — didn't survive this then what would happen to him?

Abby struggled to stay awake, but the cold was making it difficult. She'd hobbled around on her sore feet in circles in that small space for at least an hour, trying to keep her blood flowing and to warm up. Abby relied on her memories to keep her company, the one of the night she and Jordan had gone to the Governor's Ball in his mansion.

Making her way back over to the mat, she sat back down against the wall, crossed her legs, and pulled her arms back inside her shirt. That night was so fresh in her mind that she recalled every detail as if she were living in that moment all over again.

Abby was introduced to politicians, celebrities, and professional athletes, all of whom seemed to revere Jordan, or at least what he represented. And maybe it was just her, but he seemed to stand a little taller than everyone else, his shoulders a bit broader, perhaps. Even the Texas governor paled in comparison to tall, handsome, and regal Jordan Gatewood.

She was a curiosity, even though people were too polite to say it. But it was obvious that Abby was an outsider, not a regular fixture on the social scene in Dallas.

That was his world, and those people were his tribe. For the first time, Jordan was showing her what it was like to be him, a glimpse into his whole life and not just that part of him that took her to nightclubs, his ranch, or out to get ice cream.

"Are you all right, sugah?" He bent slightly to ask her.

She smiled. "I am," she said softly, squeezing a bit closer to him. Damn! She loved it when he called her "sugah."

"Let's go get some air," he suggested.

"Air is good," she said, sounding like a cave woman.

More people reached out to Jordan as he led a winding path through the mansion with her closely in tow. But he dismissed them with a curt smile, a nod, and a grunt of something that sounded like "Good seeing you." Finally, they were outside in the courtyard that was just as crowded as the inside of the mansion, but Jordan took hold of Abby's hand and searched until he finally found a marble bench hidden behind a giant rosebush on the other side of one of the smaller fountains.

Jordan pulled off his jacket, draped it over Abby's shoulders. Abby inhaled deeply, drawing in the scent of him coming off that tuxedo jacket.

"I must admit," he began, "you're holding up better than I expected."

"Well, you notice I ain't saying too much."

"Feeling shy?"

"No." She shook her head. "Just trying not to embarrass you."

Jordan knitted his thick brows. "There's absolutely nothing that you could say or do that would embarrass me, love."

"Oh, there's plenty," she quipped.

"Examples."

"Well, the governor's wife?"

"Yes?"

"Terrible calluses on her heels," Abby said, grimacing. "You'd think that woman would have a standing appointment with a pedicurist seeing as how her husband is head of the state and all. I wanted to pull her aside and recommend a great pumice stone that I found on Amazon that she could use in the privacy of her own home," she continued. "You know, because maybe she doesn't like people touching her feet or something."

He chuckled.

"Some people can be like that, Jordan," she said in all seriousness. "They don't like strangers touching them, and I get that."

"Anything else?"

She thought about it for a moment. There were lots of things. Suddenly, she smiled. "When we met Floyd Dawson, the running back?"

"Did he have calluses on his heels, too?"

"No. But my brother Wesley is a huge fan. I mean big *big* fan, in a stupid kind of way. My sister-in-law, Eva, told me that he still sleeps in that man's jersey during football season. Sleeps in it, Jordan. And I was this close" — Abby pinched her thumb and forefinger together — "to asking him for his autograph and telling him about Wesley's obsession. But if I'd done that and Wes had found out about it, he'd have been so wounded."

"Yeah, we don't want to wound Wes."

"I've exercised magnanimous restraint tonight," she said proudly.

"And I appreciate it."

"I could walk out of here with a dozen autographs if I set my whole country self loose on these people. But I'm being careful."

137

He chuckled.

A man like him could be with any woman he wanted. Abby had caught quite a few of them glaring and rolling their eyes at her, and then looking at him like he was a Texas-size T-bone steak. When the two of them were alone together, he was just Jordan, her handsome, brooding boyfriend who smelled good and made her stomach turn flips every time she locked on to those mysterious dark eyes of his. But when she read about him on the Internet or saw a story about him on the news, it didn't seem possible that she would even know someone like him.

"You never said anything about my dress," she said, finally broaching the subject.

She'd hoped that he loved it as much as she loved wearing it, but since he hadn't mentioned it, Abby prepared herself for the worst.

Jordan's gaze immediately dropped to her cleavage. Never in a million years did it ever cross her mind that she could wear a spaghetti-strapped dress without a bra and have her titties sitting firm like rocks.

"I've hardly been able to keep my eyes off you," he said admiringly. "I thought that you'd have guessed that not only do I love your dress, sugah, but I love you in the dress."

Abby smiled and blushed. "Thank you.

That's the answer I was hoping for."

"No, thank *you.*"

"For what?"

Those penetrating eyes of his bore into hers, and Abby could literally feel herself melting like a candle all up against him.

"For agreeing to come to this with me. For looking absolutely beautiful in that dress. I'll start there."

"It's not as hard as I thought it would be, actually. Being here, I mean. It's the fanciest thing I've ever been to in my life, and I thought I'd hate it, but it doesn't suck."

He cocked a thick brow. "Sounds like my chances for talking you into moving in with me are getting better. Odds moving in my favor?"

He was adorable in his persistence but highly unreasonable. Jordan broached the subject of the two of them living together every chance he got.

"You already know what I'm going to say," she said softly. "We've had this discussion dozens of times and the dialogue never changes."

"Because you're being stubborn."

"Because you and I both know that me moving here would mean giving up my business in Blink. Because we both know that even if I didn't give it up, I couldn't run it from Dallas.

Because I'm not the type to sit around eating bonbons all day, or lunching with those high-society types, or whatever — while you're at the office being fabulous and conquering the world."

He looked unconvinced. In the time that she'd known Jordan, Abby had come to realize a few things about him. Jordan had lived privilege his whole life. He knew absolutely nothing else and wasn't accustomed to not getting his way.

"You're here more than you're in Blink, Abby," he reminded her. "And it's becoming increasingly difficult for me to keep up with the two-hour commute each way to see you."

"But it's working, Jordan. Right?"

"Like I said," he concluded, "you're being stubborn."

No. She was being realistic. She was being careful.

"I'm not an impulsive person," she reminded him. "It goes against my nature."

"It's not an impulsive request," he said sincerely. "I am in love for the first time in my life and I want — no, I need — to have you with me, Abby. Preferably all the time. That's all."

Good Lord! Was he making her light-headed again? Seemed like the space around her was spinning and she was sitting still. Yes. Abby was definitely caught up in a dizzying moment.

He smiled as if he knew it. "Tell me you're thinking about it," he continued. "During the week, we'd stay at the penthouse. I'd be right downstairs in my office, baby. On the weekends, we could go to the ranch. When I traveled, you could come with me."

Jordan had been practicing his argument. And his offer was becoming more and more tempting. Being away from him for more than a few days was becoming harder. It was always so hard to leave him, and she could never seem to get back to him fast enough. That practical side of her kept rearing her ugly little head, though.

"I swear," he continued, "I'd spoil you rotten if you'd just get out of my way and let me."

Abby had always prided herself on being levelheaded and rational. But for the first time in her life, she sort of hated those personality traits.

"I don't think I'd know how to let you spoil me, Jordan," she reluctantly admitted.

"You could start by not telling me no all the time," he offered. "You could trust me."

"I do trust you," she responded quickly.

"With you. With all of you."

And that's the part that scared her the most. Jordan wanted her absolutely and completely, accessible and available at all times. There wasn't anything wrong with that, because she wanted him too, but just because you want something doesn't mean it's necessarily good for you. He had big expectations. But Abby wasn't so sure that she could live up to his expectations or that she really wanted to.

"You're taking too long to respond," he finally said. "What does that mean?"

Abby leaned in close and kissed him tenderly on his sexy lips. "It means . . . I don't know what it means."

Jordan sighed and his disappointment was obvious. "I'm not giving up. We'll have this conversation again," he said, helping her to her feet. "And again, and again, until I finally wear you down."

And he was doing just that.

"Let's get out of here," he said, taking hold of her hand. "I'm ready to go make love."

" 'Bout time," she said without hesitation.

"Good night, Jordan," Abby shivered and whispered to herself as a warm tear escaped down her cheek.

■ ■ ■ ■

Day 2

■ ■ ■ ■

In My Dawn

It was four in the morning. Jordan had just finished swimming laps in the pool and was physically and emotionally exhausted. Fear was his greatest enemy. It pressed against him like a cement wall, threatening to crush him, but he couldn't allow it. He pushed back, and would keep on pushing until he held her in his arms. Jordan physically willed his heart to beat slow and steady, taking deep breaths to calm and settle his mind and emotions. Abby had become the sun in the center of his universe, and he would die if her light went out.

He leaned back on the sofa outside on the terrace of his penthouse, staring out over the lights of Dallas.

"Call Wells," he commanded. His voice-activated communication system immediately dialed the number.

Jordan hadn't expected that sonofabitch to answer, but this call, like all the others, needed to be made.

"I'm not going away," he said when the call went to voice mail. "You call me and you tell me something — what you're doing, where you've been, what you've seen, what you think you know," he finished, and took a sip of his coffee. "End call." The system responded accordingly.

Faces, familiar and unfamiliar, flashed in his mind. That feeling that whoever was behind this wasn't a stranger nagged at him. Paranoia had him convinced that he was being watched, studied like a cell under a microscope. What were they hoping to see? A crack in his façade, perhaps? Were they waiting to catch a glimpse of him in a weak moment? To someone out there, this was a game.

They knew enough to understand how much she meant to him and that losing her could destroy him. Jordan had affirmed that for them in his response to that picture the woman on the phone had sent him. It was a knee-jerk reaction, a very uncharacteristic one, but it was an honest one. He had no idea if acting as if he didn't give a damn about some random woman in a photograph would've played in his — Abby's — favor. They might've killed her sooner. The question remained, though, how did anyone know that she'd be in Blink that day? Jordan hadn't even known. Had she been followed?

"Call Phyl."

She picked up on the second ring.

"Hey, boss," she said, sounding as if she'd been sleeping.

"Good morning," he responded unemotionally.

"What's up?"

"I asked for information on the Dakota Pipeline investors yesterday."

"Yes. I've managed to find out some things, but I'm still looking."

"Send me what you have."

"Sure. Now?"

"Please."

"Okay," she agreed. "You'll have it in a few minutes."

It wasn't in his nature to wait. Jordan had hired Wells to find Abby, but he wasn't about to idly sit around on his hands while seconds ticked by on the clock until that happened. Jordan had to find out who was behind this. For his own sake, he had to focus his attention on finding the source. Doing nothing would drive him insane.

He closed his eyes and searched for that wavelength traveling through the air from her to him. They were connected at the soul level, and he should've been able to track her down like a blood-hound. But he felt helpless.

They promised she'd be safe, but he didn't bank on that promise. Abby was bleeding in that picture and if — when — he found her, when he got her back, he'd fucking make them pay for what they'd done. Rage. More than fear, more than anguish, it was rage that flowed through his veins as reckless as fear if he weren't careful.

Two hours later, Jordan was showered, dressed, and sitting in his office at his computer studying the information that Phyl had e-mailed him. There were no surprises in her report. Jordan already knew of these corporate investors on the project. He had to take a different approach with this information. Which investor would benefit most from his involvement? Who held a grudge against him? Was this about money? Instinctively, he knew that it wasn't. This was personal. It was about Jordan.

His telecommunication system alerted him to an incoming call from his personal assistant, Phyl Mays.

"This is Jordan," he said out loud, activating the call.

"Hey, boss," she said. "Just want to let

you know that the helicopter's ready and Jake will be there to pick you up to take you to the launch pad in half an hour."

"Thank you."

Aesop wrote, "We often give our enemies the means of our own destruction." Had Jordan given them Abby simply by openly showing his love for her? And was it really so obvious that she was his weakness, more than his wife, Claire, had been? More than the last woman he'd openly dated, Robin, had been? Abby was that crack in the armor he'd never believed he'd ever have. And someone else had noticed.

"Mr. Gatewood," the man said, holding open the car door for him half an hour after he'd spoken to Phyl.

"Jake. How are you?" Jordan responded absently, climbing into the backseat.

"Good, sir. We'll be there in twenty minutes."

He dialed Wells's number. The call went straight to voice mail, much to Jordan's irritation. Jordan hung up.

He had a long day ahead of him, beginning in Houston. He had to keep up appearances for an event that he'd committed to months ago, but Jordan would not sit by idly waiting on Wells. If Jordan found her first, that mutha fucka would have to walk

away from the arrangement he'd made with
Jordan empty-handed.

A Little While Longer

It was morning and the room was gradually warming a bit, but Abby's hands and feet still felt like ice. She tried not to think about being back in her own house, in her bed, curled up underneath warm blankets. Or even better, curled up against Jordan's chest. She tried not to think about that, but when she did, an unexpected and slight smile spread over her lips. Of all the places she could be in the world, that was probably her most favorite. Jordan's broad shoulders and chest, with his huge arms cocooning her, was heaven on earth for real. The soothing drumbeat of his heart echoed through her even now.

That someone like him could come into her life at all was a miracle. But that's how she knew that it was meant to be. Abby thought back to the day she first saw him coming into the house she'd just bought.

"I loved you the moment I saw you," he'd

told her a few months back.

"Impossible," she said. "I did not make myself very lovable that day."

He smiled. God! When he smiled . . . "You may not have, but that did nothing to deter my intentions."

"Which were . . . ?"

"To make you love me back."

Abby took a deep breath and renewed her faith in him. She had to, because it was the only thing she had to cling to — that, and finding a way out of this place. She was an engineer, a problem solver. They had her locked in a box, but that didn't mean that she couldn't find a way out of it. He would find her, and she would meet him at the door when he did. Abby wasn't used to playing that damsel in distress role. She'd reminded herself of that after she'd finished all that crying at sunrise.

Once again, Abby heard noises from the other side of the door. A key turned in the lock. The door pushed open and it was the woman again. Her first thought was to try to rush her like before, but no. This time, the woman had a gun tucked in the belt around her waist. The woman stepped just inside the doorway, knelt down, and placed the sandwich enclosed in a plastic bag on the floor along with another bottle of water.

"Eat," she said, slowly standing up.

Abby knew that they'd be more careful because she'd nearly gotten away the first time, but for some reason, she didn't expect a gun. Guns had a way of dampening the spirit of an escape and Abby had been taught that most people didn't point guns at people unless they intended to shoot them.

The woman's hair had been pulled back this time into a braid. And she still had on that mask. Time. Abby needed to calm herself and to take advantage of this time with her. She couldn't be impatient. She couldn't be impulsive because her life truly was on the line now.

"I'm not telling you again," the woman said.

Abby heard a slight shakiness in the woman's voice. Whoever she was, she was as afraid of Abby as Abby was of her. Abby started to stand up.

"No," the woman told her. "Stay off your feet," she warned.

Abby slowly slid across the floor on her behind until she was close enough to reach the sandwich and water. Was she really going to eat this mess? She had to if she wanted to take advantage of this time, this opportunity to look for even a sliver of a chance to get the hell out of here. She stared at the package, flipping it over in her hands until finally she pulled apart the sealed seam, then smelled the contents. Would they try to poison her if they were expecting to be paid money for her return? She twisted off the cap on the bottle, raised it to her nose and smelled that, too.

"Hurry the hell up," the woman snapped.

She was thirsty. Reluctantly, she pulled the sandwich from the plastic bag, lifted up and examined both slices of bread, and did the same thing to the single slice of ham. It looked fine, but —

"For crying out loud!" the woman exclaimed, stepping over and reaching down to take the food.

"No!" Abby jerked back, startling the woman, who immediately reached for her gun and pointed it at Abby. "I just . . . You can't blame me," she said, instinctively raising her hand in front of her as if she could actually stop a bullet. It was a dumb thing to do and she slowly lowered it. "You know you can't."

The woman stepped back inside the doorway and waited.

Abby took a cautious bite and chewed slowly, carefully, until she eventually swallowed. She was hungrier than she'd thought and immediately took another bite, chewing faster this time. She'd eaten about half of the sandwich when she finally gagged.

"Don't you dare," the woman threatened.

Abby took a drink from the bottle to help keep her food down. Crying? Why the hell did the tears decide to come now? They came because there was no mustard on this sandwich, and because she couldn't be sure that there wasn't poison in it or in this water. Because this bitch was standing over her with a gun, forcing her to eat. The tears came because she was here in this place away from her home, away from Jordan, her family. No one knew she was here. No one knew how to find her. She pushed the other half of the sandwich away and finished what was left in that bottle.

"That's all," she said, shaking her head, disgusted. "I can't eat any more."

Abby wiped away the tears and slid back across the room over to the mat, drew her knees to her chest, and prayed that she could keep that food down. As she'd eaten, Abby looked for signs of that key, but the woman must've shoved it into the pocket of her jeans.

"I . . . I need to use the bathroom," she reluctantly said.

It was the truth. Abby had to pee. The

woman noticeably tensed. She hesitated for a moment as if the thought never occured to her that Abby would ever have to use the bathroom. Abruptly she left the room, closing and even locking the door, returning a few moments later with a small, dirty plastic bowl.

"In the bowl," she said simply.

"What?" Abby asked, stunned.

"You pee in the bowl."

Abby hesitated, half expecting the woman to laugh and tell her that she was just joking, but she wasn't.

"I have . . . to stand up," Abby told her.

The woman waited as Abby rose to her feet, reluctantly pulled down her shorts, squatted, and relieved herself in that bowl while the woman waited and watched. The humiliation of the situation weighed on Abby almost as much as the fear that these people would kill her.

Abby finished relieving herself and reached for a napkin in the sandwich bag to wipe herself before pulling up her shorts. She picked up the bowl and held it out to the woman.

"Take two steps," she instructed Abby, "and put it on the floor and then get back in that corner."

Abby did as she was told.

"Do you think I can get a blanket?" Abby asked shakily.

The woman collected Abby's trash and that bowl.

"It's so cold in here, especially at night," she explained.

The woman took a pensive stance, but she looked as if she wanted to hurry to leave.

"Please," Abby said, swallowing her pride. "Or some sweats? Socks?"

The woman stared at her for several moments before leaving without saying another word and locking the door behind her. Abby stared at the door, specifically, at the extremely narrow gap between the bottom of the door and the floor. The seams between the door and the wall were practically nonexistent. Practically. Was there a way to wedge it open in a way that the woman wouldn't notice?

A few minutes later, Abby heard the key again and the woman opened the door wide enough to stick her arm through it and drop a thick blanket on the floor, then quickly pulled the door shut again and locked it. Abby stared at the blanket crumpled on the floor like she was looking to find the meaning of life in that thing. The fact that the woman had brought it to her definitely did mean something. It meant that she had some empathy and that she didn't want Abby freezing to death. She was feeding Abby, giving her water, and now she'd given her a blanket.

Of course she picked it up carefully and shook it out, half expecting to see a snake wrapped up in the damn thing. But there was nothing. It was just a blanket. Not much bigger than a throw, but it was better than nothing. And she appreciated it. Abby examined the construction, hoping to find something on it, anything, that she could possibly use as a door jamb. She went back over to the mat, sat down on it, and tried to come up with 1,001 different ways to use a blanket to save her life.

I GOT MY PATIENCE

Gatewood had called. *"I'm not going away. You call me and you tell me something — what you're doing, where you've been, what you've seen, what you think you know."*

Plato didn't answer because he didn't have anything to tell him and because he didn't dig the way the dude was sweating him. How the hell a cat like that had ever managed to stumble across an Abby was beyond puzzling. The two of them weren't exactly like peas and carrots. But then, who was Plato to question chemistry?

"Something's wrong with Shou Shou," Marlowe said, sitting down at the breakfast table next to Plato.

Plato heaved a forkful of buttered grits mixed with scrambled eggs into his mouth. Shou, Marlowe's aunt, gave Plato's big ass the shudders. That old woman was blind as a bat, but she had a way of knowing things and doing things that should've been impossible for her to know and do. Beautiful honey-gold Marlowe furrowed her lovely arched brows and glanced at him, worried and expectant.

Gatewood had asked him if there wasn't someone in his life he'd die for or fight for. And he was looking at her. She was looking at him, too, waiting for him to respond appropriately.

"I'm supposed to ask, 'What's wrong with her?' " he said.

"Exactly." She smiled. Oh, those pretty lips of hers were mesmerizing. "Belle says she's been quiet the last few days."

"And that's a bad thing?"

"Shou's never quiet. She's always got something to say."

He took a bite of bacon.

"Belle said that Shou called her in the middle of the night but hardly said more than a few words to her," she explained, concerned. "When Belle asked if she should come over, Shou told her not to, but Belle went anyway."

"And?"

"Physically, she was fine. But she seemed distant, according to Belle. Like she had something on her mind, but she couldn't say what it was."

Plato had no idea why Marlowe was coming to him with anything to do with Shou Shou. He kept his distance from the old woman, as much as possible, which she didn't seem to mind.

"You've been quiet, too," Marlowe continued.

He certainly had been. Plato was working, and the cardinal rule agreed upon between the two of them was that when he was working, he would keep her out of it and she wouldn't try to get in it. She knew the drill.

Marlowe stared knowingly at him. "Are you going to be leaving soon?"

Typically, his job took him out of town. Sometimes, out of the country, away from home and her. Abby Rhodes was her friend. And Plato found himself perched precariously between one hard-ass rock and the proverbial hard place. Keeping a part of his life secret was his way of keeping his lady love safe. Plato never knew who or what he might run up against in his line of work, and he wanted to make damn sure that none of it ever boomeranged back around to her. Basically, the less she knew about certain facets of his life, the better.

This was different. This was personal for her, but even now he felt it best not to mention that he was searching for her friend who'd been abducted from her house less than twenty minutes from this one.

"I could be," he answered, purposefully leaving it at that.

He was considering getting away from the house, maybe renting a room in Clark City or something, just to ease the pressure of trying to keep his mouth shut around Marlowe about Abby, or to keep her from using that whole sixth sense thing of hers to somehow figure it out. A part of him believed that maybe Marlowe or that crazy aunt of hers could look into a crystal ball and tell him where Abby was, making this job a whole lot easier. But then again, he needed to hold to his oath, that keeping Marlowe safe meant keeping her out of his business. And even if he did ask them to read his palm or stare into a crystal ball or read tea leaves, what if they still came up empty? She'd know too much and she could panic and do or say something to the wrong people. Blink was small. And he was convinced that somebody in town, maybe even somebody who knew Abby, was somehow involved.

Marlowe stared at him as if reading his mind.

"I love it when you look at me," he said warmly, "except when you look at me like that."

"Like what?"

He shoveled more food into his mouth. "Like you're trying to see something that you've got no business looking for."

"There you go again, being paranoid," she said softly, reaching across the table and taking hold of his hand. "I'm just looking at you, baby."

Marlowe cast spells. Especially when it came to him. He was convinced of it. Why else would he have strayed so far off his beaten and destined path to end up here, in Blink? Beautiful and bountiful breasts pressed against the material of her blouse. Was it his imagination, or were her nipples hardening right before his eyes? Was his dick swelling in response?

"You are vexing me, sweetheart," he said with warning as Marlowe laced her fingers with his.

She chuckled and he wondered if he should take that as confirmation. Plato could forgo what was left of his breakfast, carry this curvy woman up the stairs to the bedroom, and make lazy love to her until he was utterly empty.

Abby needed him to find her.

He finished his coffee. "I'm working, baby," he said, tenderly kissing her head as he reluctantly stood up to leave.

Disappointment shadowed her face. He could live with that for now. But what he couldn't live with was not finding Abby Rhodes alive because he opted to postpone his search for her and make love to his woman. Plato walked out of that house with a dick so hard it hurt.

"It's customary in my line of work for my employer to give me time to resolve the issue I've been commissioned to resolve," he explained to Gatewood's voice mail.

This dude was understandably desperate to get his woman back safe and sound. But sweating Plato was not the answer.

"I will be in touch when I have a reason to be." He abruptly hung up.

The truth was, he had nothing. More than a day had passed and he still had no idea where to even begin to look for this woman. Her truck was missing along with her. So whoever had taken her wanted to make it look as if she wasn't home. The blood on the walls was likely Abby's. That matchstick he'd found could've been something. Could've been nothing. He drove back to her house once more. He was in and out in five minutes with no new clues to speak of.

Plato sat in his car and studied the photograph of Abby. After some consideration,

Plato texted it to a number in his phone, then followed up with a call.

"Wonder Boy!" he exclaimed. "It's me."

"Who?" the young lad responded.

"Me."

"Oh. You sent me something."

"I did."

"Wow," the dude said. "She looks to be in dire straits."

"She is. I need you to take that photo apart and find me some clues."

He sighed. "It's gonna cost you a couple of grand."

"Fine."

"And I suppose you need it in a hurry."

"Look at her. Of course I need it in a hurry."

Again with the sighing. "I'll see what I can find."

"Do that," he said, hanging up.

RUN THIS GAME

Jordan had been asked to be the keynote at the Texas Coalition of Business and Corporate Leaders annual brunch. If he hadn't agreed to speak at the event, he would have sent his apologies and opted out of the invitation. Needless to say, his paranoia had risen to new heights. Jordan shook hands and nodded acknowledgments with dozens of people on his way into the banquet hall filled with close to a thousand attendees.

Most were strangers to him, but Jordan recognized a few faces: Marshall Walsh, CEO of Variant; Amanda Coefield, who headed up Coefield Construction; and Brandon Degan, who sat at the helm of Degan Oil and Gas Refinery, started by his father, Lars. He smiled and made small talk where needed, but he met each gaze with laserlike intensity, forcing himself to appear unbothered and not at all concerned that the woman he loved might already be dead.

Sitting through speech after speech, poking at overcooked eggs and undercooked bacon, Jordan did everything he could to act like he gave a damn about being here. Even managing to force himself to swallow a bite of toast.

"We are honored to have as our keynote today a man who really needs no introduction, but I'm going to give him one anyway," the woman at the podium said, smiling.

The crowd laughed as she went on to read Jordan's accomplishments from the time he'd taken the helm at Gatewood Industries to now, thankfully leaving out his long list of failures and very public but personal tragedies. Applause filled the room as he made his way up the stairs and across the stage to the podium. Every move he'd made the past few days had been with robotic purpose. It took everything inside him to make himself look and sound convincing, to inject humor and sincerity in a way that looked and resonated as genuine.

Hiding the truth of the chaos and turmoil churning inside Jordan drained him. But he had to stand tall, to appear to be the man they all believed him to be and not the one unraveling inside because the love of his fucking life had been snatched right out from underneath his nose. It had taken him a lifetime to find Abby. Jordan had resigned himself to the fact that he had done so much shit in his life that the gods would deny him the kind of peace and love and contentment that came packaged in her. He figured that Karma had had enough of his antics and had shoved emptiness and loneliness in his face to last the rest of his life, and then, out of the blue, in Blink, Texas, of all places, there she was. She was everything he'd never had and always wanted and needed. To go back to a life without her in it was unacceptable and impossible.

"Thank you all," he said warmly, eventually wrapping up his speech. "Enjoy your breakfasts." Jordan even managed to smile, but it nearly killed him to do it.

He located the organizer of the event, explained that he had another meeting to attend, and left through the private entrance out to his waiting car. Jordan climbed in the back, and for the first time all damn day, he took a breath.

The first thing he did was check the voice mail left to him by Wells. Jordan immediately called him back. This time, he answered.

"I guess you got my message," Wells stated flippantly.

"And you got mine," Jordan retorted.

"I got nothing to tell you."

Jordan ground his teeth together. "What the hell have you been doing?"

"My job."

Jordan waited for him to elaborate.

"I went to the house yesterday," Wells reluctantly continued. "She put up a fight, but other than that, I've got nothing."

Jordan's heart felt as if it had dropped to his stomach like a rock.

"What are you planning on doing next?"

"It doesn't work like this, man," Wells warned. "You can't expect me to do what I need to while you're riding my ass like I'm a gotdamn horse."

Reason and logic understood what he was saying. But logic had been swept up into a vortex of desperation. Nothing this man was saying resonated.

"What's your next move?" Jordan demanded to know.

Wells sighed. "When I figure it out, you'll be the first to know," he said, abruptly ending the call.

Jordan immediately called back, but of course that fool didn't pick up.

A few minutes later, his executive assistant, Jennifer, called. "You'll have an hour after we land before you have to get to your next meeting, Jordan," she said. "Did you eat at the brunch? If not, I can order you some lunch if you'd like."

Suddenly a question flashed in his mind. Could she be involved in this? How long had she been working for him? A few years? Jennifer knew his schedule better than he did. But she didn't interact too much with Abby. Phyl did, though. Jordan immediately felt ridiculous for even considering that Jennifer or Phyl could have anything to do with Abby's abduction, but then again, he'd have been a fool to not consider all the possibilities. Phyl knew more about him than even Jennifer. She knew where he'd be on any given day at any given time. She knew Abby. Phyl was the last person Abby had spoken to before she'd left the penthouse and headed back to Blink.

"Jordan?" Jennifer asked uneasily. "Are you all right?"

He was anything but all right. "A ham and cheese sandwich from Wanda's." Wanda's was a deli a block away from Gatewood Industries.

"Fries, coleslaw, or chips?"

"Just the sandwich," he eventually said. "And were you able to get me those financials I asked for?"

"Yes. I sent them to your in-box ten minutes ago."

Ending the call, he began to contemplate

just how close Phyl and Abby had become. Besides Jordan, Abby spent more time with Phyl than with anyone else in Dallas. Was it possible that she'd mentioned her trip back to Blink to Phyl? Jordan's thoughts were beginning to make him uncomfortable.

A few weeks ago, Jordan got a call from Phyl.

"We've been to three stores, and she won't buy anything," Phyl said in a whisper over the phone.

Jordan was in the middle of a workout with 225 pounds pressed above his chest.

"This can't wait, Phyl?" he asked irritably and out of breath.

"I just don't know what to do, boss," Phyl admitted. "You said to take her shopping. Well, I've been trying and she won't shop. So I'm stumped."

"Text me . . . the address where . . . you are and wait . . . for me."

Half an hour later, Jordan walked through the door of some women's boutique in downtown Dallas, still wearing shorts, a sweaty T-shirt, and sneakers.

"May I help you, sir?" a woman asked, greeting him.

Phyl waved to him from across the room, and Jordan headed back in her direction. He was just about to ask Phyl what the hell was going on when Abby came out of the dressing room wearing a form-fitting strapless, shimmering gold gown that stopped him dead in his tracks. Apparently, she didn't see him, though, as she stepped up on the center stand in front of the mirrors, followed by an anxious saleswoman who looked like she'd fallen in love with Abby in that dress. Hell, Jordan was in love with Abby in that dress.

"Shoes," the woman muttered nervously, rushing over to boxes strewn on the floor in one corner of the room, then knelt and slipped high-heeled sandals onto Abby's feet. Then the woman stepped back, clasped her hands together, and gasped.

Abby stared at her reflection like she was seeing herself for the first time. "This is so . . . Wow," she said, in awe of her reflection. Jordan didn't want to move. He didn't want her to know that he was there, not until he'd finished soaking up the breathtaking view of this woman. It all worked. It was all perfect. She was perfect.

"How much is it?" Abby blurted out, breaking the spell for every damn body.

The woman suddenly looked like she was going to be sick.

"Oh, boy," Phyl muttered, shaking her head.

It was obviously time for Jordan to step in.

He walked up to where she was standing. The shoes and the fact that she was standing on that platform put her at eye level with him, and he appeared as if by magic when she turned back around from asking that ridiculous question to the saleswoman to face the mirrors.

"Oh!" she said, startled.

Jordan stood close enough to kiss.

"What you are you doing here?" she asked, after composing herself. "Did Phyl call —" She turned to Phyl. "Did you call him?"

Phyl came out of hiding. "I had to. You're driving me crazy, Abby. We've been out here for hours and the only thing you bought was a belt."

"It was on sale," Abby mouthed.

"I like this," Jordan said, ignoring the conversations around him and staring at Abby's lovely breasts swelling at the top of that dress.

"You shouldn't be here, Jordan," Abby complained.

"You should get this one," he continued, ignoring her protests. "Yes. You definitely need to get this."

She leaned in close. "The dresses in this place cost more than I paid for my truck when it was new."

He nodded. "It's prettier than your truck," he said indifferently.

She looked appalled. "I cannot justify spending this much money on a dress that I can probably only wear one time. That doesn't make any sense. I keep telling Phyl that if she'd just take me to Nordstrom Rack, I could buy a whole wardrobe for less than I'd pay for some of these dresses."

"But you're not spending the money on this dress," he corrected her. Jordan met her gaze with his own. "I am."

"Yeah, well, just because you have money to spend like that doesn't mean you should."

"I hardly think that I need you to tell me how to manage my money, Abby," he calmly explained.

She looked offended and rightly so. But she couldn't help herself. Abby was thrifty, and so was he. It was just that his thrift threshold was a lot higher than hers.

"Let me do this for you," he said, and softly kissed her between her eyes. "You're making one hell of a sacrifice for me by moving out here with me, Abby," he reminded her.

"I haven't actually agreed to move yet, Jordan."

"But you're considering it," he responded with a slight smile. "So consider this a thank-you gift. Just get the dress, sweetheart. Don't worry about cost. If I couldn't afford it, you wouldn't be here."

"You know I'm blue jeans and T-shirts, Jordan. As beautiful as this dress is, it's hard for me to justify randomly buying something like this when I don't know when or where I'll wear it."

"You can't wear jeans and a T-shirt everywhere we go, Abby. And we'll find a place for you to wear it. I'm sure something's coming up," he said, looking at Phyl, who nodded.

"How about I put this back until we do," Abby shot back.

"But I really do love this on you."

Abby gave his argument some thought and quietly rescinded her protests. "It is pretty."

He smiled. "It's gorgeous and you're gorgeous in it."

She blushed and smiled. "I think I do, too, but . . ."

Jordan leaned in and kissed her lightly on the lips.

She was uncharacteristically over-the-top feminine. It was cute and he almost laughed, except that he would've ruined the moment and he didn't want to do that.

Abby batted those pretty eyes of hers. "There is another one that I liked, too," she said sweetly. "I can't decide which one I like better."

He shrugged. "Then get both."

Abby bit down on her lower lip. "And the

shoes, too?"

Jordan grinned. "And the shoes too, dahlin'. In fact, you can get the whole damn store if you want to."

She looked like she didn't believe that he'd meant it, but he did. Jordan kissed her one last time. "I'm going back to my workout," he said, leaving.

He walked past Phyl and paused briefly. "You good?"

She nodded and sighed. "Yeah. I think I can handle it from here."

YOU WORK ALL DAY

Richardson was a half hour outside of Clark City. DJ had asked James and Naomi to meet him at a Whataburger just off the main road cutting through the small town. He and James had been sitting there for fifteen minutes before Naomi rushed in like she'd been blown in by a tornado.

"Sorry," she said, breathless, glancing at both men. "I had to get my kids off to school and wait for Thomas to leave for work."

James looked at DJ, but DJ pretended not to notice. His brother had been dropping subtle hints about Naomi's involvement. He didn't know her, so he didn't trust her. But James wouldn't have trusted any woman. As far as he was concerned, the only thing a woman could do for him was give up that ass and make him a meal. They were half brothers, related by their father. James had been raised in a totally different household from DJ, because DJ would've have gotten a foot in his mouth by his momma if he'd had the courage or stupidity to express that shitty attitude around her. James's mom obviously didn't give a damn about James's low opinion of women.

Naomi settled into the booth, pushed disheveled blond hair behind her ears, and looked anxiously at DJ, who covertly handed an envelope underneath the table.

"We each get thirty thousand now," he explained.

James grimaced. "That's it?"

Naomi stared back at him. DJ sighed. "That's thirty thousand more than she was willing to give us at all. I told her we wouldn't do it without some kind of payment up front. We'll get the rest when it's over."

Nay took a deep breath and seemed cool with that. DJ had told Naomi and James that they'd get five hundred thousand dollars each for doing this. DJ had lied to them, though. He was going to pocket a whole million when this was all said and done. In his mind it made sense that he should get more. After all, he'd been the one who'd agreed to do this. He'd been the one the woman had approached first, and he was the one who'd organized all of this —

including watching the woman's house and setting up how and when they'd take her and where they'd keep her. DJ was in charge. So he believed that he should get the most money.

He looked at Naomi. "Is she eating?"

Naomi shrugged. "Sort of. I mean, yeah."

"Well, which is it?" James abruptly chimed in. "Sort of or yeah?"

She glared at him. "She's eating."

"Don't you worry about her part, James," DJ reminded him, stepping to Naomi's defense. "All you and me have got to do is wait this out. We've done our part for now."

After Nay had nearly let that woman escape, DJ couldn't help but admit to himself that Naomi was a weak link. If he hadn't shown up when he did, just to check on things, she'd have gotten away and hell would've broken loose on all three of them.

"For now." He shrugged. "What's left for us to do, DJ?"

"We wait," he said simply. "It ain't hard. Nay checks on her twice a day, keeps her fed, and you and me just hang tight, J."

"And at the end of this?" James asked. "What happens when Friday rolls round, man?"

"We let her go." DJ shot back.

"Dead or alive?" James asked, leaning

across the table.

"Alive," Naomi said defensively. She looked around the room to see if anyone might have heard her.

"Exactly," DJ confirmed.

The smirk on James's face was meant to be unnerving. "Maybe I'm the only one who doesn't believe in Santa Claus and the Tooth Fairy. Doesn't make sense to just *let her go*. That's not real-world thinking, D."

"That's how it's gone be, man. It's not up for debate. We ain't killers." He mouthed the last word. DJ leaned back and shook his head. "Man, chill with that, J," he said, disgusted. "I told you what's gonna happen. Now leave it alone."

"Seriously, DJ, you cannot be that naïve, man," he said gravely.

"It's got nothing to do with being naïve. The only reason we're doing this" — he remembered that he was sitting in a public place, leaned forward, and lowered his voice — "is because I was promised that she wouldn't get hurt."

"She's been hurt," James said, looking too damn smug.

"Hitting women is a punk move, man," DJ said, challenging his gaze.

Naomi shifted in the seat next to DJ. Her man was like James. He had no qualms putting his paws on a female.

"Punk move or not, it helped us to get her little ass out of the house and into that car."

"Are we done?" Naomi asked. "I need to get to work."

DJ nodded, and Naomi picked up her purse and took off.

James waited for Naomi to leave before continuing this conversation with DJ. "I'm gone make a suggestion."

"I don't need your suggestions," DJ retorted. "I need you to be cool and do what I tell you to do."

"Hear me out," he insisted. "Maybe whoever is behind all this did tell you to just let her go when it's all said and done."

"That's exactly what she said. We let her go, or we don't get shit."

"Don't be stupid, DJ," he shot back. "That woman you've been talking to, the one who put this together, she's safe. You don't know who she is, and me and your girl, Naomi, definitely don't know. But little miss, locked up in that room? She knows us."

"She hasn't seen your face, man," DJ said, losing patience.

James was too damn volatile, always looking to make something harder than it was. Complicating things. DJ was starting to think he'd made a mistake asking him to be a part of this.

"But she's heard my voice, and yours, and Naomi's. They got technology, man. Think about it. All of a sudden the three of us come up with some crazy-ass money out of nowhere. This broad tells the police every damn thing about what's happened to her, and they start to put shit together."

"Then leave town after you get yours."

"Yeah, that's not obvious," he said sarcastically.

"Then don't spend it, James," DJ said coolly. "Sit on it. Business as usual. Don't draw attention to yourself."

"You tell your girl to do the same thing?" he asked, meaning Naomi.

"Why you so hung up on Nay, James?"

He sighed and leaned back. "She's shaky," he said casually.

"Shaky? What the hell does that mean?"

"Looks like she's about to jump out of her skin. First sign of trouble and she'll lose it."

DJ studied his brother. "Honestly, I'm more worried about you losing it."

His expression told DJ that he'd taken offense. Heavy silence hung in the air between them for a moment.

"This is your show, bruh." James

shrugged, standing up to leave. "We'll play your way if it means getting my money, but I think you need to put some thought into what I'm telling you."

James decided to leave, and DJ was still sitting there five minutes later. James had a flair for the dramatic. Nobody was going to kill that woman. It had been made clear to DJ that when all this was over, they were to drop her off at some agreed-upon place and leave her there — alive. DJ wasn't a killer. He wouldn't have agreed to this if that's what that woman on the phone wanted.

His supervisor was going to let him go. DJ had been late with one too many deliveries, and he was walking a hair-thin line between having a job and being unemployed. He hadn't told Nia or anybody. It wasn't like he couldn't find another job, but he wouldn't find another one that paid him what he made driving trucks. And they needed the money. DJ had his own dreams. He was sick of driving and being away from home for days, even weeks, at a time. This money was going to allow him to buy his family a house and help him to get his own business off the ground. Fuck working for anybody else. This money was going to set them up and set him free to be his own damn boss, maybe invest in some trucks and hire drivers to work for him. And it would be easy. All they had to do now was keep that woman safe and fed, and then return her after they got paid. Half a million in a week. Shit. Easy.

I SHOULD BE GONE

Naomi rushed into the kitchen carrying bags of groceries moments before the school bus pulled up in front of the house dropping off her boys. It was four. Thomas would be home by five.

"Y'all wash up," Naomi said to her sons, coming into the kitchen. "I need you to get started on that homework and get it done before dinner."

"Mine's done," TJ, her older son, said, reaching for a cookie in the cookie jar.

Naomi absently slapped his hand. The twelve-year-old stared back at her, and for a moment, the way he hesitated and glared at her, she thought she saw his father coming through. But she couldn't flinch. This was her son.

"Not until after dinner," she warned him.

He slumped away with a chip on his shoulder that made her uneasy. TJ was getting to be a big boy who'd seen things he shouldn't have seen at his age, and they were starting to rub off on him. He was the reason that Naomi had agreed to do this. She needed that money to save herself and her sons. They were starting to believe that the kinds of things that went on inside their house were the norm, and it was going to be up to her to unteach them everything that they learned from watching their father. Naomi was not going to let her boys grow up to be monsters like he was.

It had taken her longer at the store than she'd planned. Naomi put a pot of water on the stove to boil for potatoes and seasoned and put a chicken in the oven for baking, then started to cut up a salad. She was worried about that chicken. Worried that it wouldn't be done in time.

"Shit!" she muttered, dropping potatoes into the pot. The water splashed and burned her hand.

Naomi was rushing. She was nervous because she had hoped to make a quick run to the bunker to feed that woman before Thomas got home. It'd be nearly impossible to do it after dinner. Thinking about that woman, she hurried and put a sandwich together, grabbed a bottle of water, and put them both in a brown paper sack on the counter. She hadn't thought this through well. Could she trust those boys at home alone with that chicken in the oven for half an hour while she ran a quick errand?

She glanced at the clock on the microwave. It was almost four thirty. It'd take her fifteen minutes to get there. Another ten for the woman to eat, and then another fifteen coming home. The thought occurred to her to stay home. It wouldn't hurt that lady to miss a meal. If Thomas came home and she wasn't here, he'd . . . Naomi took the bag off the counter and was just about to push it to the back of the refrigerator when her doorbell rang. For some reason she quickly raced to answer it before one of her boys did. Standing on her porch was DJ's brother, James.

Her heart caught in her throat as she pulled the main door closed behind her and stepped out onto the porch, glancing nervously around at the neighbors.

"What are you doing here?" she whispered anxiously. "Where's DJ? Is something wrong?"

He grinned. "Calm down. Ain't nothing wrong."

"You are not supposed to be here," she said angrily. Naomi was on the verge of tears. "You can't be here, James. You just can't."

"You need help?" he said all of a sudden.

"What?" she asked, confused.

"Did you take her the food?"

She shook her head. "No. No. I can't. My husband will be home. I can't do it tonight. Now, please go! He can't know that you were here."

"Let me do it."

Her heart beat a thousand miles a minute. But no. She was . . . this was her job.

"You don't have to." She swallowed, nervously glancing over his shoulder. "Just go, James."

He didn't want Naomi involved. And if she wasn't, then there'd be more money to be shared between James and DJ.

"I think she'll be all right for one night," she said, turning to go back inside.

"I don't mind," he said, speaking calmly. "She's got to eat, Naomi."

Naomi recalled earlier today. The woman had been able to eat only half the sandwich. They'd promised those people to keep her fed and safe. If any of them expected to get paid, the woman needed to be taken care of. Naomi didn't have time for this today. She needed to think this through better and to find a way to make it work for her and to keep Thomas from getting suspicious.

"You're wasting time, Naomi," he said,

glancing back over his shoulder. "I could've been gone by now."

He was right.

"I just need to figure out a better schedule for myself," she said, turning to him. "But I can do my part, James."

He nodded. "Yeah," he said, sounding unconvinced.

She rushed into the house and came back moments later with the bag she'd packed and handed it to him. "Don't come back here," she scolded.

"Key," he reminded her. "I need the key."

She reached into the pocket of her jeans and shoved it into his palm. "Leave it on that shelf next to the door when you leave. I'll get it in the morning."

Seconds later, he was off her porch and headed back to his car. When she went back into the house, her oldest son, TJ, was standing at the foot of the stairs.

"Who was that, Momma?"

A chill ran up her spine. He had no business asking her that. She didn't have to answer him, but Naomi stared back at the mirror of her husband's demeanor and unwittingly dipped into a familiar place.

"Man from work," she began to explain. "One of the drivers. He's new and he needed to me to remind him of which rig he'd be pulling off in tonight."

Was it her imagination? Or did he look like he didn't believe her? The boy walked back up the stairs to his room.

Like father like son? If so, then she might already be too late to save this boy.

The beatings had started before the two of them had gotten married. She was a freshman in high school when she met Thomas. He was a junior. The first time he hit her wasn't long after the two of them started having sex. Naomi was fifteen.

"I love you, Nay," he'd whispered to her the first time they made love. He stared into her eyes with those big brown, soulful eyes of his. *"I love you more than my life."*

Before he came along, she'd never even kissed a boy. But that night, the way he'd held her, and the careful and patient way he made love to her, made it impossible for her not to believe that he loved her.

"I love you too, Thomas," she murmured, pressed against his chest.

And she meant it with all of her heart and soul.

The first time he'd hit her had been an accident. They'd been together for six, seven months. Naomi was giddy about something. She was young, happy, and silly sometimes. Looking back now, she couldn't remember what had her acting so silly, but he was grumpy. Which wasn't unusual. Thomas was having problems keeping his grades up and his father was giving him a hard time about it because the football coach was threatening to suspend him from the team.

He apologized to her, profusely, as soon as it happened. Thomas had slapped her across the face so hard that she fell to the ground. But he hurried to her side to help her up and pulled her close to him, then apologized over and over again, rocking her back and forth until she finally stopped crying.

"It won't happen again, Nay," he promised. *"I promise. I didn't mean it."*

She went back into the kitchen knowing that if her son made mention of the man at the door, then tonight was probably going to be a long one.

MUCH TOO MUCH

That white woman, Nay, was a waste of space, unnecessary, and a potential liability. But DJ was too stupid to see it or he felt sorry for her ass. James had seen it. She was scared to death of being caught with James standing at her door. His guess was that her old man was knee-deep into that ass of hers. She was so desperate to get him off her porch that she'd have probably handed over her firstborn to him if he'd pushed the issue.

James followed the rules. He'd brought the sandwich and water to that woman in the room, set it in the middle of the floor, and waited for her to come and get it. He even kept on that dumb-ass ski mask, too. It wasn't like this shit was hard.

"I know you're hungry." He motioned to the food and bottle of water. "Go ahead," he coaxed her from the corner of the room. "Eat up, baby girl."

She was even prettier than he remembered, beautiful dark chocolate skin, big brown eyes, and a mouth ripe for kissing and a few other things. She was tiny, much smaller than he'd remembered, well, in most places. Parts of her were . . . damn!

She plastered herself against that wall behind her, making it clear that she didn't trust him. But he hadn't given her a reason not to. James had entered the room as cool and chill as possible, making slow and deliberate moves to keep from spooking her. He'd really come here to satisfy a curiosity that he had.

"We promised to make sure you were all right until it's time to let you go," he explained. "You can't be all right if you don't eat."

Lovely wide eyes fixed on his, and James melted a little inside. Full, soft lips pursed together, and then parted. She knelt down on her hands and knees and crawled out of that corner just far enough to reach for her meal and pull it back to the blanket spread out underneath her.

She ate cautiously, keeping her eyes on him the whole time, but she was starving and ate so fast that she gagged.

"Slow down, sweetheart," he gently warned her. "It ain't gonna sprout legs and run off." He chuckled.

Tiny but thick. All she had on was a pair of shorts and a T-shirt. No bra. *Panties? Not likely.* It was odd seeing her again. James watched her, putting her into perspective for the very first time. Lovely. Soft. A rich man's woman. How in the hell had that man found her? And would he actually give these people what they wanted to get her back?

DJ had a heart of gold. He was everything that James wasn't and never would be. He was kind, a good man, a family man. And he wanted to believe that this pretty woman would walk away from all of this and go back to her sugar daddy and go on living her life. But DJ was playing at the dirty end of the pool this time. The people who'd put all this together had no intention of letting her live. They told DJ what he needed to hear to get him to do this, but James knew better.

"Believe it or not, we've met before," he said as soon as she finished eating.

Ms. Rhodes looked as surprised to hear it as he was to admit it. James wasn't supposed to talk to her, but he couldn't help himself. Few women in this life caught and held his interest, but this one did, and she was beyond anything he'd ever experienced before and he wanted to relish every single minute of the time he had with her.

"How do we know each other?" she asked softly.

It took every bit of restraint in him not to tell her. He wanted to, though. And he wondered if she'd remember him. Had he left as big an impression on her as she had on him? He doubted it.

"If I told you that" — he paused and grinned — "I'd have to kill you."

The look on her face was priceless. James had only said that shit for effect. She was already scared. He'd just scared her more with a joke.

"Your name is Abby," he told her.

He damn near burst out laughing at the shock on her face.

"Who are you?" The question trembled in the back of her throat.

He sighed. James worked delivery and had dropped off some lumber for her once at a house where she and another dude were putting up a deck.

"You need a hand with that?" she'd asked him, starting to follow him from the backyard and out to the truck parked in the driveway.

"Nah, I got it," he said.

"How about I give you one anyway," she

joked, and helped him to unload all that lumber.

"My name's Abby, by the way. What's yours?"

"Call me James."

"I will do that."

He'd thought of asking her for her number before leaving, but that big man hovering over her gave him pause, so he left, never thinking he'd see her again. As fate would have it, here she was.

It was nearly impossible to ignore those beautiful titties pressing against the fabric of that shirt. She saw him staring and folded her arms across herself. Was she really worth all this effort? Why? he wondered. A beautiful woman, yes, but beautiful enough to pay big bills for? He tilted his head to one side, then the other, trying to get a different kind of perspective on Miss Abby, maybe to see something in her that only a man with millions of dollars in his bank account could see. Or maybe he was looking at this from the wrong perspective.

He slowly stood up and so did she. James stood six one. Ms. Rhodes was a foot shorter. She couldn't have weighed more than 130, maybe 140. She backed so far into that wall behind her that she'd probably left a print of herself on it.

He just wanted a closer look. Just a look.

Don't put your hands on her, James, he warned himself.

He wasn't allowed to touch her, and for some reason knowing that made his dick hard. She sucked in air as he got close, close enough to —

He hovered over her, raised one arm over her head, and leveraged himself with it against the wall. "Damn," he whispered at the energy he felt warming between the two of them. She gave as much as he did. James lowered his gaze to the V neck of her shirt; then he bent slightly until his lips were close to her face. What he wouldn't give to suck on those lips of hers.

"I think I see it," he whispered, staring into her eyes, eyes filling with tears. James lowered his face to the crook of her neck and took a deep breath, held it, and released it slowly. "Smell it on you, too."

James hated perfumes and colognes on women. They didn't need it because they had their own natural scents that appealed to the core of a man. Those tears ran like track stars down her pretty cheeks. Oh, she was shaking, trembling like a leaf in the wind, but James still hadn't laid a finger on her, and he wanted to. He wanted to so bad.

He straightened up and took a step back,

then eyed her up and down. "Of course he'll pay whatever they ask him to. Won't he, sweetheart? Because you've been good to him. I'll bet you loved him with your whole self." James licked his lips. "Am I lying?"

Sweet Abby and her hidden treasures, her sweet gifts. His dick bucked in frustration. What he wouldn't give to taste what that rich motha fucka had become addicted to.

"Life ain't fuckin' fair. Is it?" he said introspectively to her. "It landed you here for fucking and falling in love with the wrong dude. Every woman's dream. Rich as hell and able to give you the whole world if you asked him for it. Or you could end up here, a pawn, being traded for some cash." He laughed. "Cash for ass. That shit would be funny if it weren't true."

She didn't laugh.

"I wondered about you the first time I saw you. Wondered how it would be to get this close to you." He laughed. "And now here we are."

James took one last, lustful look at her before finally turning and heading for the door.

And then he stopped. Shit. What if this was his last chance? His only chance? Fuck DJ and his rules.

"Aw . . . what the hell?" James groaned,

turned around, walked back over to her.

"No!" she said, pushing at him, kicking, and trying to swing. "Get — No!"

He grabbed hold of her wrists, pushed her back into the wall, pressing all of him against all of her, and pressed his lips against her lovely mouth, laughed, and took a quick step back.

Damn! He loved a good fight. James stared at her and then reared his head back slowly, closed his eyes, and licked his lips. "Thank you. Thank you for that, sweetheart. You've got my heart racing, girl and I think I'm in love."

She had his heart pounding like bass drums. He wasn't supposed to touch her, but how could he not? James backed away slowly, keeping her in his sights the whole time. He swallowed, knowing deep down inside him that he wouldn't be able to control himself around her. He couldn't. And he didn't want to.

"Maybe I'll see you tomorrow, Ms. Abby."

He closed the door behind him and locked it. And then he stood there for several minutes, listening to her sobbing and praying.

"Oh, God. Oh, dear God."

THE WORD CAME TO ME

"All the top oil, gas, and refinery players from around the world are listed as investors, of course," Jordan's assistant, Phyl, explained, sitting across from him at the table in the restaurant. "Some chemical and energy corporations, and some of the major retail businesses."

Phyl Mays had been Jordan's personal assistant for nearly two years now, and he'd come to trust her when it came to just about every aspect of his life. The thought that she could have betrayed that trust unnerved him. A staunch negotiator and businessman, Jordan prided himself on being able to read people. He'd asked her to come to dinner with him to study her, to look into her eyes as she spoke and to make sure that she looked into his. He wanted to trust his gut that she wouldn't be involved with the kind of people who had taken Abby. God help her if she was.

The lovely redhead looked back at him with vibrant green eyes as she spoke. "Out of all the investors that I was able to find, there was only one who seemed odd to me."

He hadn't told her what he was looking for specifically from the information he'd asked her to gather for him, but Phyl was exceptional enough to not need explanation.

"Which one and why?" he asked.

She shoved her dinner plate aside and took a sip of her wine. "This corporation called Variant?" She shrugged. "Ever heard of it?"

He nodded. "I have."

"Well, they're all gung-ho about synthetic and alternative fuel sources. You know? Like, for example, instead of dredging up oil from underground or fracking or whatever, they're into burning corn or spinach or whatever," she said flippantly, waving one hand in the air. "You know? Organic shit."

"So why would they be interested in the pipeline?" he surmised.

"Exactly."

The pipeline, if given the green light, stood to make billions. Investing in the project, for anyone, could make them a fortune. But not all money was good money as far as Jordan was concerned. That pipeline would erase a treaty and impact the Sioux nation in ways that would keep him awake at night. Considering some of the things he had done in his career to get ahead, his feelings about the pipeline surprised him more than anyone.

Suddenly, the server appeared at their table. "Would either of you care for dessert?" he asked pleasantly.

Jordan was exhausted but doubted he'd be able to sleep.

"Just the check, please," he said, looking up from the table and across the room in time to see Senator Sam Addison standing near the main entrance, staring at Jordan. When Jordan met his gaze, he expected the man to come over to the table, but instead the senator broke eye contact and quickly left the restaurant.

Phyl cleared her throat to get his attention. "Boss, I would like a piece of cheesecake." She shrugged. "If it's all right? I can take it home."

She stared at him, looking more like a six-year-old kid than the assistant he'd come to depend on.

"And a slice of cheesecake for the lady, please," he said to the server.

"To go," she quickly added, smiling at Jordan.

■ ■ ■ ■

Less than an hour later, Jordan was in his penthouse, freshly showered, nursing a vodka tonic, and standing on the terrace off his bedroom looking out over the city. It was the beginning of June. The days had been warm but the nights unseasonably cool. What he did manage to eat at dinner still weighed in his stomach like lead. His eyes were tired and burned from lack of sleep.

He didn't believe in coincidences. At a time like this, he couldn't afford to. The first time he'd met Sam Addison, according to Addison's recollection, was at a Variant event. The last time Jordan had seen him, until tonight, was at the Governor's Ball in Austin. It was the same night he and Abby made their first official appearance together in public, and Addison was there when Abby entered the room. Seeing him at the restaurant tonight set off an alarm in Jordan. He had had a feeling that he was being watched, and now he was sure of it.

"You can rest easy, Wells," Jordan said, an hour and third drink later, wearily over the phone. "I'm doing your gotdamn job for you."

"Meaning?"

This sonofabitch was supposed to be a miracle worker. Wells was the first and only name circulated, passed along in elite circles among men and women of wealth and influence to solve impossible problems, resolve insurmountable issues. To say that Jordan was disappointed and unimpressed was an understatement.

"What have you found?" Jordan asked, rubbing his tired eyes.

Her. Jordan willed his thoughts to the universe and silently prayed that Wells would tell him, *I've found her.*

"So far," he said and sighed, "I haven't found much. An emblem in the photograph you sent me. It's barely visible and on the jacket or something that your lady was sitting on."

"An emblem?" Jordan said curtly. "A damned emblem?" He caught himself starting to raise his voice.

"I told you it's not much, but it's a start."

Jordan chuckled bitterly. "What part of 'we've got less than a week to find her' don't you understand, man?"

Wells didn't answer. Jordan half expected him to hang up, but he didn't.

Jordan leaned back on the sofa and swallowed what remained in his glass. "I've got a lead of my own," he finally said.

"Tell me what it is," Wells said. "I'll check it out."

Jordan shook his head without thinking. "No. You keep doing whatever it is. I'll check it out."

"That's not how I work, man," Wells said with warning. "This is a courtesy call and nothing more. I'm just giving you an update. You need to stay out of my way and let me do this."

"That's the problem. You don't seem to be doing shit."

Again, the other man was silent.

"If I find out anything here that can help you to find her, I will let you know," Jordan said, extending an olive branch of sorts.

"If you want her found alive, you'll let me do my job. Whatever it is you think you know, what you do could put your woman's life in jeopardy, Gatewood. This is the only warning you'll get from me."

"Noted," he grunted, and abruptly ended the call.

A few minutes later, he placed a call to Phyl.

"Hey, boss," she said, sounding like she was eating.

"I need background information on Sam Addison," he explained. "He's a senator."

"Okay," she said hesitantly. "Anything in particular I should be looking for?"

"Any and all connections to Variant."

Phyl paused. "I'll see what I can find."

How'd they know she'd be there? Who knew that Abby was going home? Jordan didn't even know until the morning she'd left. As far as he could tell, she hadn't even planned it. Had she told someone? Skye, her best friend, maybe? Maybe she'd mentioned it to her father or one of her brothers, and if any of them knew, then they might have mentioned it to someone else.

If Jordan called them asking about Abby, he'd send up red flags to those people, which he certainly didn't need. They'd insist on involving the police, in a sense signing her death warrant.

Exhaustion took over and Jordan eventually went to bed and started to drift off to sleep. Memories of Abby's kisses grazing his lips aroused him, the sensation of her warmth pressed down on top of him.

"Pretend I'm not here," she whispered between kisses.

"Impossible," he groaned.

"Then pretend that you don't mind the fact that I am."

"I absolutely don't mind."

"I love how you taste." She dipped her tongue into his mouth.

Jordan reached for the back of her head, wrapped one arm tightly around her waist, and pushed his tongue into her mouth. He would not let her be coy with her kisses. That just wasn't fair.

A HONEYCOMB TREE

Another night in this cold and dark room. The blanket helped. She wrapped her mind around that small comfort the way she wrapped that blanket around her body, giving herself permission to be just a little grateful for it.

Tomorrow was a promise and another chance for her to get out of this place. Abby would've loved to close her eyes, even for a moment, rest, and let her guard down, but she couldn't afford to do that. Not while the bitter taste of that asshole's lips still lingered on her mouth.

She'd never felt so violated, so helpless. But then, that's all she'd felt since they'd broken into her house and snatched her from it. Miss Independent, self-sufficient, and capable, Abby had never known what it was to not be in control of her own life, of her own body. And now here she was, sitting on this cold floor, wrapped in a dirty blanket feeling every bit a victim and victimized by some bastard who'd left her feeling grimy and weak.

No one who knew her would recognize this version of Abby. That man had stolen something from her and taken it with him when he left. He'd stolen some of her courage and her fight. If he'd wanted to do more to her, he could've and Abby would've been helpless to stop him. The realization had been gnawing at her gut since he'd left, but it was the truth.

She swallowed and drew her knees tighter to her chest. "Stop it, Abby," she whispered. "Think of something else," she quietly willed herself. "Something good."

She couldn't lose hope. Abby couldn't let that fucker win — her body, mind, or soul. The longer she gave him space in her thoughts, the more power she gave him and the more he stole from her. She closed her eyes and took herself someplace else.

It was one thing for a woman's family to meet the new love of her life for the first time. It was another thing for them to meet him for the second time after finding out the truth: that he was a Dallas billionaire who was almost as famous as Denzel Washington.

Low-key and normal. Just steaks, potatoes, and maybe a salad. Nothing fancy. They could even eat outside on the covered and heated patio, just to drive home the point that this gathering was really nothing elaborate. Abby wanted her people to feel at ease and Jordan to just be, well, Jordan. Not mogul Jordan, or CEO Jordan, or billionaire Jordan.

The fact that they were meeting here at his mansion big enough to hold every last one of their houses and still have open floor space left over didn't have to be a big deal as it needed to be to her family if Jordan could just be the Jordan he was when he and Abby were alone.

Lucas Bedlam. Abby stood on the balcony above the patio watching Lucas Bedlam direct his staff in prepping the outdoor kitchen for dinner. Jordan sidled up behind her and planted his hands on either side of the railing, cocooning her between his arms, and then leaned in and kissed the side of her neck.

"I thought we were going to keep this simple?" she asked, watching Lucas Bedlam inspect freshly sliced vegetables.

"We are," he assured her.

Without meaning to, she scowled. "Doesn't he have a reality television show to film?"

Jordan sighed. "I guess not tonight."

Lucas Bedlam was the head judge on one

of those competitive-cooking shows that aired all around the country, maybe even the world. And Jordan had hired him to come here tonight to grill steaks for her family. This was not keeping it simple and low-key.

Abby turned in the tight confines of the space of his arms and stared into that handsome face. "He's a television star, Jordan, who showed up here with an entourage. I thought you and I'd just throw some steaks on the grill, chop up a salad, and peel the plastic top off a container of grocery store potato salad and serve it all up on some nice paper plates."

Jordan furrowed his thick brow as if he'd never heard of such a thing. "Nobody grills a steak better than Luke."

Two different worlds. Sometimes, the line was mercifully blurred so that she hardly even noticed that he was oysters Rockefeller and she was hamburgers and fries. And then there were times like this.

A car horn honking alerted them that their visitors had arrived. Jordan smiled. Abby suddenly lost her appetite. When she'd first introduced Jordan to her family, she introduced him as Jordan Tunson because that's the name he'd given her when the two of them first met. It wasn't until later on that she found out what his real name was, but the last thing she wanted or needed, or rather, the last thing he needed, was for her nosy family to know who he really was, so she just ran with Tunson.

Recently, though, they'd seen Abby on the cover of *Texas Society* magazine, wearing an expensive European-made evening gown, with her hair and face all done up, and coming out of the governor's mansion with Jordan, so she figured it was probably past time to have this gathering.

"That's them," she murmured and swallowed.

He straightened his stance and took hold of her hand. "Then let's not leave them waiting."

It wasn't a question of *if* she was going to be embarrassed this evening. It was more a question of *who* would be the one to embarrass her the most: any member of her family, or her man.

Jordan stood in the expansive foyer, wearing jeans and a casual pullover sweater. He looked like he should've been the cover model for *GQ.* He was beautiful, but in this case, she sort of wished he could tone down some of that gorgeousness to look more regular.

Abby hugged her stepmother and then her father. "Hey, Birdy. Hey, Daddy."

"Hey, Peanut."

She'd asked him not to call her that.

Birdy's rich brown eyes locked on to Jordan, her chin dropped slightly, and she stopped right in front of him and stared at him like he was Idris Elba or somebody.

"Hello," he said to Birdy gawking at him.

Of course she didn't say anything.

Abby nervously cleared her throat. "Daddy, you remember Jordan."

Her father raised his chin, and not just because Jordan was taller than him. It was his commanding chin raise establishing him as head of something or other. He held out his hand for Jordan to shake.

"It's Gatewood," he stated for clarification, staring Jordan in the eyes. "Not Tunson."

Jordan smiled slightly. "Correct," he said, shaking her father's hand.

For what felt like a good twenty minutes to Abby, but was probably actually closer to twenty seconds, the two men silently shook hands. It appeared to be some kind of man standoff whose meaning she really couldn't decipher.

"Hey, Eva. Hey, Wes," Abby said, hugging her older brother's wife and then him.

"Peanut," Wes said, and winked.

Rau, her other brother, standing behind Wes, sang that song from *The Jeffersons* television show about moving on up under his breath. Abby glared at him and rolled her

213

eyes, then reintroduced Wes and Eva, and finally her best friend, Skye, and her man, David, to Jordan.

"You didn't bring the boys?" Abby asked Skye.

She had two sons from her first marriage whom Abby adored.

Skye looked appalled. "Hell, no," she whispered to Abby. "They'd terrorize this poor rich man. He ain't ready, Abby."

"Peanuuuut!" David wrapped his arms around her, picked her up off the floor, and laughed.

"Don't call me that," she whispered in his ear.

He laughed even harder.

A polite Rhodes clan was a thing of beauty and awe to behold. For the first hour, everyone was on his or her best behavior. And then they sat down to eat.

"I have to say," her father began in that tone that made her feel like she was ten years old again. He wiped his mouth with his napkin, then leaned back in his seat and looked at Jordan. "I find it quite unsettling to have been lied to about who you really are." His glance bounced back and forth between Jordan and Abby. It kind of weighed heavier on Abby for some reason, though. At least, it felt like it. "Not a good way to make a first impression."

He looked back to Jordan for a response.

Jordan nodded slowly and thoughtfully. Abby swallowed the food in her mouth, but it kind of hung up in her throat for a moment. Jordan Gatewood was not accustomed to being challenged in any way. He said what he wanted. He got what he wanted. And over the last six months, Abby'd learned that he pretty much didn't take too well to having to explain himself.

"I had my reasons for not being forthcoming, Walter."

Abby looked at her brothers, who both looked back at her. Walter. Rau's eyebrows shot up as if to say, *Wow.*

"I didn't want to draw attention to myself because I hadn't planned on staying in town and" — he looked at Abby — "and I had no idea that I was there to even make an impression on my woman's father."

"Oh, my God," she heard Skye mutter.

Jordan turned back to her father. "But you're absolutely right. It wasn't the best way to begin a relationship."

From that point on those people hurled questions at Jordan like rocks.

"How many acres you got here?"

"Do you own more than one house?"

"How many cars you got? What kind?"

"Did you raise the meat we're eating now on

215

this ranch, or did you buy it at the store?"

"Is that the guy from the cooking show throwing down on that grill?"

"Do you really have as much money as they say you have?"

And then a statement came through that made everybody shut up. And it came from Walter Rhodes.

"She's my baby, Jordan. And if she ever comes to me crying because of something you did, you'll never see her again."

Abby didn't know whether to pass out or jump across the table into her father's lap and hold on to him for dear life. All eyes then fell on Jordan. But his fell on her.

"Understood."

In and out of a restless sleep, Jordan lay with his forearm covering his eyes, trying to keep his worst fears at bay, trying not to think of what she must be going through right now this very moment.

It had taken him a lifetime to find her. Jordan still wrestled with the truth that a man like him did not deserve her, but by some ridiculous twist of fate, she was his. Jordan had dismissed the man he'd been before he'd met Abby. He had been given a brand-new chance at something he'd never had, at something he never even realized he'd needed. She was his soul mate, the pulse of his soul. Abby Rhodes with all her quirky little ways balanced him, and losing her was not an option.

As he lay there, a random thought came to mind, one he'd never given much time to before, but now it came to him as clearly as if it were happening all over again. It was a conversation.

"I'd imagine that a man like you would have his choice of women," Walter Rhodes lazily stated while Jordan lined up his next shot on the pool table.

Abby's family had come to his ranch for dinner for the first time and Jordan was being grilled about his intentions toward the man's daughter like he was a teenager.

"I checked you out on the Internet, man," Rau added. "You've been with some hotties."

"Seven in the corner," Jordan said before taking the shot.

Even the father of his first wife, Claire, hadn't interrogated him the way Abby's clan was doing now. Jordan wasn't quite sure what it was they expected him to say, but he found it amusing that they were setting up questions the way all of them tried setting up pool shots.

"She's not very . . ." her father started and then stopped.

"Experienced," Wes continued. "Abby's

always been into the books and math and shit like that."

"She's had boyfriends," her father continued. "Just not many."

"Four in the side," Jordan said.

"Look, man," Rau said. "Just don't play no games with her," he blurted out. "Abby tries to act tough. She acts like shit don't bother her, but it does. She's sensitive."

Jordan made his shot and looked at each of them. "What are you expecting me to tell you?"

They looked at each other, then back at him. Wes took the lead. "Tell us that she's not just —"

"Do you intend to marry her?" her father asked abruptly.

"Yes," he said without hesitating. "Eight, right corner."

Abby's whole family had that accent. And they all had so much to say, with no qualms about talking over one another, shouting to the point that Jordan would think they were arguing, until boisterous laughter broke through, indicating that though the discussion may have been heated, it was also amusing. His family had never been so animated, with so many personalities clashing like wrecks on a highway and yet blending together and sounding like a chorus in perfect harmony.

She wore a simple pink knit maxidress, padding around the house in her bare feet. Jordan watched in awe as she effortlessly engaged with each and every family member, slipping into her role as Peanut, baby girl, little sister, and best friend. Jordan felt a bit resentful that he had to share her. Abby seemed to sense it, because she made her way over to him almost at the exact moment when he was beginning to miss her warmth.

"Hey, baby," she murmured, planting a sweet kiss on his lips and then taking her seat in his lap and staring deep into his eyes. "You holding up okay?"

"I'm tougher than I look, Peanut."

She rolled her eyes. "They can call me that because they can't help themselves. But I don't want you to call me that."

"But it suits you," he teased.

She sighed. "Thank you for doing this."

"I had to. I need to ensure that Walter has a better impression of me and that he trusts me with his little girl."

Sudden tears appeared in her eyes. "I trust you," she whispered.

"With all of you?"

Not just her body. Not just her mind, but her

soul. Did she trust him with her life?

She nodded. "Every part."

DAY 3

ALL THIS COLD DESPAIR

Sleep had come in small packets off and on through the night. Abby couldn't allow herself the luxury of rest. The one time she'd probably slept the longest, she'd awakened startled, kicking and screaming at that man who'd assaulted her yesterday. Knowing that he had a key and could come into this room anytime he wanted was terrifying. They were on a schedule, showing up twice a day with food and water. Her biggest fear would be that he'd be the one showing up this morning.

"You know how to fight, Abby," she reminded herself out loud.

Her two older brothers, who didn't exactly pick on her, had taught her a thing or two about defending herself.

"One thing you got to remember," her brother Rau had told her, *"eyes is eyes. Eyes are vulnerable and soft. Go for the eyes if you can, and if you do decide to kick him in the*

*nuts, make sure you kick good and hard, hard
enough to damn near kill him, because if you
don't, you're just gonna piss him off."*

She shuddered at the thought of that man
touching her again. She didn't want to think
about what he could do, what could happen. But damn! How could she not think
about it? She sat with her back against the
wall and dared to ask herself the obvious. If
they wanted money from Jordan, why was
she still here? Abby had been here going on
three days now. If all they wanted was
money, why hadn't they let her go? Unless —

"Don't," she commanded herself, inhaling
her frustration. "Don't even think that."

Jordan would've given them money if
they'd demanded it from him for her safe
return. Abby was not going to give in to a
lie. He loved her and the police were looking for her, she surmised. They probably
wouldn't want him to pay right away. Jordan would have to stall them for a while to
give the police a chance to find her and to
catch these bastards. She imagined an army
of cops out there searching for her, questioning any- and everybody in the county, while
Jordan was worried sick over where she
could be. He'd be angry, pissed that some

asshole had had the nerve to put their hands on her.

She almost laughed at the image of him standing in the middle of the living room of his penthouse scowling at detectives and Phyl, barking orders, demanding that they do their damn jobs, get off their asses, and find her. They'd have to talk him out of leaving and looking for her himself and it would take everything in him to back off, but only if he wasn't satisfied that they weren't doing everything they could to find her.

If they hurt her, I'll kill them! he'd yell to somebody, everybody.

And he'd mean it. She couldn't lose faith in him. Just like he'd touched her soul, she'd touched his. What they had was more than love. There wasn't even a word for it. It was force unlike anything imaginable. Abby desperately needed to remember that, to hold on to it and know that nothing in the world would keep him from finding her before — Abby was going to be all right. She was going to walk out of this room alive and back to Jordan. That's all that mattered. She was going to survive this.

"No matter what," she reassured herself.

These people weren't going to break her. She wouldn't let them. Abby was strong. She stared down at the three items on the mat in front of her. That fool had left without taking them with him. A brown paper bag. A clear plastic sandwich bag. And an empty plastic water bottle. She was an engineer, and engineers were problem solvers, born to create, design, and manipulate. There was seemingly no way out of this room. But Abby never did believe in the impossible. She'd find a way. She'd make one.

Abby was so lost in her thoughts that she almost missed the sound of the outer door opening and closing. She quickly hid the items underneath the blanket balled up and shoved in the corner behind her. Her heart jumped into her throat at the sound of the key turning in the door. Jesus! What if it was him? She almost started crying again when she saw that the woman had returned.

The woman squatted and placed the bag and a bottle of water on the floor like she'd done all the previous times and waited while Abby slowly crawled over to get it and take it back to the mat. She didn't have an appetite, but Abby knew better than to not eat. She had so many questions.

"How long are you going to keep me here?" She dared to ask the first one.

"Eat."

She had on that black ski mask, but Abby

couldn't help but notice a cut down the center of her bottom lip. The woman caught Abby staring.

"I've got to pee."

"I said eat," she demanded more forcefully.

"Did he do that to you?" Abby asked, forcing herself to bite into that sandwich. She chewed and made herself swallow it. "The one who came here last night?" Her voice cracked as she stared up at the woman.

She didn't answer, but Abby noticed the strange way in which she bent one arm across her midsection.

"Did . . . did he hit you? The man who — ?"

"I said eat, gotdammit!"

Abby twisted off the cap to the bottle of water and gulped down half of it before placing it on the floor and taking a bite of that sandwich.

"Hurry the fuck up," the woman yelled.

The woman cringed. She was in pain. If he had beat her, Abby couldn't help but wonder why. But she knew that asking would get her nowhere.

"Will you be back later?" she did ask. "Will it be you? Not him?"

The woman pulled a gun from behind her

and pointed it at Abby. "You're done," she said.

Abby shook her head and took another bite of the sandwich. "No," she said with a mouth full of food. She immediately followed it with a drink of water.

The woman used both hands to steady the gun aimed at Abby. "Push it back over to me," she demanded.

When Abby didn't immediately comply, the woman took a step toward her.

"Now!"

She did as she was told, then quickly scooted back to the corner.

"I really do have to use the bathroom," Abby insisted.

To Abby's horror, the woman gathered up Abby's trash and abruptly left the room, locking the door behind her.

"Please!" Abby called out. "I need to use it!"

Moments later, the key turned in the lock again and the woman shoved the dirty bowl into the room, then closed and locked the door again.

"One minute," she said through the door to Abby.

"Tissue?" Abby reluctantly asked.

Again, the door opened, and a single tissue from one of those packs you carried in your purse floated to the floor.

A few moments later, the woman returned to remove the bucket.

"Will you be the one coming back later?" Abby asked before the woman slammed the door shut behind her.

"Just don't let him come back," she called after her. If he'd hurt that woman like that, then what would he do to Abby? "Just you. Okay?" she begged. "Just you. Please don't let him come back!" she yelled, slapping the palm of her hand against the metal door. "I just want to get out of here." She sobbed, slowly sinking to her knees. "Please, let me go!"

She didn't know how long she stayed there before going back over to the mat and pulling the bottle and bags from underneath it. Abby stared at each of them long and hard, until she finally calmed down enough to focus.

"Now. What the hell can I do with a plastic bag, a bottle, and a brown sack?" She shrugged. "Maybe nothing," she said, sounding defeated enough to get on her own nerves. She took a deep breath and focused. "Maybe something," she said, determined.

BACK TO THE LAB AGAIN

Plato had warned Gatewood. If the motha
fucka insisted on meddling in this problem
he'd hired Plato to solve, he could end up
getting his lady love killed. After their phone
call last night, Plato could've left the man
to his own devices, but the fact remained
that he knew Abby. He liked Abby for what
he knew of her. Marlowe loved Abby.

Plato made the call while he waited in the
car for Marlowe to finish getting ready so
that they could go to her crazy aunt's house.
The phone rang once before Gatewood
answered. "This is the one and only conversation you and me are going to have about
this," Plato abruptly began the conversation. "I am not a member of a team, man.
You commissioned me to find her, and
that's what I'm doing."

"Is that what you're doing?" Gatewood
responded with an attitude. "Because it
doesn't appear to me that you're doing any

damn thing, Wells. This is day three and you've got a fuckin' emblem. That's all you've managed to get, and it is not enough."

"I get it, Gatewood. You snap your finger and the sun rises and sets. That's the kind of shit you're used to."

"Yes. That's the kind of shit I'm used to."

"Gratification ain't always so instant," Plato told him. "Believe it or not, I do know what I'm doing."

"Then show me."

"You back up off my ass and let me find her. But if you insist on taking your happy-go-lucky rich ass out there and stirring the pot of all the wrong people, you might as well consider her dead now."

The man was silent.

Plato understood. If Marlowe was the one missing, he'd be all over that shit, turning over every stone, knocking down every damn wall in his path to find her. He knew where Gatewood was coming from, but dammit, this dude needed to back up and let Plato do what he needed to do, which was to find Abby Rhodes.

"Let me find her before you go off running rampant with a temper tantrum, Richie Rich," he reluctantly reasoned. "Once she's back with you, you can go knocking heads against walls, man, but until then, stand the fuck down."

Plato hung up.

Truth be told, a man like Plato had no business trying to live a so-called normal life in a pimple on a gnat's ass town like Blink, Texas. He taught trigonometry at the local community college. He mowed grass. Changed the oil in his woman's car. Sat down to eat dinner with her every night at six. Made delicious love to her every chance he got. And damn near forgot that in the course of his life, he'd killed more people than she could count on all her pretty little fingers and toes. Being in love with a woman was one of those luxurious liabilities that a man in Plato's position could ill afford to have, and yet his dumb ass was head over fuckin' heels.

"Shou hasn't been feeling well for a couple of days now," Marlowe said to him on the way to her aunt's house.

Plato absolutely did not like being around that old woman, a tiny thing, frail and blind, who had a way of making all six feet four inches, 240 pounds of him feel like a bug she'd squash under her shoe if she could do it without Marlowe noticing. She scared the shit out of him with that hoodoo vibe she had going on. He never believed in that nonsense until he met Shou. The old woman didn't trust him with her Marlowe. She didn't like him. She'd made that point clear enough every chance she got, so he made sure to keep his distance.

"I'll wait in the car," he told the lovely Marlowe after they pulled up in front of Shou's house.

She looked at him. "Don't be like that, baby."

Good Lord, those eyes of hers were hypnotic, amber gold, big and bright. She was his weakness.

"I've got a call to make, sweetheart," he explained.

Marlowe waited for him to elaborate, but not long. She knew better.

"At least come in and say hi when you finish?" she asked, batting those long lashes at him.

He salivated at the sight of her plump ass as she climbed out of the car to go inside and made a mental note to make love in slow motion to her when they made it back to the house.

"Wonder Boy," he said over his cell phone. "You called?"

Plato never did know this kid's name. He came recommended by a former associate and had impressed Plato with his ability to find out any- and everything about any- and everybody whenever Plato asked, no questions except the pertinent ones.

"So that file you sent me." He sighed lazily. "The one with the lady in dire straits and all tied up?"

"Yes?"

"That same emblem that's on that jacket or whatever she's sitting on is also on the tip of the blindfold. I almost missed it, but of course I didn't," he explained, sounding smug as always.

"Of course."

"It's a crown inside a triangle. Belongs to a machine parts distributor called Crown Distributors, headquartered in Memphis, Tennessee. They ship parts all around the world, machined parts mostly related to farming equipment, big rigs, even trains."

Memphis? Was this search really going to take his ass all the way to Memphis? As if reading his mind, Wonder Boy chimed.

"They have a warehouse in a town called Nelson." He paused. "Ever heard of it? It's in northeast Texas."

"Anything else?"

"Who do you think I am? Some sort of genius, all-seeing, detail-oriented motha fucka who can tell the make of the vehicle she's in by the seat she's sitting on or something?"

Plato smiled. "That's exactly what I think."

"Toyota Highlander. I know this because I used to have one back when I was in high school."

"I thought you still were in high school," Plato quipped.

"I'd laugh if that was funny. That was last year."

"Is that it?"

"Damn, man. You could at least sound impressed."

"I'm gushing, bruh," Plato said before hanging up.

Plato had no idea how long Marlowe had planned on staying, but he looked up Nelson on his cell phone and saw that it was a forty-minute drive and he was anxious to find that distribution center and check it out. He walked in to find Marlowe sitting across from Shou, holding the old woman's hands in hers. That house felt like an oven. It was chilly outside, but not cold enough for her to have the heat turned up to kiln levels.

"You're not running a fever, Auntie," Marlowe explained with concern.

"Because I'm not cold. My hands are,

though. And my feet won't get warm."

"What'd the doctor say?"

"He didn't say nothin' 'cause I ain't gone see him."

"Shou," Marlowe said, frustrated.

"I'm allergic to peaches." The old woman turned her face to where he was standing. If he didn't know better, he'd swear that that old woman could see him. "I'm allergic to peaches, damn you!"

"I know you're allergic to peaches, Auntie," Marlowe said, concerned. "You haven't had any. Have you?"

Shou shook her head.

"Marlowe," Plato said, "how long do you plan on staying?"

"Where you going?" Shou blurted out to Marlowe, grabbing hold of her hand.

"I've got to make a run, baby," he said to Marlowe, being careful not to address Shou Shou directly.

"You know I don't much care for you," Shou stated simply.

"But I care for him, Auntie," Marlowe interjected.

Shou turned, frowning, to Marlowe. "Then I guess that settles it."

Marlowe stood up and came over to him. "How long are you going to be?"

"I can be back in a few hours."

Marlowe walked him to the door and stood outside on the porch with him. "You know it doesn't matter what she thinks."

He smiled. "As long as she doesn't stick pins in a doll that looks like me, I really don't care. She ain't the one I'm here for."

Marlowe stood up on her toes and planted those succulent lips of hers against his. "I'll see you when you get back."

Wednesday afternoon and Crown Distributors was teeming with people. The facility, a large gray one-story building, was surrounded by an eight-foot-tall security fence, with a parking lot big enough to hold a few hundred cars. This was Plato's best and only lead, and he wasn't feeling too optimistic about it. He sat parked outside it, watching cars and trucks pulling in and out of the place. He went ahead and made the assumption that Abby Rhodes's kidnappers were employed here, now or in the past.

Plato had been given five days to find her. Today was number three and he didn't have shit. He took a deep breath and blew it out slowly. His specialty was hunting down people for reasons other than to save them. Plato was not a search-and-rescue kind of dude. In theory, it shouldn't have mattered, but because he was frustrated, this time, it did.

Blink, Texas, was surrounded by two other cities. This one, called Nelson, and another one called Clark City, small towns overlapping each other until one blurred into the other. She could've been in any of them.

He quietly concluded that skill would have very little to do with finding this woman. What Plato needed was some good, old-fashioned luck or a miracle.

He truly did not want to make this call, but Plato felt that he had no choice. He called Gatewood again.

"I'm in a town called Nelson."

A long pause.

"What's in Nelson?" Gatewood finally asked.

"A lead. Crown Distributors. Ever heard of it?"

"No."

He had nothing else to give the man, but pride wouldn't let him concede that fact. "I need to know if it's affiliated with Gatewood Industries in any way."

Again, the brotha was quiet.

Plato had to offer him something else. So he gave him the last morsel. "They took her in a Toyota SUV. She's somewhere between Nelson, Blink, and Clark City."

Gatewood sighed. "I'll see what I can dig up on that distributor and get back to you," he said before abruptly hanging up.

Two days to find a pretty, little needle in a big-ass haystack. He'd done more with less. Time wasn't on his side, but he wasn't about to let a silly little thing like that get in the way of progress.

Cut Other People Open

The emotional exhaustion was beginning to take its toll on Jordan. His patience was tissue paper thin and other people were starting to notice.

"Hey, Jordan," one of the heads of his engineering group said, coming into Jordan's office. "Sorry this is late. I got held up in a meeting."

"I needed it half an hour ago," Jordan snapped back unapologetically.

"A . . . again, my apologies. I hope it's still useful," he said, holding out the portfolio.

"It's not," Jordan responded without bothering to take the document.

"I'll hold on to it. You might need it later."

The man stood there like he was expecting some kind of attaboy pat on the back, but Jordan had nothing for him.

"I'll e-mail you a soft copy as well," he

said, clearing his throat before finally leaving.

Jordan's executive assistant, Jennifer, appeared in the doorway. "I had the valet bring your car around like you asked," she told him. "The senator's assistant called to say he's on his way to the restaurant."

"Thank you, Jennifer."

On the ride down in the elevator, Wells's warning echoed in Jordan's head: *"If you insist on taking your happy-go-lucky rich ass out there and stirring the pot of all the wrong people, you might as well consider her dead now."*

Of course the man was right. Every second of every day since she was taken threatened to derail Jordan and turn him into a raving maniac. He couldn't afford to lose control — for her sake. He couldn't afford to fall apart. But that thought that he might not ever find her, might never see her again, skirted across his mind constantly. And what would he do if he lost her? Who would he become without her in his life? Could he go back to living the way he had before he'd met and fallen in love with Abby? Living. More like existing.

Jordan understood the risks involved in meeting with the senator if he was, in fact, involved in any of this. Then again there was the chance that Jordan was wrong about him and that he knew nothing of Abby's abduction. Too many coincidences had struck him as odd, though, and he needed to see for himself if even the slightest bit of suspicion that he had about the man could be true. If there was even a remote chance that the sonofabitch could lead Jordan to Abby, he couldn't let it slip past him. Time was running out, and Wells was no closer to finding Abby now than he was the night Jordan reached out to him to find her.

He'd had Jennifer contact the senator's office, inviting him to have drinks with Jordan. The man accepted immediately.

"Needless to say, I was surprised by your invitation," Senator Addison said as the server set their drinks down on the table.

Jordan silently studied every movement, every nuance of him, hoping to latch on to a clue that he might actually know about Abby's disappearance. He had to be careful not to give away any sign whatsoever that he was suspicious of him though.

"Well," Jordan said casually, "when I noticed you leaving the restaurant last night, I saw it as an opportunity to maybe sit down and have a drink before you left Dallas. "We cross paths quite a bit in our social circles. And yet we don't really know each other personally."

The senator responded with a wry smile. "I'd have stopped at your table and said hello before I left last night, but I noticed that you were involved in what looked to be an intense conversation with a very lovely redhead."

Jordan nodded. "My assistant. Yes. We were wrapping up some business."

Addison's expression made it clear that his idea of business and Jordan's idea of business didn't exactly align where the lovely redhead was concerned.

"So what's lured you away from D.C.?" Jordan probed indiscreetly.

"My granddaughter's recital," Addison warmly replied. "She's a prodigy, actually. Plays the piano better than Mozart, and she's only ten."

"A proud grandfather, I see."

"Indeed." Addison smiled. "She's the love of my life and I don't care who knows it."

The love of his life. Jordan could see in the man's eyes that he meant it. Love, true love, shone transparent in a man, and Jordan had no doubt that the love he had for Abby shimmered on him like pixie dust. Addison had seen it, Jordan surmised, thinking back to that night at the Governor's Ball. Addison, and whoever the hell he was working with, had known the moment that Abby walked in, that she meant more to Jordan than any other woman he'd ever been with publicly.

The man stared back at Jordan strangely, and Jordan realized this his expression must've piqued Addison's curiosity, so he decided to change the subject.

"So, mind if I ask you about a rather hot topic?"

Addison shrugged. "I'm listening."

"What's your personal position on the pipeline protests?"

Addison sighed heavily. "Is that why you invited me for drinks? To get the inside skinny on the political stance of this highly controversial issue?" he asked sarcastically. "Planning on investing?"

"What makes you think I haven't, Senator?" he asked simply.

Addison met and held Jordan's gaze. "I'd know if you had," he said with confidence, and then shifted in his seat and sighed.

"It's a heated issue right now, heavily affecting an industry I'm a part of. But no. I'm not interested in investing in the program."

The man looked unconvinced. "Then it's really not any of your business where Congress stands on the issue," he said, trying to sound polite, but Jordan hadn't missed the bite in his tone.

Tread lightly. Had he given Addison the idea that he suspected his involvement in Abby's abduction? Was he that transparent?

"And here I thought you asked me here purely to establish a friendship?" Addison chuckled.

"Is it even possible for politicians to have friends?" Jordan coolly asked.

Addison seemed to seriously ponder the question. "Perhaps not," he said rather soberly. "I suppose the intention is to have just one less enemy." He smiled and raised his glass in a toast before taking a sip. "How's that pretty lady friend of yours, by the way?" He locked gazes with Jordan. "The one wearing the pretty blue dress at the ball?"

Jordan's gut tightened. His heart pounded.

"Safe," he said for some reason, intensely studying Addison for reaction. Fuck! Had Jordan just shown his hand?

The man furrowed his brows. "A curious response."

Jordan forced what he'd hoped was a convincing smile. "A knee-jerk response. Actually, she's fine."

"Someone special," he said, pausing and waiting for Jordan to respond. When he didn't, Addison continued. "Then again, maybe they're all special in their own way."

Again, Jordan didn't give him the benefit of a response.

"Ever think you'll marry again?" Addison asked, motioning to the server to bring him another drink.

"I'd like to think so."

"Maybe do a better job of it the next go-round."

The deviant glimmer in his eyes warned Jordan that it was Addison now casting the line.

"An intelligent man learns from his mistakes."

"An arrogant man just tells himself that he does and just figures out a different way to make them."

The senator pulled his cell phone from the breast pocket of his blazer when it chimed. "Ah, unfortunately, I must cut our visit short, my friend." He looked up at Jordan, smiled, and finished what was left in his glass and then stood up to leave. "Thank you for the drink and for the unusual conversation. It's been enlightening."

Jordan watched the man leave, worried that he might have slipped up and just sealed Abby's fate.

■ ■ ■ ■

As he was driving back to his office, his phone rang. Jordan didn't recognize the number on the screen, but he couldn't risk not answering it.

"Jordan," he said over the car's intercom system.

The extended pause set his heart racing.

"Mr. Gatewood," the woman finally responded. "It's been a few days since we last spoke and I felt it necessary to give you a call to see how you're holding up."

Rage surged through his veins. Confirmation? He and Addison had just parted ways ten minutes ago, and now this woman calls? If Jordan wasn't sure of it before, he was sure of it now. That bastard was in on this and he'd put this woman on alert, sending a message to put Jordan in check. Was that what this was? "Let me speak to Abby," he demanded.

He had to hear her voice. He had to know that he hadn't fucked up and that she was alive.

She sighed. "That's not possible."

She wasn't dead. Jordan forced the thought from his head. He felt weak, but he couldn't give in to it. "How do you expect me to move forward with your demands without proof that she's alive?"

"You'll have to take my word for it."

"Fuck your word!" he exploded. "I need to know that she's alive. I need to know that she's all right or you can shove that gotdamn contract up your ass."

Silence from her end of the line. Jordan couldn't be sure that she just didn't hang up on him.

"I need to see her," he said firmly. It was as close to begging as he dared come. God! He hoped he hadn't fucked up.

"The contract will arrive to you on Friday as planned," she explained.

Dread weighted in his stomach like lead, but Jordan needed to stand his ground. "Don't ignore me," he warned. "Don't you dare."

"You'll receive it via e-mail in-box, sign it, electronically is fine, return it immediately, and wire the funds to the account provided in the body of the e-mail."

"You don't get shit from me unless I know that she's alive and unharmed."

"You seem to think that you're in the position to bargain."

"I know I am," he said with convincing bravado. "If she's been harmed in any way, if you've — You show me. Show me that she's alive. I want to talk to her."

"I can't let you do that."

A lump the size of his fist swelled in his throat.

"I'll forward another picture," she told him.

"Date-stamped."

"Of course," she said before hanging up.

He needed to be ready, just in case. "Call Mike Bernstein," he said out loud.

The phone rang through his car speaker and his accountant answered. "Mr. Gatewood," he said cheerfully. "It's been a while."

"It has."

"What can I do for you, sir?"

After a brief pause, Jordan told him, "I need you to get a hundred million dollars ready to transfer."

"Whoa! That's a lot of money. From your personal account?"

"Yes."

"You opening up a new account?" he casually asked.

"Something like that."

"Where do want me to transfer it to?"

"I'll let you know in a few days. Just, get it ready."

"Mind if I ask you for a bit more information?"

Mike worked for Jordan, and for good reason. He was more careful with Jordan's money than Jordan was.

"Yes."

An uneasy pause rested between them. "I'll wait to hear back from you."

"Thank you," Jordan said before ending the call.

I Got the Antidote

Half an hour after Naomi had come back from her lunch break, James called asking for the key, offering to take food to the woman again.

"I know it's hard for you to get away in the evenings," he explained when he called. "You take care of her in the mornings and I'll hook her up in the evenings. Keep that old man of yours from getting suspicious."

"What'd you do to her, James?" Naomi had asked, knowing that James didn't give a damn about Naomi's well-being.

That woman was terrified of him coming back. Naomi didn't know him the way she knew DJ, but he didn't seem too cool.

"I didn't do shit to her. I took her the food and water just like I was supposed to, or rather" — he paused — "the way you were supposed to."

The critical tone was meant to cut into Naomi, and it did. DJ had entrusted her in the daily care of the woman, but she'd let James take advantage of the fact that she hadn't properly planned to do the job she was supposed to do. If she wanted that money, she couldn't afford to slip up again.

"I'll take care of it, James," she finally said. "It's my responsibility."

The sounds of that woman's cries coming from the other side of that door echoed through Naomi's mind. Naomi had no idea what he'd done to her, and she didn't want to know. Men were animals. She knew that better than most, but they couldn't afford for her to be hurt. DJ had said that they wouldn't get a dime if anything happened to her.

"I'll be by there in an hour," James finally said.

"Why?" she asked, panicked.

"I'll see you at noon."

"You coming here?" she asked, concerned.

"Yeah."

"What for? Do I need to call DJ?"

Naomi couldn't let James have that key again.

"Not unless you want him to know that you haven't been able to keep up your end of the bargain, Nay," he said coolly, but the underlying threat was definitely there.

"I'm holding up my end fine, James."

"Yeah," he said condescendingly. "I'll tell you what. Meet me at the rest stop off the highway at Exit 38."

"The highway going to Paris?"

"That's the one."

"No, James. There's really no need."

"Fine. Then'll I'll just swing by your place again. It ain't no big deal."

Naomi responded quickly. "No. Not my house. At the rest stop. It'll have to be after I get off work." James wanted this key in the worst way, but Naomi couldn't give it to him. She'd have to find a way to make him understand that.

James was abusive. Naomi had seen it in his eyes the first time she'd met him. He had the same look in him that Thomas had. Dark, hollow eyes pretending that there was a soul hidden inside them somewhere. She'd stared into those eyes last night at the dinner table. Thomas always had a way of finding things out without asking questions directly to Naomi. Now that the boys were older, he manipulated them for information he wanted to know.

Her older son hadn't volunteered that he'd seen Naomi talking to James, but somewhere between talking to the kids about school and baseball practice and telling Naomi how his day was Thomas had subtly and masterfully worked in a way to get their son to get her into trouble.

"Don't your momma look pretty today, boys?"

The boys shrugged.

"Makes me wonder if I need to worry," he said, reaching across the table and taking hold of her hand.

Warning. It shot through her like an arrow.

"You know you don't have anything to worry about, baby." She smiled her best smile and forced her food to stay down.

Did he know? Had he seen James at the house?

"Y'all would tell me if another man was hovering around too close," he said, looking at the boys. "Wouldn't you?"

Her younger son kept his gaze lowered and pensively shoved a piece of broccoli into his mouth. Thomas held her hand tighter. Naomi made eye contact with TJ.

"Sure would hate to have somebody steal you away from me," Thomas said, glancing at Naomi, and then locking on to the older boy.

"You're being silly, Thomas," she muttered.

He squeezed her hand, hard enough to send a message.

"Am I?"

"What'd you know good, Junior?" he asked, referring to the older boy.

Thomas had seen James. Naomi didn't

know how, but he had to have seen him. She tried swallowing the dread swelling in her throat, but it stuck there.

"Just somebody from her work," her son said, glancing nervously back and forth between his parents. "That's all."

Lie, Naomi. Lie as if your life depends on it, because it surely does.

"Oh, you mean James," she said suddenly, trying to pull back her hand, but Thomas wouldn't let it go. "He's a new driver." She stared her husband in the eyes so that he could look into her soul to see that she was telling him the truth. "He was driving by here, on his way home, I guess, and saw me and asked if I remembered which rig he had to take out today. He didn't stay long."

Thomas pretended to believe her, but she knew that he didn't. She knew that he'd make sure that she understood that lying to him was unacceptable. No matter what, though, she had to keep this secret or die trying.

Ten minutes after leaving work, she spotted James sitting and waiting for her at the park bench underneath a huge tree far enough off the main highway not to be seen clearly by cars passing by.

"Why you trying to make this so hard, Nay?" he asked, incredulous, as she stopped and stood in front of him.

"Why do you want that key so badly?" she challenged.

"I'm just trying to do you a favor, girl. That's all."

"DJ said that she's not to be hurt," Naomi reminded him.

James shrugged. "I know what DJ said."

"What'd you do to her, James?"

He slowly lowered his hand and cocked his head to one side. "What the fuck you talking about? What makes you think I did anything?"

For some reason Naomi thought better of telling him about how the woman begged her not to let James come back. If he knew she'd said that, it might make him angry enough to really hurt her badly enough for DJ to somehow find out. Naomi telling him would be like adding fuel to a fire.

"We don't get paid if you hurt her. I can't . . . I can't walk away from this without that money."

Naomi was too damn close to being able to buy her freedom for this silly asshole to mess up now.

"She say I did something?" he asked, giving her the side eye. "That bitch lied on me and you believed her?"

Naomi just stared at him. James stopped

being defensive.

"Your old man give you that?" He motioned to the bruise on her cheek starting to darken underneath her foundation. "I think I can guess what you need that money for."

"I think we all need it," she said, swallowing. "I'll stick to my part of this bargain, James. I said I'd see to it that she ate, and I will. You don't need to worry about it."

"But what if I want to worry about it, Nay?"

The threat coming from a man like all men held the same stench, and it all made her stomach turn.

"Maybe we should talk to DJ about this," she said, returning a threat of her own.

He threw his head back and laughed. "Is that supposed to scare me?" James shook his head in disbelief. "You and DJ holding hands, skipping along through the woods chasing kittens and puppies if you think that whoever's behind all of this is gonna let that woman live when it's all said and done."

"Why else would they want us to keep her safe if they had no intention of letting her live, James? Of course she's gonna be set free. They'll get what they want. We'll get our money and —"

"And drop her off at the nearest Dairy Queen. Maybe give her a few quarters so that she can call the police or that rich motha fucker of hers to come to scoop her up. And then all of this will be over with. We'll have our money and every one of us will scurry off like roaches when the lights come on. Is that it?"

She shrugged. "Yeah, that's pretty much it."

"Until she tells them about us."

"What's to tell? She's never seen our faces, James. She has no idea where she is or who we are. She can't tell anybody anything about us."

"She knows that there are three of us, one white woman and two brothas."

"I'm mixed."

"What-the-fuck-ever. She knows that you've got blond hair. She knows how tall I am and the sound of my voice."

"Those things don't mean anything. She can't point any of us out in a lineup."

He licked his lips. "I know that you'll be a ghost as soon as you get money in your hands. The cops will put it together, Nay. And when they find you, they'll find me and DJ. They find DJ, they might just find the people who hired us. It's not that hard, Nay. She's a witness."

James was not the voice of reason in this situation. Even if he was right, Naomi couldn't afford to get caught up in thinking about shit like that right now. The only way she could handle this was one day at a time, and the only reason she'd agreed to do this, besides the money, was because DJ assured her that the woman wouldn't be killed.

"No matter," she told him definitively. "I'll take her food."

The way he looked at her made Naomi take a step back.

James held out his hand again. "Or I could show up at your door today at around five thirty."

Of course this dirty bastard would play dirty games. If Thomas found out that James came back, every hope she'd ever had of saving herself and her children would be gone.

"My husband will be home," she murmured, more to herself than to him, her plans for escape dangerously balancing the actions of this fool sitting in front of her.

"I know," he said, stretching out his arm and waiting for her to place the key in his palm.

Hold Your Nose

Belle was sleeping in the other room. She'd been staying with Shou Shou since she'd started feeling poorly. The hush of night fell around her, and Shou should've been asleep, but she was wide awake, sitting up in her bed, more anxious than she'd been about anything in a very long time. Sleep should've come hours ago, but lately, she'd gotten her days and her nights mixed up. That sometimes happened to the blind, but it hadn't happened to Shou in years. Her nerves were bad, only she didn't know why. It was as if someone had shot a jolt of electricity through her, flooding her with unsettled energy.

She'd tried not to let on how nervous she really felt, to keep Belle and Marlowe from worrying too much. The doctor had said that her blood pressure was fine and that Shou was healthier than just about anybody else she'd ever seen at her age. She was into her seventies now. But what was ailing her wasn't physical. It was spiritual. Warfare. Her ancestors were restless, jostling around each other trying to put order to chaos. Whose?

"Y'all need to tell me," she murmured earnestly to the spirits.

Did it have anything to do with one of her girls? Shou absently wrung her hands together in her lap.

"Marlowe." She mouthed her niece's name over and over again. "That one always did give me the blues. Lord knows Belle ain't got no business to worry me. Never does."

Her lovely Marlowe with her soft and willing heart was vulnerable to the world's ugly ways. She called herself being in love with that man called Plato. Shou never liked him. His spirit was filled with shadows and warnings. He held part of himself back and away from Marlowe and from anybody who threatened to get too close.

"She don't listen," Shou said, shaking her head. "Too damn hardheaded. Stubborn and silly."

Marlowe would fall in love with a rock if it rolled the right way. That crazy girl just wanted Plato. Didn't matter how he came to her or when.

"Is it her again? Is she who's got me worrying so?"

Shou sat and waited for the ancestors to confirm her suspicions that her niece was the cause of all of Shou's turmoil, but they were quiet.

She thought about Belle, Marlowe's cousin and Shou's other niece, sleeping quietly in the other room. LuLu Belle she used to call her when she was just a little girl. Sweet and unselfish, Belle never asked for nothing, but she gave. Oh, she was generous to a fault, with everything except her heart. Shou feared that love would never come for Belle because she ran from it, had been running her whole life. Belle never wanted a man to come into her life because she was afraid he'd break her heart. Shou'd tried to tell Belle that she'd been breaking it herself since she'd first come into this world.

"My hands and feet are always cold," she said to her ancestors. "Nothing I do seems to warm 'em up." Sudden tears filled her eyes. "I'm afraid." Her voice trembled. "But of what, I just don't know."

An authentic, unexplainable fear filled her inside and wrapped around the outside of her like a blanket. It had been gradually building, growing stronger with each passing day. On the surface, Shou had no reason to be afraid, but this feeling was unnatural and spiritual. It was the worst kind because it came at her from all directions with no good sense of what was causing it.

The last time she'd felt this way was when Marlowe's twin, Marjorie, got sick. She hadn't even gone to the doctor yet, but Shou knew before anyone that death was coming for her. She knew and didn't tell anybody and it did. By the time Marjorie went to the doctor, they told her that she had only months to live. Shou Shou had already known it, though. The memory prickled on her skin.

The flavor of a peach filled her mouth all of a sudden. It was as if she'd actually taken a bite of one. Shou smacked her lips and swallowed the sweet, sticky nectar of the fruit washing down her throat. Panic immediately filled her.

"But I'm allergic to peaches," she said dreadfully.

What if death was coming for her? Peaches made her break out in hives and closed her throat. The last time she'd eaten one had been more than thirty years ago, and oh, that peach sure gave Shou Shou a fit. And it was the best peach she'd ever eaten, too. The juice from it ran between her fingers and down her chin. She ended up in the hospital because of it.

All of a sudden, the *spirits had her*!

A rush of warm air filled her room and washed over Shou's body, pushing breath back into her chest and pressing heavy against her. She felt herself floating — flying until suddenly she stopped and felt twigs and dry leaves crunch beneath her bare feet.

She jerked, startled by the sight of a dark and commanding figure of a man with no face. Shou had vision in her spiritual walks. Never clear vision, though, blurred shadows mostly and this one was no different. But she knew who he was instinctively; she knew that he was Marlowe's man, Plato. Black from head to toe, featureless, big and bold. She handled him well enough in the real world. He was scared of her here. But Shou was seeing him in the spirit world, his true self.

"I'm allergic to peaches," she blurted out in defense, as if he were personally going to force her to eat one.

He needed to know that. For some reason she didn't understand, he needed to know that Shou was allergic to peaches and that she would not stand by and let him force one into her mouth.

The scent of ripe peaches filled the air.

"So sweet," she repeated, turning in slow circles and inhaling the scent. "But Lord, no! I can't eat 'em. I can't."

It was as if someone had taken her and dropped her into what her version of hell would be. The smell of them peaches was strong enough to taste. The hair on her arms stood up as welts began to swell on her skin.

"I ain't ate any!" she yelled angrily. "I ain't even touched one!"

But the smell was overwhelming. It was in the air all around her, thick like marmalade, so rich she could taste it on her tongue.

"No!" she spat.

Shou felt the muscles in her neck constrict; her windpipe began to close in on itself. She began to claw at her neck, gasping and coughing, desperate to catch pockets of air to fill her lungs before it was too late.

"Auntie?" Belle's voice startled Shou back into this present moment, still coughing and trying to catch her breath.

"It's all right. Just a bad dream, Auntie Shou. I got you."

The urgent need to tell him that she was allergic to peaches was too overwhelming to ignore.

"Get me the phone, Belle," she recovered and told her niece.

"Auntie Shou, it's late."

"Get the phone, girl. Now."

Belle took the phone from the nightstand and handed it to her. Shou fumbled with it until she found the button to push to dial Marlowe's number. Her hands were shaking so terribly she feared she'd drop the phone.

"Hello?" Marlowe answered groggily.

"Is he there?" Shou asked, her voice shaking.

Every nerve in her body was on edge. If that bastard was going to try to kill Shou with a peach, he needed to know that she was on to him. That she'd be watching him, and that he'd have one hell of a fight on his hands if he thought he could get rid of her so easily.

"Aunt Shou?" Marlowe asked, confused.

"Put him on the phone, Marlowe," she demanded.

"What? Who?"

"Your man, girl! Put his ass on the phone."

"Calm down, Auntie," Belle said, soothingly rubbing Shou's arm.

Shou slapped her hand away.

"Yeah," he finally said huskily.

"I'm allergic to peaches," she said angrily.

"What?"

"I'm allergic to peaches, gotdammit!"

"Why're you telling me this?"

" 'Cause you need to know. You keep yo'

distance and you keep them peaches away from me. You hear me? I mean it. You keep them peaches away from me!"

Shou abruptly hung up and shoved the phone back in Belle's general direction.

After a few minutes, Belle, feeling that Shou had calmed down enough to sleep, left and went back to her room. But Shou wouldn't get any sleep tonight. Not until that bastard understood who he was dealing with. Not until he took his damn peaches and shoved them up his ass. That devil would not take Shou without a fight.

COULDN'T FAKE IT

"Go on, baby girl," James said as tenderly as he knew how, sliding the white paper bag on the floor toward her. "Got you a burger and some fries." James then slid the soda over to her. "None of that boring-ass shit that old girl's been giving you to eat."

Pretty brown eyes locked on to his and James quietly fell in love. He wasn't a bad dude, and he wanted her to know that. It wasn't hard to see that she didn't trust him, though. But he got it. She was scared, and him hiding behind this mask wasn't helping.

He remembered the first time he'd seen her, weighed down with steel-toed boots and a utility belt. There's no hiding pretty no matter how hard you tried. But she didn't pay him no mind. Barely even glanced at him when she asked him what his name was and offered to help him unload his truck. She thanked him when they finished. Smiled when she did it. Almost like she might actually remember him, but he knew that she wouldn't.

"I swear it's good," he assured her with a smile. "Just take a few bites. You don't have to finish it."

Reluctantly, she opened the sack, pulled out the hamburger, and took a small bite, but she never took her eyes off his. James liked that. Watching her eat, he couldn't help but think about the magic she spread all over that man of hers that probably drove him crazy. Why else would James, DJ, and Naomi be hired to go through so much trouble taking her and keeping her? Whoever he was, the people behind all this believed that he was crazy enough about her to pay to get her back, way more money than the three of them were getting. *Are you worth it, sweetheart?* he wanted to ask.

"I'm not supposed to know your name," he said softly, "and of course you can't know mine."

It was just the two of them in this small room. James played this game in his head, the one where he would try to do the right thing. DJ had his rules that he expected James to follow. Bullshit rules that didn't mean a damn thing. James played along, though, in his mind. He was the good guy.

In reality, he could do whatever the hell he wanted to her and no one could stop him.

"Is this a courtship?" James posed the question more to himself than to her.

She stopped eating. He wanted her to trust him. He wanted to impress her and to sway her into relaxing just a little bit with him here. He could be her savior. Couldn't he? James could be the one to set her free if she could somehow convince him that he should. It was an odd thought for him to have, and he had no idea why it even came to mind, especially when he knew the truth. He knew it better than any of them. Her fate was sealed and James was the only one with the courage to think about it.

James would be the one to kill her because DJ was too chickenshit to do it, and Nay was fuckin' useless. James would do it because he was the only one who could do it. The revelation struck him like a punch in the gut. So, he owned her. Didn't he? He held her life in his hands and that meant that she, in some way, belonged to him.

"I don't want any more," she said softly, putting the hamburger back in the bag and pushing it over to him.

He sat across from her on the floor for several minutes wondering how he'd do it. Something quick. A bullet? When she wasn't looking. A bullet when she thought she was free. Damn! That'd be fucked-up. Wouldn't it?

"How much money did they promise you?"

Her question caught him by surprise. Miss Abby squared her shoulders and challenged him with a look.

"I beg your pardon?" he asked, surprisingly proud at the courage she seemed to have all of a sudden.

"I can get you more than what they said they'd give you." She swallowed. "I assure you — I can."

She was serious. James leaned his head to one side and studied her.

"Whatever they've promised you, I can double it. Triple it."

Of course she was thinking she would get it from that rich motha fucka.

"And no one would ever have to know," she told him. "You could take the money and disappear. Go where you want. Do what you want. I can make this happen," she said, with all the confidence of a queen.

Of course, James had to consider this offer. The money DJ had promised him was nice and all, but it didn't take a genius to know that it wasn't enough to last for the rest of his life. Her man could set James up

for forever, and the idea was far too tempting to just dismiss it.

"I just need to make a call," she continued
softly. "One call and you can have more
money than you ever dreamed of and no
one would ever have to know about this."

James took a deep breath and let what
she'd said sink in. This was a deal just for
him. Not DJ or Naomi, but just James.

"You know it's a good plan," she said.
"You win if we do it this way. You win. Be
smart about this."

After a long pause, he finally spoke. "A
phone call?"

She nodded. "Yes."

He could be a rich man, too, with a whole
collection of chocolate beauties like her at
his beck and call if that's what he wanted.
And all he'd have to do is let her make that
call. James raked his hand over his head and
let that idea take hold. Basically, he'd be
flipping a finger to his brother and Nay, and
riding off into the sunset free and clear of
this. Or she could be setting him up.

"Who would you call, sweetheart?"

She damn near choked holding on to her
man's name.

"I ain't no genius." He shook his head and
sighed. "But I ain't a complete fool, either."

"I know you're not."

"Stop," he commanded, and pointed at her. "You call him. He has my number and takes it to the police. I seen my share of movies. They trace this number to me and then track it to a cell tower somewhere around here and find you."

"Then get another phone," she suggested desperately. "One from the convenience store. They can't trace that to you."

"But they would be able to find you, and then we'd all be up shit creek."

"I won't tell —"

"No, you won't," he said, pressing his finger to his lips. "Sounds good, though. Damn! How much would he pay me for you?"

She shook her head slightly and shrugged. "Let me make the call. He'll pay whatever you want."

All of a sudden, James laughed. "What the hell did you do to him, girl?" he asked absently, staring mesmerized by this woman.

For all her lovely promises, he knew that there was no other way for this situation to play out than the one ending with her dead.

"Then let me give you the number and you can call from any phone, anywhere."

Did she know she was living on borrowed time? Did she know that his face would be the last one she'd ever see again? Killing was intimate and he wanted to know her.

"How'd he find you?"

She glowered at him and then anger turned to fear. Which was only right. James scooted closer. She tried to disappear into that wall behind her to separate herself from him. He studied her, wondering what she might've looked like all made up and wearing fancy clothes.

"Where'd you meet him?"

Men like the one paying for her could have any woman they wanted. Why had this one chosen her? And why did James give a shit? She was just going to die anyway.

Tears glistened in her eyes.

"What's so special about you?" he asked. James nodded his own affirmation. "I mean, you look good and all, but you're just some bitch outta Blink. What's so special about you, Miss Abby? Why would he pay all that money to get you back?"

Deep down she had to know how all this was going to end. He reached for her. She was close enough to touch, but she shrugged away from his fingertips, recoiled like a snake. James couldn't help himself. He laughed.

"Where the hell you think you gonna go, baby?"

"Just leave," she said shakily. "Please."

It was her rejection of him that fueled him. It made him want her even more, just because she had the nerve to think he couldn't. James abruptly reached out to her, grabbed her by one of her ankles, and pulled her to him.

"No!" she screamed, kicking with her free leg, but he grabbed hold of that one too, pulled her off that mat and across the floor and onto his lap. "Oh, God! No!"

James laughed, pinning her thighs against his sides with his arms, and twisting both her arms behind her, pinning them to her back. Her soft breasts pressed against his chest. And his dick doubled in size and pressed painfully against his zipper. Oh, she fought. And the harder she fought, the harder he got.

"You getting me all worked up, baby girl," he said, nuzzling his face in the crook of her neck and inhaling. "Mmmm." He kissed her there. "Shit! You feel so damn good."

"Stop!" she screamed at the top of her lungs. "Don't do this! Don't do —"

"Hush now," he said, clamping her wrists in one hand and slowly raising her shirt with the other. "Aw, shit," he murmured, cupping one breast in his hand, kneading it in his palm, raising the nipple to a ripe, dark peak.

They were bigger than he first thought, and his mouth watered to taste one. James licked his lips, lowered his head, and wrapped his lips around that sweet little berry. She bucked against him, but he held on tight. James made love to that thing, licking and nibbling on it like it was candy. Her petite, curvy little ass fit him like a glove. He had her all to himself. Nobody was going to hear her cries. Nobody was going to save her or stop him from doing whatever the fuck he wanted to do to her. Her rich man was nowhere to be found. She belonged to James. He knew that now, more than ever.

In one effortless motion, he raised up on his knees and pushed her down on her back onto that mat, and nestled between her legs.

"Damn, I been wanting you so bad," he groaned, slipping his hand between the two of them. He shoved the material of her shorts to one side and slipped his fingers between the warm, moist folds of her pussy. "Shit, girl. Fuck!"

Nothing mattered anymore. Not promises to DJ or threats to Naomi. Keep her safe. Keep her safe. Who would know? Even if she said anything to Naomi, who the fuck cared? Her cries got lost in a vacuum as James fumbled to unhook his belt. And then his phone rang.

It'll stop! He ignored it. He wanted to ignore it.

She screamed all up in his gotdamned ear.

"Fuck!" he grumbled, reaching into his pocket to get to that fuckin' phone.

He looked at the screen and saw his brother's name on the screen. James looked into her face. She was crying like crazy. But he had to take this call.

He climbed off of her, grabbed what was left of the food and drink, and left, locking the door behind him. His dick bucked in protest as he braced himself on the other side of that door. The phone stopped ringing, but then DJ immediately called back. He'd keep calling until James answered.

"Yeah," he said abruptly.

"Where you at, man?" DJ asked. Music played in the background. "You were supposed to bring the ribs."

Ribs? Fuck! James was supposed to have met DJ and the fellas at a friend's house to watch a basketball game. "Yeah, man. Yeah," he said, trying to compose himself.

"Don't tell me you laid up with some woman?" DJ asked teasingly.

"You know how it is, D."

"Yeah, I know how it is. But we need ribs, man. Get them and come on."

"On my way."

James stood at that door for several minutes before his hard-on dissipated enough for him to walk straight. He was at the door before he remembered to leave the key for Naomi. James walked back and placed it on the shelf; then he leaned against the door and listened to the soft sobs coming from the other side.

SEE DISHONOR

"Senator Addison." Brandon greeted the senator with a handshake arriving at his father's home, as the senator appeared to be leaving.

"Ah," the senator said, greeting him with a warm smile, "young Mr. Degan. It's good seeing you."

"You too, sir." Brandon glanced at his father, standing in the doorway. "You're leaving?"

"Yes," he said, shoving his hands into his pockets. "Just stopped by to check on the old geezer since I was in town."

Brandon's father huffed. "I'll show you old on the golf course the next time I make it to Austin," he threatened.

The senator laughed. "You got lucky last time."

"And what about the time before that?" Lars Degan asked with a smirk on his face.

Addison groaned. "In any event, I'll be in

Washington for a few weeks representing this great state of ours, but I'll be in touch," he said, raising his hand in the air to say good-bye as he left.

Brandon followed his father inside and closed the door behind him. His father was the reason Sam Addison had been a seated senator for three terms now. Addison had been his father's attorney for years, before deciding to run for office, and Lars Degan was the first to get on the Addison bandwagon, contributing heavily to his campaign. The two were as thick as thieves, old and dear friends who would do just about anything for each other.

"Reputations are fragile things," Brandon's father said, standing at the massive window of his study and looking out over acres of his land. "Especially for men like us." He sighed slowly, deeply, and then turned to face Brandon sitting across the room from him.

"Everybody's protesting every damn thing these days," Lars said, taking his seat behind his desk. "You have to wonder how anybody's able to get things done anymore when every move a man makes is considered a sin against God, nature, and mankind." He shook his head.

Brandon had studied his father his whole life, going out of his way to take heed of every action, every word. And yet being conscious not to digest those things about the man that he found to be the most reprehensible, like his racism, misogyny, and endless affairs. His father was the man he'd looked up to and even feared, but he never wanted to be like him, and yet he found himself in the position now of becoming exactly that.

"This pipeline will have the name Gatewood all over it after he signs those contracts," he reminded Brandon. "And just like that, his righteous black ass will become public enemy number one, his golden reputation tarnished. The indigenous will hate him and blame him. Liberals will shun him. Investors will pull out of business dealings with him, and magically" — his eyes twinkled as he stared at Brandon — "that empire of his falls."

The old man gloated as if this whole idea of getting Gatewood to invest in the pipeline was his idea. And like the good and devoted son he was, Brandon let him believe that it was. Or was Brandon just too damn cowardly to stand up to his father?

"When did you say he'd have the contract?" Lars probed.

"In two days."

"What's taking so damn long?"

"Verbiage," he simply stated. "Gatewood will be the lead investor, but we have to be sure that he gets no return on his investment and that there are no loopholes to allow for any. And if Congress does shut down the project, we have to be sure that there's no way he can recoup losses. We're pushing this to get it done so quickly, but it has to be an airtight contract, Dad, one that will hold up in any court, because he will try to fight it, and if we're not careful, he'll win."

Lars sighed. "He'll try. I'm sick of that sonofabitch winning," he said with disgust. "Right now, we have all the leverage," he said as an afterthought. "As long as he believes she's alive and that we have her, he'll do as he's told."

"She is alive," Brandon responded with an unexpected air of surprise at his father's statement.

Lars glared at him. "Still?"

"Yes, sir. Why is that a problem?"

The hardened expression sent a cold warning to Brandon.

"She is, as you say, leverage. We need to keep her until the very end," he said carefully. "It's the sensible thing to do."

Brandon didn't like thinking about the fate of Abby Rhodes. "He's asked for proof that she's alive. I had a feeling that he might, so keeping her safe plays in our favor."

Lars nodded slowly. "Good. Send him his proof and then do what you have to do."

Brandon made a call to Bianca as soon as he left his father's house. "Have one of them photograph her and then send it to him."

"I'll have it to him by morning," she said before hanging up.

Brandon rode in the back of his limousine to company headquarters, gathering his thoughts on the man he'd become. Had it happened overnight, or had he been groomed for this since he was born? It was strange. He had always been aware of his father's manipulative ways, and yet he'd always fallen into place with them, sort of like a twig floating on the surface of a river rushing downstream. Through the years, he'd promised himself that he'd break free of his father's influence and become the man he knew that he could be. But despite that promise, Brandon now realized that he was indeed his father's son, and that he'd inherited some of the man's worst qualities, despite his best efforts not to.

Jordan Gatewood had always been someone Brandon had admired: strong, powerful, and confident. He'd always considered Jordan fortunate that his father had died and Jordan was left to run the company on his own, his way. Julian Gatewood might've started Gatewood Industries, but Jordan had overshadowed his father long ago. And he'd done it on his own terms, in his own way, to hell with Julian's ideas or ideals.

He was a man standing on the precipice of destruction now. Jordan was about to lose everything he'd worked so hard to build, and he was about to lose the one thing that meant more to him than even his corporation or his reputation. Love, the kind that was true and pure, and was nearly impossible to come by. Brandon knew that better than anyone. He'd been married and divorced twice and had never been convinced that either of his wives loved him for who he was. It was his money that they loved. Brandon saw how Jordan looked at Abby; he saw that what the two of them had transcended money and status. It was old-fashioned and sweet and enviable. Brandon could take Gatewood's business, his money, and not lose a minute's sleep over it, but to take her from him — Brandon would probably never forgive himself for that. She was innocent in all of this. Abby Rhodes was guilty only of loving the wrong man at the wrong time. For her to have to die because of it, because of a silly old man with a silly grudge, reserved a special place in hell for the Degan family.

Too Afraid to Lose It

Abby shivered in the corner of that cold room, with her knees to her chest, covered by the blanket the woman had left her. Abby listened for any sounds coming from outside warning her that he might be coming back.

She'd been naïve to believe that rape looked a certain kind of way. Ultimately, though, no matter how it presented itself, rape was violation, pure and simple. He'd raped her. She'd been sitting here for hours coming to terms with the fact that it was true. No, he hadn't penetrated her with his penis, but he'd still taken from her, her body, and her will, without her permission. Rape was stolen power, freedom, and choice.

Pride always overshadowed ignorance when it came to her and how she viewed the world. Abby was an engineer. Her very profession, her nature at its core, was ruled by science, mathematical equations, and absolutes. How could she be so smart and yet be so dumb at the same time? A penis was a weapon in rape. But so were fingers and tongues and force. She couldn't have stopped him no matter how hard she'd fought or screamed. And that revelation shook her to the core.

She let her eyes close, only for a moment, but she knew that he wasn't finished with her. Bile rose in the back of her throat at the thought of him touching her again.

She had been left shattered after he left. A part of her turned in on herself, trying to void her mind, body, and soul from the residual of his touch. But after some time, the truth gradually settled in, forcing her to begin to accept the one thing she'd been fighting against since they'd taken her from her home.

Would they really let her go? Tears fell as hope sank to someplace dark inside her. Abby had always been a realist, facing the challenges in front of her head-on, prepared to take on whatever came her way. Would they let her go, or was Abby going to die?

She didn't want to die. And she didn't want that man to come back and put his damn hands on her. She didn't want to spend one more night in this cold and dark room. She didn't want to keep eating food that got stuck in the back of her throat. Abby wanted more than anything to be home, to be with Jordan and in his arms. Oh, God. The thought of never seeing him again, of never seeing her family again, was devastating.

She'd spent years working with men, trying to get them to understand that being a woman didn't make her less valuable than any of them, or weak or inadequate. And because she was a woman, she worked doubly hard to earn their respect and to get them to have as much faith in her abilities as she did. Abby had stood toe to toe to men half a body taller than her, cussing them out until they looked like they would cry, proving the point that she was no pushover. It had taken years to gain the respect of her peers, but she'd done it. What would any of them think of her now, seeing her cowering in the corner of this room, shivering and vulnerable? Abby had been afraid since they'd taken her, but he'd left her feeling something more than fear, a disgusting and ugly thing with no name.

If this was just about money then why was she still here? Had they even contacted Jordan? He had to know that she was missing. They spoke every single day, several times a day, especially when they weren't together.

Of course, he'd give them money if he knew, if they'd told him that that's what they wanted. Wouldn't he? Abby shook her head against doubts starting to creep into her thoughts. She had money, too. Not as much as he did and she had no idea how much they'd demanded for her safe return, but Jordan wouldn't hesitate to pay it. And she'd pay him back. Maybe not overnight, but damn if she'd be bought and sold like property. He just needed to do what had to be done to get her out of here.

The tears fell. "I'm so scared, Jordan," she whispered.

She could count on one hand how many times she'd been crippled by fear in her life, and this was most certainly one of those times. They were never going to let her go. If somehow she couldn't find a way out, or if by some crazy long shot of a chance Jordan couldn't meet their demands, she knew deep down that she wouldn't get out of here alive. And she could sit here in the dark crying about it, or she could try to figure out a way to save her life.

Sometimes, finding the solution to a problem was as simple as shifting perspectives. Abby had been looking for flaws in this predicament from one angle, the most obvious one. So far she'd been wrong.

Maybe, it wasn't that woman who was the crack in the façade of this crew. Maybe it was him. While that idiot was being led around by his dick she had to keep her wits about her and to find a way to use his weakness against him. What was his weakness? It was Abby.

She pulled the flattened plastic bottle out from underneath the mat. The seams on that door were too tight to even slip a piece of plastic through, but maybe she could use it as a wedge to keep the lock from engaging completely after it was closed. She needed to soften the material; using heat and pressure, she needed to open the bottle until it was flat, like paper. That would take time and it would help her to stay awake.

LOVE, PLEASE LET ME BE

It was after two in the morning and Jordan
sat slumped on the side of the bed, feeling
every second of his age. May 18, Jordan
turned fifty and he'd celebrated the mile-
stone with her.

He stood on the balcony of his stateroom,
freshly showered, dressed, and looking out
over the Mediterranean, watching the sun set
as the yacht he'd chartered slowly pulled into
port in Malta while Abby slept soundly in bed
behind him. Coming to terms with having lived
half a century was beyond surreal. Jordan
remembered a time, not so long ago, when
he considered anyone who was fifty a senior
citizen. He didn't feel old, though. He felt as if
he was getting his second wind, ready to
embark on the next half of his life, the half
that mattered because she was a part of it.

"What time is it?" she asked sleepily.

He turned to face Abby sitting up in bed,
holding the sheet against her with one hand

and rubbing sleep from her eyes with the other.

"Doesn't matter, dahlin'," he said, making his way over to her and sitting on the side of the bed. "We've got all the time in the world."

Jordan leaned in close and kissed her. He had promised her once that he wanted forever with her, and not just a lifetime. He'd never been so certain about another human being in his life.

"You smell good," she said, flashing that gorgeous smile of hers.

"You smell like us." He grinned.

Abby laughed. "Everybody probably thinks we fell overboard."

Everybody was the ten other people, people he didn't mind spending a week with, whom he'd invited on this trip to celebrate his birthday.

"Yeah, well, I'm going to head down to let them know that we've been here all along."

"Okay," she said, planting a sweet peck on his lips. "I'll be down shortly."

"No rush, sugah."

"Darlene Johnson."

That was a name he hadn't heard since his freshman year in college.

"Darlene Johnson?" Jordan repeated, looking back at the man like he'd lost his mind.

Jordan and Ron Davis had played football together and became hard-and-fast friends the first time Ron tackled Jordan after he'd made a catch causing him to fumble. Ron went on to play pro ball for fifteen years before finally retiring.

"Why the hell are you bringing her up?" Jordan asked, incredulous.

Ron laughed. "You got stupid over that girl."

Jordan immediately became defensive. "I didn't get stupid."

"Nah, man. You got dumb. Only girl, until now, that I've ever seen you get dumb over."

Dumb? Was he dumb over Abby?

Ron seemed to have read his mind. "I remember you stalking Darlene."

"Bullshit."

"You stalked her, Jordan. Followed her to every class."

"I walked her to her classes, Ron. That's not stalking."

"You walked her to class and skipped your own, waiting on her to get out of hers, so that you could walk her to the next one. Even waited for her to finish cheerleading practice and debate practice. That's akin to stalking, at the risk of your education, I might add."

"She liked it," Jordan retorted.

"Her friends tried talking her into reporting you to campus security."

"But she didn't."

Ron's wife, Laura, shook her head and laughed. "Still, that does sound like stalking, Jordan."

"Can I help it if I was attentive?"

"Obsessive is more like it," Ron shot back.

"I was young. What? Eighteen?"

"And bold. She was a junior."

"What?" Laura asked, stunned.

Jordan grinned. "I rocked her world."

Ron laughed. "Aw, c'mon, man. She rocked yours, which is why you were put on academic probation for that semester."

He laughed too, remembering Darlene and all those things she taught him how to do in bed. Jordan nodded. "Boy, was she worth it."

"I take it you plan on asking her to marry you?" Ron asked, turning serious.

Jordan happened to look up at the deck above them and noticed Abby making her way to the staircase. Without answering Ron's question, he walked over to the bottom of the stairs and waited for her. Jordan had spent all afternoon in bed with this woman, and yet seeing her now was like seeing her for the very first time.

Abby wore a long multicolored dress, with a split stopping midway on her thigh. It was cut into a low V, highlighting full, round breasts, and the material clung to her shapely figure, singing praises to every lovely curve. Her short hair was parted on one side, sleeked down, and brushed back.

"Don't you look beautiful," he said to her.

"Thank you, baby," she said, smiling and toying with the collar of his shirt.

"I'll take that as a yes," Ron called out to him from the bar, raising his glass in a toast.

Once they were in port, a limo was waiting for the twelve of them. While everybody else talked about whatever, Abby stared out the window, marveling at architecture that seemed to be a fusion of Roman and maybe British influence, but sprinkled with a taste of Greek. They ended up at a restaurant called Tarragon. Jordan damn near ordered the whole appetizer section off the menu. Calamari, trout carpaccio, tiger prawns, lamb shoulder, some kind of ravioli.

Of course the wine flowed like Jesus was in the kitchen personally changing it from water coming out of the tap, but Abby opted for sparkling water.

"You all right, baby?" he asked when she did.

"Oh, I'm good," she assured him.

For dinner, Jordan had a black Angus fillet and Abby ordered the lobster.

After dinner, the driver took them to a city called Bugibba, and Jordan led them up the stairs to a gold-painted door. The music bellowing through the room sounded ancient but had been infused with what sounded like hip-hop. Tall, arched, and ornate cathedral ceilings had to have been at least fifty feet high and looked like they'd been hand-painted by Michelangelo. Silk and satin draped from them, and across tables and chairs — and there were belly dancers. Jordan turned to her and smiled. He knew how much she loved belly dancing.

Abby stayed plastered to him the whole night, gazing into his eye

"Happy birthday, my love," she whispered.

Jordan kissed her, but immediately noticed something concerning in her expression.

"What's wrong, Abby?"

She swallowed nervously. "Would you . . ." She paused and then took a deep breath. "Would you want to have a baby with me?"

Jordan cocked a thick brow and let what she'd just asked gradually take root.

"Yes. I would like to have all my babies with you."

Abby turned her face away from everyone around them so that none of them could see the tears forming in her eyes. He studied her for a moment, realizing that the question might not have been rhetorical.

Jordan whispered in her ear, "Are you pregnant?"

She nodded. "Sort of."

■ ■ ■ ■

DAY 4

■ ■ ■ ■

He's Chokin'

Marlowe had spent all night at her aunt Shou's house. The old woman was going crazy or something, having irrational fears about peaches and a deep-rooted belief that Plato was trying to kill her, so he figured it was best for him to keep his distance and let Marlowe and Belle sprinkle holy water on the old woman or something until she snapped out of whatever it was she was tripping over.

Three days into looking for Abby Rhodes and Plato had absolutely nothing to go on. He'd hoped that Crown Distributors would lead him somewhere, but it didn't. Hundreds of people went in and out of that place all day long. It wasn't like Abby's kidnapper was wearing a T-shirt that read "Hey, yo! Pick me! I got her, man!" Gatewood hadn't called him — yet — but he expected to hear from him at some point today. Tomorrow was D-day. And that dude's head was likely ready to explode, and understandably so. Plato's was throbbing, too.

He'd never failed to deliver on an assignment before. Plato had always managed to come through with whatever it was he'd been hired to do, claiming property, gathering information, or making bodies disappear — living or dead. It had never dawned on him that he could fail. And to fail in this? Well, this was . . . personal. He'd never had much of a conversation with Abby, but she was nobody who should've been anybody in this type of situation. Abby Rhodes was a victim of circumstance in Gatewood's world. Plato couldn't help but think that the man should've left well enough alone. He should've stayed away from that woman and left Abby Rhodes where he'd found her. In that respect, Gatewood and Plato were alike. Plato should never have latched on to Marlowe, either.

He wasn't a fan of the man, but Plato couldn't deny that the two of them traveled in dark circles and they had both been drawn to the light of sweet country love, which neither of them deserved. The Abbys and the Marlowes of the world were innocent to the demons that Plato and Gatewood toyed with. Gatewood had put Abby at risk simply by being who he was. He'd pissed off the wrong people. Or he had something that they'd wanted. The brotha was enviable, living in his ivory tower and staring down his nose at everybody he'd stepped on to get there. Somebody didn't like it.

"More coffee?" the waitress asked, hovering over him.

Plato had left the house early this morning since Marlowe wasn't home and opted for breakfast on his own.

He nodded. "Thanks," Plato said when she finished filling his cup.

Out of the corner of his eye, he saw a tall, thin, blond woman coming into the place. She sat down at a table near the window across from a brotha staring at his cell phone.

The bacon was good here. Smoked? Thick cut. Eggs were a little runny for his taste, though. That couple, the blond woman and the brotha, were in his line of sight, so without even trying, he watched them while he ate. Animated. Her. Not him. Like she was angry with him, fussing but keeping her voice down so that no one could overhear. She was pissed, but that cat sitting across from her didn't give a shit. The dude finished his food, set his phone down on the table, leaned back, pulled a matchstick from his shirt pocket, and stuck the wooden end in his mouth, like a toothpick. He waited patiently, letting her rant until she'd finished saying whatever it was she'd needed to say before she got up and stormed out of the place.

A few minutes passed, and Plato was about done. Dude across from him paid his bill and got up and left, too. Plato contemplated his next move. Where the hell was Abby? In Blink? Nelson? Clark City? Was she even in this dimension anymore? Where the hell was her truck? Plato gave the waitress a twenty.

"I'll be back with your change."

"Keep it," he said, leaving.

Did he need to go back? Back to the beginning, to Abby's house? As he was leaving, he held the door open for an old woman hobbling in on a cane.

"Hey, Peaches," the waitress said when she saw the woman. "How you been?"

Peaches?

"Thank you," the old woman said, nodding at her and smiling.

Peaches couldn't have been more than four and a half feet tall. Reddish-brown skin, white hair, and round.

"Oh, I been trying to keep these old bones

of mine loose." Peaches laughed heartily and waited for the server to pull out a seat for her to sit down at an open table.

"Thank you, sweetheart."

"James just left. Did you see him?"

"I did. Saw him outside."

"Well, your food will be ready in about ten minutes. Want some coffee while you wait?"

"You keep yo' distance and you keep them peaches away from me. You hear me? I mean it. You keep them peaches away from me!"

Dismiss it. Plato didn't have the luxury of entertaining coincidences. Especially dumb ones related to fruit and old women. He took about four steps before he stopped. The thing was, Shou Shou wasn't just any old woman. He would never openly admit it, but he believed she was magic or a witch or maybe even a mean, little fairy. He turned back toward the restaurant and stared at fat Peaches sitting near the window.

Peaches had just walked into the same restaurant he'd had breakfast in. Shou was allergic to peaches and had been adamant about making sure he understood as much. Peaches. Not a thing, but a person? Had she been trying to tell him something? He walked contemplatively back to his car,

305

climbed in, then immediately shook the ridiculous theories of Shou Shou and her allergies out of his head. Damn! Was he that damned desperate, or what?

Plato shook his head and started the engine of his car. Before he pulled away from the curb, the old lady came out of the restaurant carrying a bag.

"Mornin', Ms. Gooden," a man said, walking up and hugging her. "It's been a while."

"Oh, it has, Mr. Braxton. How's yo' wife?"

"Her sugah's been acting up. Had to increase her insulin, but other than that, she's fine. We was just talking 'bout you the other day."

She reared back. " 'Bout me? Why?"

"Talkin' 'bout that cobbler you used to make." He grinned. "Oh, Lord, that was the best cobbler."

She laughed. "That's what people still tell me."

"You ever think about opening up again just to make cobbler?"

"Naw, my arthritis is too bad."

"Well, tell somebody else how to make it."

"Now, I ain't never been one to give away my recipes," she joked. "That's a recipe I'ma take to my grave."

"Well, that's pure selfishness." He laughed.

"Write it down so I can give it to my wife. We won't tell nobody."

"I might just do that," she conceded slyly. "Long as she keep the name the same. Can't give it her own name."

"You named it?"

"Course I did. It's my trademark."

It was silly banter that for some reason held him captive, probably because Plato was at a loss for how to do his damn job and "peaches" had been the buzzword of the week.

"What's it called?"

"Miss Peaches' Precious Peach Cobbler," she said proudly.

He laughed so hard he nearly fell over.

"What's so funny?" she asked, offended. "That was the name on my menu. Don't you remember?"

"Nah. I just remember asking for the peach cobbler," he finally conceded.

"See. I ain't giving y'all my recipe," she huffed, and started to walk away.

"Oh, c'mon, Ms. Gooden."

"You had your chance," she said, stopping and turning back to him. "Like I said, I'm taking my recipe to the grave."

"Fine. Want me to tell Mary to call you?"

She paused for a second. "She can call me, but that don't mean I'm giving her my recipe," she said, walking off.

He shook his head and dismissed her with a wave. "Crazy woman," he muttered.

It was a humorous interchange about peach cobbler, deadly to a crazy blind woman. Shit. Plato had nothing. Not a single lead to finding Abby, and time was not on his side. So why the hell was he sitting here enthralled, watching Peaches hobble, wobble down the road, cursing under her breath and shaking her head, ready to murder that old man over a damn recipe?

Plato started up his car. "You're getting pathetic, Plato Wells. Plenty pathetic."

IF YOU'RE NOT THERE

"Wake up!"

Abby heard a woman's voice and felt a shoe bump against the sole of her foot.

"Hey, get up and eat."

She'd slept, but she hadn't meant to. Disoriented and panicked, Abby glanced at the woman and then at the food she'd placed on the floor.

"Can I use the bathroom?"

"Eat. Hurry up," she commanded.

One day had blurred into another in this endless nightmare playing itself out over and over again like that movie *Groundhog Day.* Abby stared at the bottle of water and at the bag she knew contained a bologna sandwich on white bread. The thought of eating it turned her stomach. Moments later, the woman returned with a man following behind her.

"No!" Abby blurted out, and immediately scooted back up against the wall. "You stay the fuck away from me," she yelled, with fearful tears filling her eyes. As far as she knew he was as much a rapist as the other one.

He held up a cell phone and took pictures of her.

"Are you going to eat?" the woman asked angrily.

"Keep him away from me!" she demanded.

Why she thought that woman could or would protect her was insane. She was one of them. Of course she didn't give a damn about what he did to Abby.

He took a few more pictures and then left the room.

"Eat or I leave and you get nothing."

Abby waited until she thought he was gone before reluctantly doing as she was told, swallowing as much as she could of the sandwich and water before pushing it away.

"I need to go to the bathroom."

Just like before, the woman picked up Abby's trash, closed and locked the door behind her, and returned moments later with a bucket for Abby to pee in. This time, she watched Abby relieve herself.

After she left, Abby heard their voices coming from the other side of the door.

Abby hesitantly walked over to it, and pressed her ear against it.

"That's it. Right, DJ? Just a picture. That's all he wanted?" It was the woman. "You send him that picture and he'll pay?"

DJ.

"He needed proof of life," he said in a low tone.

He? Jordan?

"We send them this, they send it to him, and he'll pay. But he needed to know that she was alive first."

"You hurry up. That bastard needs to get these people their money so that we can get ours."

"Stop tripping. We're getting ours."

"We'd better, DJ."

"Keep your damn voice down," he demanded. "And stop saying my fuckin' — She might hear you."

"I don't give a damn what the fuck she hears."

"You'll give a damn if she talks to the police."

"Like she'll get the chance."

"What the hell you mean by that?"

"Nothing," she said after a long pause. "Just . . . nothing."

After a few moments the sound of the outer door closing indicated that one or both of them had left. Abby slowly backed away from the door, stunned.

"He hasn't . . . he hasn't paid," she murmured as the revelation set in.

How the hell long had she been here? How long had he known that she was here, and he — Jordan hadn't paid them? The sounds of her crying didn't sound like they were coming from her at all. Abby collapsed on the mat, pulled the blanket over her, drew her knees to her chest, and stopped being brave, and she stopped trying to hold on to any faith that she had been clinging to in him. She'd been so stupid, so gotdamned stupid, thinking that she was ever going to survive this. This wasn't a movie. These people had no intention of ever letting her go. And Jordan — in all the time she'd been gone, he only just now started asking for proof that she was alive?

"What does that mean?" she asked, trying to make sense of all this.

He knew she was missing. He'd known it for days, but why, why wait so long for proof that she was alive?

"We send them this, they send it to him, and he'll pay. But he needed to know that she was alive first."

Three days. Four. Longer? And he'd waited? Abby became numb. Memories of the things the two of them had said to each other, of the things they'd done together, all began to dissolve in her mind and heart. She loved him like crazy and believed that he'd loved her too, but enough to stand the test of her life for his money?

"Don't you dare, Abby," she warned herself. "Don't you dare believe that it was a lie." He loved her. How many times had Jordan promised her that he would do anything for her, that she was everything to him? But he hadn't paid the ransom. That was the truth. Abby had been missing for days. And he hadn't given in to their demands.

She looked around at the four walls in this room. They could leave her here and disappear. No one would ever find her. Abby was tired, and broken inside. Nothing in her life had ever been the same since meeting Jordan, and now it would end because of him. To sit here feeling sorry for herself because he wasn't coming to her rescue was a waste of time. It didn't matter if Jordan came flying in with a red cape, looking like Superman. He was never meant to be her savior and she'd been a fool to believe that he should be.

"Since when do you depend on anybody to save your life, Abby?"

Abby sat there, gradually giving in to one of those reckoning moments. She might die here, but Abby had been taking care of herself long before she'd met Jordan Gatewood. She was resourceful, intelligent, and she'd never depended on anyone else for anything. At what point had she lost sight of those things about herself?

They would kill her. It wasn't a question of if. She sat in the corner of that room forcing herself to make peace with it.

"Everybody dies, Abby," she muttered to herself.

She had so wanted to be a momma. Abby wrapped her arms tight and low on her stomach to hug a child she'd never lay eyes on. She loved it already, and never seeing her baby's face would be her biggest regret of all.

"Dammit." She began to sob. "We might have to try this again in the next life, little baby."

She took solace in knowing that her baby was as close to her as it would ever get and that even as she fought she'd protect this little bugger with her last breath. Abby would not lose like some wispy, weak, helpless woman screaming and begging for her life. That bastard would be back and the next time she'd be ready for his ass.

" 'Faith is the bird that feels the light when the dawn is still dark." ' Abby softly repeated the quote from poet Rabindranath Tagore that had always resonated deeply to her. Now it seemed brutal. But still, faith was all she had. Abby might surprise him and her and somehow find a way out of here. That was faith. She might land one, good clean blow to his nuts. That surely was faith.

She was exhausted, but Abby was resigned now to her fate. She had absolutely nothing to lose, because she'd lost it all, except for her dignity. Her pride. Her whole life people had underestimated her, and she'd come through time and time again to prove them wrong. The odds were not in her favor that she'd live through this, but she'd never needed odds on her side before.

LIKE A POOR MAN
LOOKING FOR GOLD

"Senator Addison's assistant said that he'd be flying to D.C. tomorrow," Jordan's assistant, Phyl, said, sitting across from him in his office.

Jordan was convinced that Addison's leaving on Friday was no coincidence.

"I didn't find any relation between Crown Distributors and the pipeline project at all," she continued. "However" — Phyl glanced up at him — "I did find a connection between the senator and Variant."

"Connection?" Jordan asked

"It wasn't easy, because I don't think he wanted anyone to know, seeing as how he's a public servant and this would probably violate all the lines of conflict of interest. I mean, politicians can't opt into stuff like that. Can they? Since it's all political and stuff now."

"What'd you find?" he asked impatiently.

She sighed. "His nephew, well, actually a

step-nephew, is a vice president at Variant over their production division. Again, it's weird considering that they're all about alternative fuels and saving the environment, why invest in an oil pipeline? We can't be the only two people who are asking that question. Right?"

"How much has Variant put into the project?"

"A couple of million, which is pretty low compared to most of the others."

"What's the largest investment?"

"Big oil," she said, shrugging. "Alforma has nearly ninety million tied up in the deal."

The people behind extorting Jordan and Abby's abduction wanted to make Jordan the controlling investor in name and in money, but without the power or profits, if there ever were any.

"I've been trying to get in touch with Abby, Jordan," Phyl continued, concerned. "I've left her several messages but she hasn't returned my calls, which isn't like her. Not to get too personal, but is everything okay?"

Jordan's first instinct, without even thinking, was to lie and say yes. All he could do, though, was stare back at Phyl without uttering a word.

Her eyes widened, and she seemed to

understand, as much as it was possible for her to without him revealing more.

"Is there anything I can do?" she asked, with tears filling her eyes.

Of all the people he knew, at this moment, Phyl was the only one he felt that he could trust.

"You're doing it."

The two sat in silence for several moments before his executive assistant, Jennifer, appeared in the doorway.

"Jordan," she said, smiling, "you've got a meeting in five downstairs in the Birch II conference room."

Phyl cleared her throat and gathered her things. "That's my cue to go."

Jordan stood up too and both walked toward the door.

Phyl stopped short, causing Jordan to nearly bump into her. "If you need anything else, let me know. Please?"

He nodded, genuinely touched by her concern. "I need to see the senator. Today."

Phyl nodded. "I'll get right on it."

Jordan sat in on the second meeting of an already busy day, pretending to be engrossed in the project schedule on the screen, constantly checking his phone for news from Wells. Jordan had sent several texts and left one voice mail for the man already and it wasn't even noon. Phyl had sent him a text that Addison had agreed to meet with Jordan at Addison's home later this afternoon.

At the end of the meeting, as Jordan was making his way back to his office, his phone rang. It was Wells.

"Do you need me to order lunch, Jordan?" Jennifer asked.

"No."

Jordan closed the door behind him.

"Tell me you've found her," he demanded, panic sitting in his gut like a brick.

"I can't tell you that."

Jordan slumped down in his chair. Wells was a waste of fucking time. Without saying another word, Jordan hung up. Addison was the key. He knew it. Too many arrows pointed back at the man for Jordan to ignore. It was about money. That's all. Jordan had briefly entertained the idea that someone had had a personal vendetta against him, but no. This was greed, pure and simple.

Addison wanted controlling interest in the pipeline project. A hundred million would give him that. Jordan didn't know how, but he figured that the man must've had a way of taking what Jordan paid and somehow clipping it to Variant's investment, giving them more shares than anyone else.

Jordan rubbed his burning eyes. Tomorrow. Friday. They'd told him he'd be receiving that contract for him to sign, with instructions on transferring funds, and then he'd be told where to find Abby. But would they keep up their end of the bargain?

His phone vibrated, alerting him to a new text message from a number he didn't recognize, with an attachment. He stared at the photograph of Abby and his heart broke. She sat on a nearly bare floor, with both hands raised defensively in front of her face, but there was no denying the look of fear and confusion in her eyes.

Jordan swallowed the fist-size lump in his throat, took a deep breath to quell the rage surging through his veins. His phone rang. It was the woman.

"You have your proof of life, Mr. Gatewood. We will not speak again." She hung up.

Abby had to know that he was searching for her and that he wouldn't stop until he found her. If it was money they fuckin' wanted and his name on a contract, then so be it, but they'd better give her back to him in one solid beautiful piece.

Phyl had sent Jordan Addison's address,

and half an hour later, he drove like a man possessed, gripping the steering wheel tight enough to crush the damn thing.

He had to calm the fuck down. Jordan couldn't go into this meeting enraged, or he'd blow it. Addison couldn't know that Jordan was on to him, but Jordan had to somehow get him to reveal Abby's location or give him some hint of it before leaving town. This was his last and only chance to save her.

When he arrived, he was let into Addison's Fort Worth home by the housekeeper, who led him through the expansive house to the backyard, where he found Addison standing on a small putting green.

The man glanced at him before taking his next shot.

"Two visits from the great Mr. Gatewood in two days," he said sarcastically. "I'm starting to believe that you might actually like me." He chuckled.

Focus. Jordan had to pull that shit from the bottoms of his feet and hold on to it with everything he had. He had to force himself not to wrap that putter around that sonofabitch's neck.

"I hear you're heading back to D.C. tomorrow."

Addison eyed Jordan suspiciously. "Well,

it's about time I get back there to do the job the good people of this state elected me to do."

Jordan had to be careful. This man might hold Abby's life in his hands.

"I'm glad I caught up with you before you left," he said casually. "I, um, came across some interesting information," Jordan carefully stated, "by chance, of course."

The senator continued lining up his shot. "Information?"

"About Variant."

The man took his shot, and missed, then turned his attention to Jordan.

"Why would you be interested in a little guy like Variant?" he casually asked.

Addison studied Jordan with the same intensity that Jordan studied him with. He hated this man and had from the first moment he laid eyes on him.

"I found it curious that a company like that would be interested in the Dakota Pipeline. I'm sure I'm not the only one."

"Well, I wouldn't know what their interests are in the project. Can't say that I've given it much thought. Why would I? Why would you?"

Jordan had one small ace in this hole. It wasn't much, but it could net the senator an inquiry by some political board questioning his relationship with Variant in a highly charged social and political issue. Weak? Yes. But that depended on how uncomfortable Addison didn't mind being.

Jordan was out of time. "Where is she?"

Addison furrowed his brow and stared back quizzically at Jordan. "I'm sorry. Who are we talking about?"

That smug sonofabitch was playing dumb, and Jordan was all out of patience for this shit.

"Where the fuck is she?" he said, taking a step toward Addison.

The man slowly shook his head. "I have no idea what or whom you're talking about, son, but I don't think I like your tone. Maybe you need to leave."

Fuck what this sonofabitch thought about his tone. Nothing mattered but answers. Nothing mattered but Abby. Anger burned like fire in his veins and everything around him faded to black except for Addison — his face, puffing and sweating, his lips bloated and purple.

A woman's voice. "No! Stop it! Don't!"

Her hands clawing at Jordan.

"Where is she?" It was his voice, begging the question over and over again, coming from someplace far away.

Jordan was out of time. Abby was out of time.

"Get — the — fuck off me!" Addison managed to say, spitting back in Jordan's face.

"I'm calling the police!" The woman screamed.

"Fuck — Jordan!" Addison's eyes bulged in desperation. "You're — killing —"

All of a sudden, it dawned on Jordan that he'd gone too far. He released the grip he'd had on the man's throat, and stumbled back, realizing that it wasn't Addison who'd just killed Abby. It was Jordan. He'd just sealed her fate.

"Get the fuck out of my house!"

The woman rushed over to Addison, who was coughing and gasping for air.

"Get out of here!" she repeated to Jordan.

He'd gone too far. *Oh, God! Abby.*

FEET FAIL ME NOT

DJ reconciled with this shit he was doing every time he sat down with his family at night to eat, kissed one of his kids, or made love to Nia. The woman they held was no worse for wear, and by tomorrow night she'd be back at home, safe in her man's arms and picking up where they left off. Maybe she'd need a little therapy or something, but she'd get on with her life soon enough. She was cool, even though she didn't know it. But he knew it, and because he knew it, DJ could sleep at night.

It wasn't like he'd gone to Craigslist searching for an ad that said, *"Looking for some dude to kidnap a woman, hold her for five days, and get paid more money than you'll probably ever see in your life."* That woman found him. Called him, like she knew that he needed the money and bad, too.

DJ had never laid eyes on her. When he saw that number come up on his cell, he

325

didn't answer it the first two times because he thought it was another bill collector, but on that third call she finally left a message that got his attention.

"Answer my call and I promise to get you the money you need."

That was all she said, and at first he thought it was some crazy trick for a collector to get him on the phone. DJ's money was jacked up. His check was being garnished for Nia's medical bills from having the baby and his hours had been cut because he'd shown up late a few times, which was fucked-up because it wasn't his fault that he'd gotten stuck in snow crossing Colorado.

"You need money," the woman on the phone had said as soon as he answered.

"Who are you?"

"I can get you money, more than enough to help you resolve your financial issues."

She sounded white. He started to hang up, but DJ was curious about how this woman had found him and why.

"You have a young family, DJ." She said his name.

"How the hell do you know my name?"

"What if I told you that you could make two million dollars in less than a week?"

This was some bullshit. "I don't run drugs, lady."

"It's about a woman."

"And I don't run people neither, so you can take your fake-ass millions and prank-call somebody else's ass."

"And what happens when you lose your job?" she asked. "How long do you think it will take you to pay off that thirty-five-thousand-dollar medical bill without that pathetic paycheck of yours? Who's going to pay you the kind of money you really need when all you have is a GED?"

How the hell did she know all this? This shit freaked him the fuck out, but DJ wasn't going to let her know it.

"Better to be fired than in prison."

"Is it better to be fired than to have millions in the bank? Is it better to be fired than to be able to provide the kind of life for your family that you've been dreaming of?"

Despite his better judgment, DJ stayed on the call. Yeah, he needed money, and that kind of money was crazy. But he had no idea who this woman was or how she knew so much about him. He didn't want any part of transporting human cargo across state lines. In his line of work, trafficking was huge and it was ugly. DJ wanted no part of it.

"There's a woman," she continued. "The

woman of a wealthy man. All you'd need to do is take her someplace, keep her hidden and safe for a week, maybe less, and then let her go," she explained as casually as if she were telling him where to drop off her laundry for dry-cleaning.

"That's kidnapping."

"It is," she concurred. "But no one will be hurt. We'll get what we need from him, and she'll be set free. Then you get your money."

How in the hell could she make something like that sound so easy? "Why me?" he asked. "How'd you find me?"

"Research."

"What made you think I'd buy into some shit like this?" he asked, clenching his jaws.

Even he found it crazy that he would even consider kidnapping. Especially when he was too damn righteous to run drugs or traffic people.

"You need this," she said, almost in a whisper.

No, he didn't need this. He needed funds, but he didn't need to commit no felonies. "What's to stop me from going to the po-po and telling them what you're asking me to do?"

"I found you because I saw that you were in trouble."

"You can't just know something like that," he

retorted.

She paused. "Everything I know about you is true. You're getting desperate and you hate that you can't do more for the people who depend on you, who look up to you. I'm offering you a chance to provide the kind of life you want for them and for yourself."

It was like she'd read his mind or something. Like she'd been watching him.

"You're a good man, DJ. A good husband and father. I'm not asking you to hurt anyone. The plan is simple. She won't hurt and in a week, you'll have everything you need for your family."

She told him to think it over and that she'd call him back the next day. Of course DJ couldn't and wouldn't get involved in no shit like that. He was broke and his family needed the money, but he sure as hell wasn't going to prison over some dumb shit.

The next day, he went to work. DJ was scheduled to pick up a haul in Chicago.

"Sorry, DJ," his supervisor told him. "Gave that one to Carl. He promised to get it back here by tomorrow night — early."

"What the hell time did he leave?" DJ asked, incredulous.

"He left at four this morning."

"You told me I didn't need to head out until eight."

He shrugged. "What can I say? Carl said he could leave earlier and get it back earlier."

DJ felt sick to his stomach at the thought of having to tell Nia that he'd lost out on another route. The last thing he wanted was for her to have to work any more overtime. Nia had gone back to work right after she'd had the baby, and it had been hard for her. Too damn hard. He was her man. DJ had promised to take care of her, and lately it seemed like it was the other way around.

DJ sat on the sofa, smoking a joint. Half an hour after he'd gotten home, his phone rang, again with an unknown number, but he knew who it was.

The woman started talking right after he said his name, and told him what she wanted him to do. While she spoke, DJ couldn't help but wonder if she had anything to do with him losing that job this morning. After she finished giving him the address of a house in Blink, letting him know that he'd have to watch it just in case that woman showed up, DJ finally responded.

"I'ma need help," he said after a long pause. "I can't be going on with my normal life and watching a damn house just in case she shows up," he ended sarcastically.

She assured him that if she could pin down the time and day that the woman would arrive, she'd let him know. But DJ couldn't do this by himself.

"Someone you can trust," she told him. "And you split the money."

He'd told James and Nay that they were all splitting up one and a half million dollars instead of two. And he didn't feel bad about keeping more of the money. Half a mil was a ton of money for anybody. It was enough to get Nay and her kids away from that asshole she was married to and buy her a whole new life someplace else. And it was enough to keep James in weed and pussy until he was sick of the shit.

DJ had already planned how he was going to spend the money he made from this. And that plan started with Nia.

"Who lives here?" Nia asked, looking out the car window at the house he'd parked in front of.

It was in Nelson, and a big old For Sale sign was planted in the front yard. He got out of the car and then hurried over to her side and held the door open for her. A dude wearing khakis and a button-down immediately opened the door as they walked up the sidewalk.

"Whose house is this, baby?" she asked again.

"DJ," he said, holding out his hand for DJ

to shake.

"This is Nia," he said proudly.

"Very nice to meet you, Nia," the dude said, grinning a little harder at her than DJ would've liked. "I'm Brian, and welcome."

DJ had found this place by accident a few days ago, just driving, trying to clear his head. It was perfect. Perfect for his family, and he was a day away from being able to drop cash on this joint and make all her dreams come true.

"I'll leave you two to look around," old dude said. "If you have any questions, don't hesitate to ask."

DJ took hold of her hand and led her through the foyer into the living room that opened up with hardwood floors and a big-ass kitchen. A sliding glass door led to a massive backyard with a tall wooden fence around it. It'd be perfect for the kids to play.

"What are we doing here?" she leaned in close and whispered.

He squeezed her hand in his. "Planning our future, baby." He looked at her and smiled.

"We can't afford this," she said, worried.

Nia grazed her fingers along the granite countertop of the center island. She didn't have to tell him how much she wanted a place like this.

"I promised you that I'd take care of you and my kids," he said, turning her to face him. "I haven't been doing such a good job lately."

"Don't, baby," she murmured, pressing her hand to his face. "It's not your fault and we love you."

Jesus! He loved her. Loved everything about her. And there was nothing he wouldn't do for her. One more day. That's it. Other than the first night, the night that they had to grab that woman and get her in the car, it had gone smoothly. DJ had been so careful, and he'd made sure that Nay and James were careful, too. In less than twenty-four hours it would all be over and he could be the man his woman dreamed he'd be.

"Act like it's yours already, Nia." He smiled. "Your kitchen. Your living room. Your yard. Your two and a half baths," he said, laughing.

She laughed too, and it was like hearing his favorite song.

"Because I'm gonna get this for you, and if this isn't the one you want, I'll find you another one, baby."

Nia wrapped her arms around him and held on tight. "You're so crazy."

Nah, he wasn't crazy. He was in love, though, with his wife and his life. And after tomorrow everything would be different, better.

"A place like this would need some fancy furniture." She smiled with tears shimmering in her eyes.

He grinned back at her. "Of course it would. And I'ma get you that, too."

Both My Hands Are Tied

"Damn, can this day go any slower?" Naomi muttered loud enough for her coworker to laugh.

"Sounds like somebody's ready for the weekend," she said to Naomi.

"You have no idea," she responded.

One more day. Tomorrow, Naomi, DJ, and James would get that call they'd all been waiting for all week and this whole ordeal would be over. Naomi would have half a million dollars that Thomas would never know about, and hopefully, she and the boys would be long gone before the man came home from work.

"Hey, Naomi," one of the drivers said, coming over to the counter in front of her desk. "Got my manifest?"

She pulled up a file, printed out a sheet of paper from it, and handed it to him. "There you go, Jack."

Naomi's life was never supposed to be like

this. She grew up in a good home, raised by loving parents with her brother and two sisters. In high school she was popular, homecoming queen and runner-up for prom queen. She'd enrolled in the junior college in Tyler and had planned on becoming a nurse. Maybe she still could become one. Naomi was only thirty-three years old. Still young enough to build a new life for herself and to help people doing what she loved.

Helping people. It seemed like an odd notion considering her involvement in all of this. The woman they had locked in that room would be all right even if James was — had — She pushed the thought from her mind. She pushed aside the sounds of that woman begging her not to let James come back into that room. He hadn't killed her. He hadn't beaten on her. She was alive. It was all that mattered when this was all said and done; maybe she'd see it that way, too.

She'd been covertly packing things this last week, things that she hoped Thomas or the boys wouldn't know were missing, clothes and shoes. She'd also packed important papers like birth certificates and shot records.

If everything went as planned, they'd be gone tomorrow. DJ said that he would call as soon as the money was wired into accounts set up for them by that woman he'd been speaking to who'd arranged all of this. She'd given them money up front to prove that she was telling the truth. Naomi had thirty thousand dollars put away in an account that Thomas didn't know about. She'd hid her bankbook in her locker here at work.

She was so excited at the prospect of finally getting away, but she had to be careful. Thomas paid close attention to everything about her, and if her mood changed or her routine changed, even if it was subtle, he questioned her about it. So she had to quell how anxious she really was. Naomi had to force herself to get home on time, make dinner, small talk, and love if that's what he wanted. She had to pretend to care about how his day had gone and to be prepared to provide details of hers down to what she'd eaten for lunch, and whom she'd spoken to at work.

"Crown Distributors dispatch," she said, answering her phone.

"Aren't you glad I didn't call you on your cell?" It was James.

She took an unexpected deep breath. "What can I do for you?"

People were always buzzing around the

dispatch office. Some of those people knew Thomas.

"You can tell me where the key is. It ain't on the shelf."

The familiar wave of anxiety that she'd felt every time Thomas confronted her about something washed over her.

"It's not time yet," she explained, choosing her words carefully, reminding him that it was too early to take food to her. "Besides, I can take care of it today. In fact, it's probably best."

He was silent for several seconds before finally responding. "Nah, now that ain't the deal we made. I'd rather it be me."

"I said don't worry about it," she said, forcing herself not to sound uptight. "It's no problem. In fact, it's my pleasure."

She knew. Naomi didn't want to know it, but she did. James was crossing a line with the woman, one that could cost all of them everything, and they'd come too far for this pervert to ruin it.

"Do I need to come in there?" he threatened.

"That's probably not a good idea," she said, forcing herself to steady her voice.

"Then bring me the gotdamn key," he demanded. "I'm in the parking lot on the east side. You've got five minutes, Nay."

Naomi didn't know this woman and she didn't want to know her. But this wasn't about the woman. As selfish as it was, Nay's reasons for wanting to keep him from that lady, especially now, were about everything she stood to lose if James went too damn far. And maybe he already had, but Naomi had to stand her ground this time. Tonight was the last night that woman would be kept in that room. James had no business going back there.

"Cassie," she said to the woman in the cubicle behind her, "I'll be right back. I'm going to get something out of my car."

"No problem, Naomi."

Naomi made it a point to make sure she didn't see anybody and that she wasn't seen climbing into James's car.

"All I want is the key."

She glared at him. "Do you understand how close we are to finishing this?" she asked angrily. "Do you understand what's at stake, James?"

Her heart pounded so hard it was a wonder it didn't shake that car.

"I look dumb to you?"

"They said she wasn't supposed to be hurt."

"And she hasn't been."

"Raping a woman is hurting a woman, James."

He stared back unemotionally at her like she was speaking a foreign language. "Give me the key and you can get back inside."

"DJ has it," she lied.

"DJ doesn't have the damn key, Nay," he shot back.

"He went with me this morning so that he could take a picture of her and send it to that woman we're working for. He kept it when we left."

James immediately pulled his phone out of his pocket.

"Who're you calling?"

"DJ," he casually responded.

"No."

He looked at her. "Then you give me that damn key or I stop by your place tonight on my way to take her something to eat."

"You're about to make half a million dollars, James," she said, shaking her head in disbelief at this ignorant man. "All you have to do from this point on is nothing."

James stared out across the parking lot.

"It's so easy," she continued. "And after tomorrow, you can have any woman you want, go anywhere and do anything. Just — go home. Go home, and tomorrow will be

340

here before you know it and this will be all over."

If James did come by her house tonight, Thomas would kill her. Naomi wasn't afraid of dying anymore. Death wouldn't bring her escape, but freedom. It wasn't her life she was fighting for, though. It was the lives of her boys. This idiot just had to leave that woman alone and go home. But it became obvious that James relished his role of fool.

James looked at her and held out his hand. It was as if he hadn't heard a word she'd said.

"You're going to mess this up for all of us," she said dismally.

"Trust me, Nay. I ain't messing up nothing because we're not letting her go. That woman DJ's been talking to, she ain't stupid. If we set her free, somehow, someway, somebody will follow that trail back to us, back to whoever put all this together, and whoever he's been talking to don't want that."

"DJ won't kill her," she said softly.

James sighed. "DJ won't have to."

Reluctantly, Naomi reached into the front pocket of her jeans, pulled out the key, and placed it in his palm and held it there with her finger. "You can't — not until tomorrow. They might want to know that she's alive."

He nodded slowly; she let go of the key, then left him in the car.

Only a special kind of desperation or fear would compel a woman to allow any kind of abuse of another woman without at least trying to intervene. Self-preservation was Naomi's excuse. Naomi hated the woman she'd become. Half a million dollars and the chance to buy her way out of her own hell was worth sacrificing someone else to hers.

"Thomas called," her coworker told her when she made it back to her work area. "Wants you to call him back as soon as you get in."

Dread washed over her. Thomas had a sixth sense about things. Did he know? Could he know?

"Hey, baby," she said when he answered. "I've been here. I just thought I left my sweater in the car. No. No, I didn't. You know how forgetful I can be sometimes. Yeah, I was hoping we could grill some burgers and hot dogs for dinner. I've got the potato salad made already. Okay. Sounds good. Love you, too."

Sickness over You

You can't be a decent human being if you have no qualms about snatching a woman out of her bed in the middle of the night for money. DJ might've been cool with thinking he was better than James, but James knew better. They were the same, except James had no problem owning up to who he was or things he'd done.

James sat on the sofa in his small apartment, surveying the shabby-ass shit of his, disgusted and like he was just now seeing the place that represented his life for the very first time. It never dawned on him that he could have more or be better in his life. He was closing in on forty, an ex-felon, having spent fifteen years in prison for robbery and assault.

Half a million fuckin' dollars. How many different ways had he spent that money in his head? And not on the things DJ or Naomi probably thought he'd spend it on, either. James was the thug. James loved to fuck and get high. But money like that didn't come around every day, and he'd figured out that if he was going to make something of his life, then this was his chance to do it.

He leaned back on the sofa and sighed.

"Kill that bitch, start a business, reinvent myself," he muttered sarcastically.

But that was how it was going to go down. Money like that could buy him a new him. So it was only fitting for James to spend this last day celebrating the old him. Gin and juice. James had been drinking since he left Naomi. He wasn't drunk, but booze flowed through his veins like blood, settling him into the truth of what he'd have to do, to the fact that tomorrow he'd be a different kind of James, one with blood on his hands and a bright future.

He took a long, slow drag of his cigarette. Nay called it rape, but that's not how James saw the dynamics of this relationship with that woman locked in that room. He couldn't see it that way, wouldn't. Because that'd make him as dumb as DJ and Naomi.

She was already dead. James had reached that conclusion even before he and his brother dragged her out of that house. James had gotten caught up in a fantasy with Abby, and he looked forward to letting it play itself out because he deserved it. He'd never taken a life before, and he wasn't looking forward to taking hers. The animal in him couldn't help himself. She was prey and that excited him in ways he hadn't believed possible. He had a crush on her. The first time he'd met her, he dug her, but she made it clear that she wasn't interested. Now it wasn't up to her.

"Doesn't that smell good?" he asked, placing the bag of food and an ice-cold soda on the floor in front of her. "Fried chicken. Fries." He grinned, moving back across the room and kneeling in the corner to watch her eat.

That smooth, pretty dark skin of hers made him lick his lips. He suspected that she tasted every bit as good as that chicken. His dick kicked at the thought of being inside her. Tonight, it would be.

"I guess you could call this a date." He winked flirtatiously. He snapped his fingers. "Damn! I should've bought some candles."

The thought of fucking her had become such an obsession for James. It was the whole scene that turned him on, like some elaborate porn movie. A woman held captive and at his mercy. She was within his grasp, but not quite. Something always seemed to stop him just as shit was about to go down, and James would be forced to leave with a vicious boner, making him even hornier for her little black ass.

Nipples pressed against her shirt, teasing him. She saw him staring and used that dirty blanket to cover herself. She was so fucking vulnerable and that shit was erotic. He felt like a lion stalking a sheep, a sheep that he knew he could have whenever he wanted. And the sheep knew it, too. That was the best part.

"Go and eat, baby," he gently coaxed. "I'll wait."

Sweet, fearful tears glistened in her pretty eyes. "I'm not hungry," she said meekly.

Was she trembling?

"Don't be afraid, baby girl," he told her, caught up in the magic that she was. "I'm not going to hurt you," he whispered.

Had she heard him? Did she believe him? He wanted her to believe him.

James stood up and walked over to her as if he were being pulled. He felt like a fish on a hook and couldn't help himself. She stood up too, and backed into the corner.

"Don't touch me!" she yelled, putting up her fists. "I fucking mean it."

The tears fell. Nostrils flared.

"Aw, baby," he murmured, taking a step toward her.

She braced her little self, lowering slightly into her knees as if she truly meant to fight him.

Without thinking, James grabbed his throbbing cock through his pants and tried to rub the ache from it. And then he reached for her.

"No!" she yelled, punching at him, landing a solid little blow on his chin.

He laughed, lunged at her, and pinned her back against the wall, kicking, scratching, and punching.

"Let me go!" she screamed hysterically. "Let me — !"

"It's going to be all right," he promised her. "I swear it is."

Small fists pummeled against his back, face, and arms as he jammed a thigh between her knees and effortlessly lifted her off the ground.

"Hold on, baby girl. I got you. I got you, Abby."

And he did. James had all of her.

Some of Us Cannibals

Hitting him was like punching brick.

"Ffffuck!" he growled, laughing and grabbing hold of her wrists.

He pressed her tight enough against the wall to keep her suspended, pulling her arms down at her sides and pinning them against her.

Disbelief and shock shrouded the sounds of her screams. Her muscles burned with adrenaline.

Fight, Abby! These words echoing in her mind took on a whole new meaning. Fight! Not just for her body or for her right to herself. Fight for her dignity. Fight to save her life.

"It's all right, baby girl. We gone do this. It's 'bout damn time. 'Bout damn time."

Somehow, he managed to free himself from his pants while keeping her arms pinned.

"Ah, yes," he said, pushing himself between her leg and the material of her shorts, groaning disgustingly in her ear and thrusting his hips against her.

The thought of him inside her made her want to vomit, and somehow, before he could enter her, Abby managed to place one hand between them as a barrier between her legs, and grabbed his penis before he could penetrate her. He stopped and started to jerk away until she started to slowly massage him. The tip of him grazed against her, but he wasn't inside her. Not yet. God! She didn't want this monster inside her body!

Deep moans rolled in the back of his throat as he closed his eyes and pushed and pulled in her palm. Abby stroked him slowly, squeezing her fingers around his shaft until he began pumping in a frenzy, lost in that repulsive world in his head. It no longer mattered that he wasn't inside her. He was fucking and she needed to keep him caught up in the filthy fantasy until he came.

As he rested his head against the wall next to hers, hot pockets of breath rushed onto her neck and shoulders.

"Aw, baby," he kept saying over and over again. "That's it. That's it, girl."

Bile settled in the back of her throat. Abby pursed her lips together to stifle her cries.

No greater crime had ever been committed against her. He had stolen from her the most sacred and intimate parts of who she was. With each moment of this degrading act, the weight of this defeat took its toll on her emotionally, spiritually. If somehow she managed to get out of this ordeal alive, she knew that she'd never be the same.

An eternity seemed to pass before it was over and semen covered her hand and spilled onto her leg.

He backed away abruptly and let her fall to the floor. "You fuckin' cheated, girl!" he yelled angrily, backing away and shoving his penis back into his pants.

And then he hit her hard enough to crack the back of her head against the wall, leaving her dazed and nearly unconscious. Abby felt him grab her by the ankles, jerk her shorts off of her, and press all of his weight down on top of her, fumbling to try to push inside her.

"Fuck! Bitch! Fuckin' — Shit!"

A phone rang several times before he finally raised up onto his knees and glared down at her. She tasted blood.

"Make a gotdamn sound and I'll kill your ass now."

"What is it?" he said into the phone. "Where?" He rubbed his hand down his face and huffed. "Right now?"

She didn't dare move or say a word. Abby held her breath. He ended the call, stood up, gathered up the food he'd brought, and left without saying a word, locking the door behind him.

Her hands were dirty. She was dirty, but Abby eventually managed to compose herself and worked feverishly to flatten the plastic bottle that sonofabitch had left days ago. They weren't going to let her leave this place alive. She knew that now. The sun had set on another day of what felt like an eternity, but she wasn't afraid. It was strange, but despite what he'd done to her, Abby felt oddly surreal, empowered and calm as she quietly made peace with the fact that her life might very well come to an end tomorrow.

Some part of her had been expecting Jordan to ram his shoulder into that door and rescue her, but Abby had no room for fantasies like that anymore. Jordan wasn't coming. He wasn't Galahad. He was just a man. And men had their limits. If she did nothing, they'd just kill her like swatting a fly. Abby was no gotdamn fly. If she was going to be murdered, then they were going to know that they'd been in a fight.

Of course that nasty bastard would be back. Maybe tomorrow, maybe tonight. Better to face that fact than to hope for anything else. Hope was gone.

Abby stared at her weapon made from a plastic water bottle. She sat facing the door, listening for sounds that someone was coming back through it. The sun had set hours ago, but sleeping wasn't an option. It would only waste time, and Abby wanted — no, she needed — to savor every precious second she had left.

She wasn't alone. Abby placed one hand on her belly and sighed.

"I love you, sweet one," she whispered. "And I don't even know your name."

Abby had peed on a stick, and the little pamphlet said that a plus sign meant that she was pregnant. That something as monumental as giving life could be determined by a piece of plastic and urine seemed almost sacrilegious. As shocked as she'd been by the result, Abby had never been so happy. And Jordan . . . She smiled at the memory of the expression on his face.

"Don't you dare," she whispered. "Don't you dare ever believe that he didn't love us."

He hadn't come bursting through that door for a reason. She'd never know what it was, but Abby refused to believe that he hadn't come because he didn't want to. He didn't come because he couldn't.

Sadness washed over her as she settled into the fact that she'd never see Jordan's face again, or taste his kisses, and lie in his arms. They'd never see their baby's smile or hear it laugh or cry. She had no idea how much she'd wanted to be a mother until she found out that she was pregnant, and even more when she saw how happy he was about being a father.

She'd rolled the flattened plastic into a cylindrical shape. On the surface, it didn't look like much, just a rolled-up piece of plastic. She knew better, though.

DJ's simple ass wanted to meet. Like, what the fuck for? James sped down the dirt road headed toward the main street in a rage. That bitch thought she was slick, jerking him off like that. He'd been so worked up that he'd cum to a gotdamn hand job and it pissed him off. But it wasn't over. She knew it. She had to. And she knew that his face was going to be the last one she saw in this life. That's for damn sure.

"Did you leave the key?" Naomi asked, rushing over to him as soon as he got out of the car as the two of them headed inside the restaurant where DJ was sitting.

He just looked at her.

She held out her hand. "Give it to me, James."

Fuck her.

"We're too close to mess this up," she said as they stopped outside the door.

Reluctantly, he placed it in her hand, but she'd be giving it back to him soon enough.

Taking over Me

"Be glad that the police aren't at your office door to arrest you, Gatewood."

Jordan sat stoically behind his desk, listening to the senator's voice mail. "My lawyers will be in touch, and if nothing else, I will sue you for every gotdamn penny you have to your name."

For the first time in his life, he stood to lose absolutely everything he'd worked so hard for: his corporation, reputation, legacy. He stood to lose his fortune. Most important, however, Jordan was about to lose the only woman he'd ever truly loved, his connection to another human being, someone in this vast world capable of rescuing him from utter isolation. He'd lived his whole life in a bubble, and only now, in this moment, was he fully aware of just how desolate it truly was and how empty it had been.

They could have their money and their contract. They could have his reputation as a businessman. But they needed to keep up their end of the bargain and send her home to him, safe and sound. If they failed to do that — if they failed Jordan would spend the rest of his life hunting them all down until he found every last of these sonsofbitches.

"God help them," he murmured solemnly.

He glanced at the time. It was after nine o'clock and Jordan had been sitting at his desk for hours, making mental assessments of all the mistakes he'd made since meeting Abby. From the moment he'd met her, he knew that she was too good for him. He never should've gone to Blink that day or to that house. And even if he had, he never should've noticed her, pursued her, because Abby had no business with him.

Jordan's life had always been filled with the unsavory residue of greed and dirty games that only people like him and Addison knew how to play, games that ate away at a person's moral core until there was nothing left. He'd played them better than most, and Karma rode him like he was a horse because of it. Jordan had debts that, until now, he'd believed might never be fully paid for trespasses he'd committed in his lifetime. He'd always expected it to come for him head-on, but for it to come for him through her was beyond anything he could've ever imagined. It was beyond cruel.

He glanced at his cell phone and saw Phyl's number come up on the screen. Jordan wasn't in the mood to talk to anyone, but reluctantly, he answered the call.

"Yes."

"Hey, boss. I know it's late. I just . . . I'm worried about Abby," she admitted. "I was just wondering if there was anything I can do."

Jordan didn't respond because he honestly had nothing to tell her.

"I know you can't tell me what's going on, but whatever you need, I mean, I'm here."

Jordan was touched by her sincerity. Phyl had been invaluable in coming through with all the information she had given him related to Variant, Addison, and Crown Distributors, but there was nothing else.

"I bought her the pregnancy test," Phyl finally admitted.

Jordan was speechless.

"Is she — ?"

"Yes," he said softly.

Heavy silence loomed between them.

"So there's no correlation between Crown Distributors and the pipeline project," she explained without him asking.

"Any connection between Crown and Variant?"

"No. I mean, Crown distributes parts for drilling and trains and big stuff like that to just about every- and anybody, but nothing stood out with Variant."

He was still reaching, still searching for something, anything that could provide a clue to lead him to Abby. As long as he was breathing, Jordan couldn't give up.

"I did find out some more interesting stuff on our good senator," she said sarcastically. "Not only is his nephew or whatever a top exec and investor at Variant, but who do you think owns controlling interest in the company?"

Jordan waited, expecting her to say Addison.

"Laurel Penbroke."

"Who is Laurel Penbroke?"

"She's a lovely old woman living in a nursing home in Santa Fe, New Mexico, who happens to be Senator Addison's stepmom. She divorced his father years ago, but old Addison's been footing the bill for her care for years now, and she, in turn, made him her primary beneficiary in the event of her death."

Jordan sat up. The implications to what Phyl had just told him were huge.

"How did you find out that he was her beneficiary?"

Phyl sighed. "I'd rather not say, but let's just say that I don't quite owe my source my soul, but if I ever have any kids, I might have to hand one of them over to the person."

Jordan's mind was reeling after hanging up from talking to Phyl. Addison was in on this. Somehow, the money Jordan invested in this pipeline would end up absorbed by Variant, the bulk of which would land in Addison's lap.

Without giving it a second thought, he dialed Addison's cell number.

"What the hell do you want?" Addison blurted out.

"Where is she?"

The man hung up. Jordan dialed his number again but got his voice mail.

"Laurel Penbroke," was all he said before ending the call.

Moments later, Addison called back. "I don't know what you think you —"

"Where the hell is she?" he yelled, his voice cracking. "You tell me where she is, or I swear . . ."

"I have no idea," he reluctantly admitted. "I had nothing to do with any of that."

"Don't do this. You want your money. I'll

give you the fuckin' money, Addison, but don't — She's not a part of this. She's got nothing to do with any of us."

He was pleading, begging for her return, for her life.

"I don't know where she is," Addison snapped. "I didn't even know she was missing until now. I had no idea. All I know is that you'll be getting a contract tomorrow with instructions on where to wire the money. That's all I know."

"Who else is there?" Jordan demanded to know. "Who else is involved?"

"I . . . I can't . . . I can't —"

Addison ended the call this time. Jordan gathered his things and hurried from his office to the parking garage. An hour later, he banged on the door to Addison's home in Fort Worth.

The housekeeper answered. "The senator and his wife are not here. They flew back to Washington this afternoon."

It was late, but he knew he wouldn't sleep. Jordan had placed a call earlier to his accountant to confirm that all arrangements had been made to make the investment. You don't just move a hundred million without having to jump through federal hoops.

His signature on that contract was the

most important part of all of this. And Jordan was expected to sign it without disputing a single word, which was why he was using his personal funds. He would not put his investors at risk like that. Besides, this *was* personal. Abby was his, and it was up to him to hand over whatever they wanted in order to get her back.

It was just after midnight when Jordan's phone rang. Finally, it was Wells. "Yes," he said, fearing the worst.

"I think you should get down here," he said.

Jordan swallowed the lump in his throat, or tried to. "What's happened?"

Was she dead? Had he found her?

"I'm not sure yet. But I think it's best if you're close. Go to her place and wait to hear from me."

"What the hell is going on, man? Don't play games with me."

"And don't fuckin' insult me. Just do what I tell you. I'll be in touch."

"Is she alive?" Jordan yelled.

Wells paused. "We shall see, man. If I'm right. We'll see real soon."

Jordan didn't waste a moment. He packed up his laptop and his gun, got dressed, and left immediately. It was impossible to quell the anxiety in his gut. Adrenaline raced through every fiber of his being, and Jordan couldn't have slept even if he'd wanted to. Wells with that cryptic shit was fucking killing Jordan. He needed to know what the hell the man had found.

It normally took on average two and a half hours to drive from Dallas to Blink. Jordan made it to Abby's house in an hour and a half. He went inside, walked to the bedroom in the back of the house, and turned on the small lamp on the nightstand. She was all in this place. Signs of her, everywhere, enveloping him, cocooning him in the spirit that was her. He used to welcome that feeling, but now, now it felt like it was squeezing the breath out of him.

He told himself over and over again that it was going to be all right. Jordan forced himself to believe that she would be found and would be in his arms soon. He had to tell himself that. And he had to make himself believe it because nothing else would do. If this house was all that he'd had left of her, then Jordan would fucking die. He'd rot inside. Shrivel up and rot and nothing would matter. Not a damn thing.

DAY 5

Better Never Let It Go

"Addison couldn't tell him anything," Brandon explained, sitting in Lars's office.

Brandon had received a phone call from Addison late last night from Washington, D.C., detailing his encounter with Gatewood in person and the last time the two had spoken over the phone earlier that evening.

"He claims he didn't confirm or deny anything."

Lars sighed deeply. "I hate politicians," he said solemnly. "You can't trust any of them. They can't even spell the word 'truth,' so how the hell can we trust them with it?"

"He didn't lie about not knowing where she was," Brandon told him.

The money they demanded from Gatewood was to go into an account belonging to some obscure company started by Addison's nephew. It was to sit in that account for several weeks before being transferred to two stateside accounts with 65 percent placed into an account belonging to Brandon and 35 percent to Laurel Penbroke. Addison stood to inherit that woman's fortune upon her death. Lars had a fondness for Addison. They'd been friends for many years, and Lars had been instrumental in raising funds to support Addison's campaign. The money made from extorting Gatewood was a campaign contribution, as far as Brandon's father was concerned. Addison had influential friends in high places in Washington, relationships that had proven to be good for business.

Would he ever tire of these games? Lars's body aged faster than his mind. On the outside, he was an old man, but inside, he was as sharp as he'd ever been and, as far as he was concerned, he was the only man living with the wherewithal to finally drive Gatewood to his knees.

"I'd heard rumors that Jordan wasn't Julian's son by blood. But even if that were true, you couldn't tell. Blood is thicker than water. Sometimes, though, it's not the blood that matters, but the conviction," Lars said, talking more to himself than to Brandon.

Today was a trying day for Lars Degan. His rheumatoid arthritis was flaring up again, making it particularly difficult for him to get around the way he liked without the aid of his walker.

"Jordan has always been committed to the legacy of his father, to the point of adopting the man's persona, his attitude." He looked at his son, Brandon, sitting across from him in the living room. "There are moments when I've had to remind myself that Julian Gatewood died years ago, but it sure feels as if I'm talking to his ghost."

He wasn't disappointed in Brandon, but oh, what he wouldn't have given for his boy to be more like Julian Gatewood's son, Jordan. Even Lars had to admit that Jordan was a larger, more imposing figure than the man he emulated. If Julian Gatewood was alive today, even he'd shrink in the shadow of his son, biological or not.

"He's grown to be more of a titan than his father ever was, though," Lars said, grimacing as he rubbed into the soreness of one of his hands. "The last time I saw him, it took everything in me not to drop down on one knee to pay homage to him, like he was some fucking god." Lars laughed at his own analogy.

Brandon smiled politely. That was his way — politeness. He was like his mother in that sense.

"I suppose that you hate the fact that I

am your father."

Brandon blinked, astonished, at Lars. "Sir?"

"Have I been a disappointment, Brandon?" Lars asked unapologetically.

Yes, he backed his son into a corner, wondering how in the hell Brandon would make his way out of it. Would he come out fists swinging? Would he stay there waiting for permission to be excused? Or would he kiss Lars's ass, say what he thought was the right thing, believing that if he was agreeable he would win his father's favor? "You're my father."

Lars waited. Brandon was stalling for time to try to figure out what it was Lars was looking for from him. Something about the way Brandon's expression changed, though, caught Lars by surprise. It was involuntary but poignant.

"I've disappointed you," Brandon continued. "I don't need you to tell me that. I know it. I've always known it."

"But that wasn't my question. Was it?"

His son's complexion flushed red. He was angry. Good.

"I love you, Dad," he finally said, swallowing. Brandon met and held Lars's gaze. "But yes. You have been a disappointment to me. You've never been the father I've needed."

"I've been the father I believed you needed," Lars clarified.

"And you've been wrong."

Lars waited patiently for Brandon to elaborate.

"All I ever wanted was for you to accept me as I am." Brandon swallowed. "To be proud of those things I did well, and not shrug them off because you felt I could've done better. You don't know me, and my guess is, you don't care to know me. Not really."

"Oh, I know you, Son," Lars finally responded. "Everything you are and everything you are not."

If young Brandon was expecting an apology from Lars, he'd best not hold his breath.

"I've never understood your fascination with him," Brandon continued, trying to mask the hurt in his eyes. "Your hate for him is as obsessive as your admiration for him. It's unnatural and it's been stifling growing up under the pressure of it."

"Shit," Lars huffed. "If you think it's been stifling to you, imagine how fucking suffocating it's been for me."

"So why hold on to it, Dad? Why hold on to that kind of obsession for over thirty years?"

Lars had never really thought about it before, but it was a valid question. He paused, then flipped back over the pages of his life until he finally reached the only answer that made sense, at least to him.

"Jordan Gatewood left me broke and damn near destitute," he concluded. "The only thing I had left after he had me escorted out of that building was my loathing for him and my admiration for how he'd pulled the proverbial rug out from under not only me but all of us who'd sworn to not rest until we'd seen him fail. It was masterful, and unexpected from someone so young and inexperienced. He'd outwitted us all, using the seeds of our combined knowledge against us and planting them in his own soil, cultivating them with such patience and care to yield his own fruit." He laughed. "I've never seen anything like it. The man is a genius and I am probably his biggest fan."

"Daddy." Lars's youngest, his daughter, Bianca, entered the room, walked over to him, and planted a sweet kiss on his forehead before sitting down next to Brandon.

She was the most beautiful thing Lars had ever created, with long dark hair like her mother's had been, and rich brown eyes that he melted in every time he gazed into them.

"The contract is nearly ready," she said, looking back and forth between the two of them. "And it's airtight," she assured them both. "Not even his Gatewood descendants could finagle a way out of this one." She smiled, and Lars's heart jumped a bit in his chest.

His beautiful Bianca was a huge point of contention between Lars and his wife. Bianca's mother was a black woman. The affair had ended years ago, but he'd fallen in love at first sight with his baby girl, and the notion that he wouldn't give his right arm for her, claim her as his own, love her, was inconceivable and unacceptable.

Bianca was the son he never had. She was never condescending to Lars, never too eager to please in the hopes of getting his approval. She was true blue, unapologetic, and possessed the backbone that Brandon lacked. She'd orchestrated every detail of this situation herself, carefully enough to not offend her brother, but she'd definitely taught him some things that Lars hoped he'd taken to heart. It had been her idea to start having that woman followed not long after she'd shown up at the ball with Gatewood. Being proactive like that was not his son's strong suit.

"The contract will ruin his name," Lars

said introspectively. "Destroy it, possibly. If anything goes wrong with that pipeline, then the blood will be on his hands as the controlling investor."

We'll have it to him no later than three," Brandon said confidently, offering his only little contribution to this unsavory scheme.

"Gatewood would take most of the risks, but his return, if any, will be almost non-existent," she assured them both. "We went through it with a fine-tooth comb."

"A hundred million dollars" — he chuckled — "well, it won't leave him broke. But it'll sting. If nothing else, losing it like this will embarrass the hell out of him. Not to mention, the whole Sioux nation will likely sue the shit out of him for everything else he owns."

Lars looked at Bianca and smiled.

"Then all that's left is the woman," Brandon added, looking sheepishly at his father.

That boy looked sick to his stomach every time the subject of Gatewood's woman was brought up in conversation. "If I didn't know better, Son, I'd think you had a thing for Ms. Rhodes," he teased.

Bianca smiled. "A little bit?" she asked, nudging him gently in the arm.

Of course he looked offended. "She really is innocent in all this."

"But according to you, she is his soul," Lars concluded. "And you don't have to kill a man's body to end his life."

"We agreed that it would be painless, Brandon," Bianca reminded him. "But the point of all of this was to make him suffer. Gatewood could recover his name, his reputation, even his money. But she's personal. Intimate and sacred. Besides, we can't afford any loose ends. The people I hired to take her are amateurs. I can't guarantee how sloppy they've been with her, and I don't want to take the chance that she could somehow identify any of them and lead an investigation back to us."

"Make the call, Bianca," Lars said, locking gazes with his son. "Let them know that they won't see a dime until I see proof that she's gone."

"We should at least wait until after the contract is signed," Brandon insisted.

"He'll sign it," Lars said confidently.

Gatewood was in love. On some level Jordan Gatewood and Lars Degan were the same when it came to that. Love was demanding and absolute. True love, that is. Lars loved his wife, but it was more of a convenience than anything. He had loved Bianca's mother beyond anything rational and reasonable. She'd broken his heart in ways he never thought were possible when she left him. But yes. He'd have done anything to keep her. Breaking Gatewood's heart would bring Lars more satisfaction than ruining his reputation or business. It would destroy the man. And that's all he'd ever wanted.

TOO GOOD AT GOOD-BYES

Naomi methodically followed the same morning routine the exact same way she'd done since the kids had started school. She was up at five, making lunches and fixing breakfast. Thomas liked a hot breakfast, usually bacon and eggs, every morning before leaving for work. While the boys dressed and her husband finished his cup of coffee, Naomi went into the bathroom to put on her makeup and then to the bedroom to get dressed for work.

"Y'all quit playing and get dressed," she heard Thomas tell the boys on the way into the master bedroom.

Thomas stood behind her and slipped his arms around her waist. "I get paid today. Maybe me and you can go out to eat."

She turned her head, kissed him softly, and smiled. "I'd like that, baby."

He couldn't know that she wasn't going to be here when he came home from work.

While she watched him leave, Naomi knew that this would be the last time she would ever see him. She drove the boys to school without mentioning that she'd be picking them up early. Normally, Naomi's next stop would be to give that woman some food and water, but she didn't think it was necessary this morning. After all, this was her last day. And besides, she just really couldn't bring herself to look at her again, especially after knowing what James had done to her and knowing what he kept saying he would need to do.

It was almost over and this had been the longest week of her life, but everything that'd happened this week, everything that she'd done, would finally set her free, and so it'd been worth it. She had to keep reminding herself of what was at stake. That woman had suffered, but Naomi had suffered too, probably for longer. Probably worse. She hoped they'd hand her back over to her man, and in time, she'd put James and whatever he'd done to her behind her. Women were strong like that. And that man would be there for her. Of course he loved her, enough to pay God knows how much money to get her back. He'd take care of her. Naomi was sure of it.

She'd finally made up her mind about

where she and the boys would go. First, she'd had to make peace with the fact that there were places that they couldn't go. Naomi couldn't go to family. Thomas would find her. She couldn't even tell them where she was, because they'd probably break down and tell him. He was convincing like that, making it seem like she was wrong and he was the victim. She'd figured out a long time ago that he'd missed his calling and should've been an actor.

Half a million dollars was so much money. It was more money than most people see in a lifetime. But it wasn't enough to fly to the moon and to never be seen or heard from again. She was going to have to use that money to pay for new identification documents. You could get them off the Internet easily enough, or even make them yourself, but either way, it was going to cost her. She'd decided on someplace far away from Texas, a place where it snowed because she knew that the boys would love the snow.

Naomi had decided on Wilmington, Delaware. She didn't know a soul in Delaware, and in her mind it was almost as far away from Texas as the moon was from Earth. Thomas would never think to look for her in a place like that. She could find an affordable place to live, get a job, maybe doing hair. She could do it out of her house so she wouldn't have to go out so much, and she always liked doing hair. She'd have to get a license first, though. But at least she could afford it.

Sitting in her car outside in the parking lot of her job, Naomi took several deep breaths to try to calm that anxious feeling filling her stomach. What was it going to feel like to be brand-new? To be free? Free to feel her feelings without the threat of her expression being met by Thomas's fist? Tears flooded her eyes at the thought. It was the simple things that too many people took for granted, things like being able to openly laugh at something funny or to curse because you stubbed your big toe. Little things like that had cost her many nights of sleep.

It was hard not to get her hopes up, but for the first time in a very long time, Naomi did have hope. It felt foreign to her, and precious like she wasn't entitled to it. And she was afraid of having it snatched from her hands, so she held it close to her heart.

The first thing she'd do after leaving Texas would be to buy another car. Thomas would track this one. She wouldn't sell this old heap; she'd just leave it somewhere. There were thousands of pieces to the puzzle that was freedom. At any given moment, one would randomly pop into her mind and Naomi would have to look at it, figure out what to do with it, and then wait for the next one to reveal itself.

Naomi had been watching the minutes tick off the clock ever since she'd gotten to work that morning. It was nearly lunchtime before the phone on her desk rang with D.J.'s number appearing on the screen. Her heart thumped so loudly it was a wonder that no one else in the room seemed to hear it. Naomi glanced at the clock on her computer. It was early. Too early. Wasn't it?

"Crown Distributors. Naomi speaking."

"We need to get together," he said in a hushed and hurried tone.

"I'm unable to do that right now," she said professionally.

Naomi's heart began racing. Was this it? Did he have her money?

"We can't wait, Nay. We've got to do this now. Just — we've got to talk."

Talk? She didn't want to fuckin' talk. All he had to do was tell her when that money had been wired and the two of them never had to say another word to each other.

"I'll have to call you back," she said before abruptly hanging up.

Moments later, the phone rang again. It

was him.

"Crown Distributors. Naomi speaking."

"This is serious, gotdammit!" He sounded scared. "We . . . we've got to talk, Nay. I can't — oh, shit. We need to talk now. You know where."

This time, he was the one who hung up. And that precious sliver of hope she'd been clinging to slowly began to seep through her fingers.

Naomi went to her coworker. "Eileen. One of my sons forgot his lunch and I need to take him some lunch money. I shouldn't be very long," she promised.

"Don't worry about it, girl." Eileen smiled. "I got you."

She couldn't shake the thought that they'd done all of this for nothing. Naomi drove through town to the burger place in the next county over, weighted down with dread. What would she do if she didn't get that money? Naomi couldn't put up with Thomas even one more day. She'd been so close — so fuckin' close! She had a little money. Maybe it was enough. Maybe it was going to have to be. Fuck going back to work. After this meeting with DJ, Naomi was going straight to the school and taking her boys and leaving this fucking town.

She pulled into the parking lot fifteen

minutes later, dried her eyes, and did the best she could to compose herself. She needed that money like she needed blood in her veins. It was the money or her life and the lives of her children.

LOSE YOURSELF

DJ damn near jumped out of his skin when his phone rang and the word "Unknown" showed up on the screen. He knew it was the woman who'd hired him. It was after breakfast and the kids were getting their shoes on for him to take them to school.

"We'll see you later, bae," Nia said, leaving to pick up her mother on her way to the hair salon.

"Bye, baby."

"Yes," he answered anxiously after she'd left.

"We've come to the end of a long and arduous road," the woman on the phone said, sounding like she was saying a farewell speech. She'd called right after Nia had left. "It's been a challenging week for you and your friends, I'm sure."

He shrugged as if she could see him. "It's been aiight. But it ends today. Right?"

"Absolutely." She sounded sexy on the

phone, sophisticated and shit.

He sighed, relieved, and cleared his throat. "So what's next?"

His heart raced. By the end of the day, DJ would have his money. They all would. And with that money came a brand-new life for him and his family. He would finally be the man Nia deserved and the man his children would always look up to.

The woman didn't answer right away and he was starting to wonder if she'd heard him, or maybe they'd lost the connection. He pulled his phone away from his ear and looked at it to see if he still had a signal, then put it back to his ear.

"You still there?"

"I'm here," she softly responded.

"So the money'll be in the accounts today, then? Or is it there already?" he asked, hopeful.

A million dollars was about to be his, and DJ was no worse for wear for it. It had been easy. Too damned easy.

"You'll get it after she's dead."

DJ was speechless. That wasn't their deal. From the very beginning, she'd told him that the woman wouldn't be harmed in any way. "W-w-wait a minute. You said that wouldn't have to happen."

"Daddy," his son said, "we're ready."

DJ got up, went into the bathroom, and shut the door behind him. "That's what you told me." Panic began to wash over him. "I wouldn't have agreed to do this if — You said for us to keep her safe and we did."

"If the police find out what you've done, you'll get as long a sentence as if you had killed her," she coolly explained. "Do you think the man paying the ransom won't use every resource to see that you get the maximum allowed by the law?"

This bitch was fuckin' threatening him. "Like I wouldn't take you down, too? Like I wouldn't tell them that you paid us to do this? If I go down, I'm taking you with me."

"And who am I?" she softly asked, and paused.

She thought he was stupid. DJ wasn't dumb. "They can trace your calls from my phone," he blurted out.

"To who? To where?"

Her number had never shown up on his phone. But DJ was sure that the police had ways of finding shit like that out. He'd seen those crime shows and he knew that they could use cell phone towers to track people.

"Choose carefully, DJ," she said, almost as if she gave a damn about him. "You can do this, do what I ask, or you can take your chances in court — you and your friends."

DJ's heart sank into his stomach.

"The money can be yours just like I promised, by the end of the day, or the police can be knocking on your door in twenty minutes."

The baby started crying. His son knocked on the door. "Daddy, we're ready."

He wasn't a killer. But if he didn't do this, all this would be for nothing. Nia would never have her house or new furniture. DJ would never be able to start his own business. And if he went to prison, who would take care of them, then? He never should've agreed to this, but James had been right. Deep down, DJ had always known that he probably was.

"Take a photo and send it to the secured e-mail address that will be texted to you. You'll get your money when I am satisfied that it's been done, DJ. I'll need the photo by three o'clock this afternoon and you'll have your money almost immediately. No later than that. I'll be waiting." And just like that, she hung up.

He was in such a fog after that call. DJ managed to get his son to school and dropped his daughter off at day care. Hours passed before he finally called Nay and then James.

Naomi was the last one to show up and she slid into the booth at the restaurant next to DJ. He and James had been there since twelve thirty, waiting on Nay, who showed up at twelve fifty-five.

"Do we have our money?" she asked in a whisper, looking at DJ. When he didn't answer, she looked at James. "Do we?"

"Tell her, DJ," James insisted. "Or do you want me to tell her?"

"Tell me what?" she asked, agitated.

"Calm down, Nay," DJ told her.

"Tell me what, DJ?"

James leaned in close to the two of them. "They want her dead," he said, almost as if he couldn't believe that this was finally happening.

"Since when have you been so excited about taking a life, man?" DJ whispered, glaring at James.

"Since half a million is at stake," he said quickly, glaring back at DJ. "I told y'all this was going to happen. You don't pay that kind of money to pick somebody up and babysit 'em for a few days."

All color washed from Nay's face. "They want her dead? So, we can't just let her go?"

"That's what they told me, Nay. I wouldn't have signed on to this if I thought that this was what they were going to ask us to do."

"But you did sign on to it," James reminded him. "And you pulled us into it. If we don't do this, we all go to prison and nobody gets paid."

"What's he talking about?" Naomi asked frantically. "What — how will they know we did this?" Naomi's eyes stretched as wide as saucers. "That can't happen," she muttered. "I can't do this. DJ, I can't do this."

"Because boss lady's going to tell 'em," James said, staring back at DJ. "She knows DJ." He shrugged. "He knows us."

Naomi looked as if she were about to cry, and shook her head. "No. No, this can't happen. That can't happen, DJ." She started to raise her voice, but he grabbed hold of her hand to calm her down. "I can't go to prison. I can't leave my boys."

"Neither can I, Nay," he said, hushed, to her. "I wouldn't have dragged you into this if I knew this is what that woman wanted. I swear to God I wouldn't have."

"I can't stay here," she said desperately. "I can't stay with Thomas." Tears started to fall.

"This is fucked-up," DJ said, leaning in

close to her and whispering. "This isn't who we are. And it's fucked-up."

Nay looked like her soul had left her body, and staring back into his eyes were hazel orbs of nothingness. "Who's going to do it?" She looked back and forth between the two men. "I can't go to prison. I won't. I need this money."

"We were felons the second we walked into that house and put our hands on her," James coolly reminded them.

"He's right, DJ," Nay said, with an expression on her face so cold that she didn't even look like herself. "I have to get out of here, and that money is the only way my boys and me can be safe."

"You're okay with taking a life?" DJ questioned, seeing the same disregard for that woman's life in Nay's eyes as he saw in James's. "You think it's going to be that easy?"

Nay swallowed. "I don't care about it being easy. It's her life or mine, DJ. The only one I care about is mine and my boys'."

James huffed. "I never believed that they'd let her go in the first place. So this don't surprise me," he said, shrugging. "Not surprised that they want her dead and not surprised that I'm gonna have to be the one to do it."

There was no argument from DJ or Nay.

James held out his hand, palm up, and stared at DJ while Naomi placed the key to that room in his hand. There was no stopping this now. DJ sat frozen in his seat as his brother stood up and left. Nay sat next to him.

"We've broken all kinds of laws, D," she sadly explained. "For the first time in my life, I'm able to save myself. You don't know what it's been like. No one knows," she tearfully explained. "But if this is the only way that I can get away from him, then I'll take it."

"And you can live with this in your new life with your new name in your new house? You can sleep at night knowing that you got all that at the expense of a woman's life?"

"Like I said. It's hers or mine. I got children to think about."

The two of them sat there for the next ten minutes in silence. Could he spend a dime of that money knowing that it had that woman's blood on it? Would he buy that house that Nia loved so much, live in it, raise his kids in it, sleep in it, knowing that she died in order for him to have it? He'd fucked up. DJ had been quietly coming to terms with that realization ever since he'd hung up the phone from talking to that woman. She'd found him, seen that he was weak, and she used him. Played his family against him, his hopes and dreams. DJ had been a fool.

"Even if James does kill her," he said quietly to Nay, "what guarantees do we have that the bitch who hired us to do this still won't drop a dime on us and get us arrested?"

Naomi leaned back, staring at him as her eyes began to water. "She — she can't do that," she muttered fearfully.

Yes. She absolutely could. DJ had made his share of mistakes, but damn. This was one he knew without a doubt that he would never be able to live with.

"Move, Nay," he said, shoving her out of the booth.

"Where you going?" she asked, following behind him. "DJ, don't!"

He unlocked his car door and climbed in behind the wheel. Nay climbed in on the passenger side.

"If you stop him, we get nothing!" she yelled through tears.

"Don't you get it, Nay!" he shouted. "We never were going to get that money!" He started the car and peeled out of the parking lot.

Naomi screamed.

HE'S COLD PRODUCT

Jordan had unintentionally dozed off several times since arriving at Abby's bungalow in Blink late the night before. He'd also called Wells too many times to count, only to get his voice mail every time. It was just after noon when he opened his eyes again and immediately checked his cell phone. Wells still hadn't called.

"What the hell am I doing here?" he questioned irritably. He went into the kitchen and started a pot of coffee. While it brewed, he strolled through the house again, noting the blood on the wall. His baby had put up a fight, but at what cost?

Jordan went back into the kitchen, poured himself a cup of coffee, and took it outside in the backyard. A random memory of Abby wearing cutoff shorts, planting flowers, and dancing and singing to Johnnie Taylor came to mind. That was the second time he'd seen her. Jordan had knocked on the front door that day, but when she didn't answer, he followed the sound of the music to the backyard and caught her off guard. That's when he told her the truth about who he was and what this house had meant to him.

"I didn't mean to startle you. I was here about a month ago," he reminded her. "You and your friend allowed me to take a tour of the house. Jordan," he said. "Um . . . Abby, isn't it?"

"Yes. I remember you."

"My father died in this house," he eventually admitted after a long pause. "Thirty years ago, he was shot and died in the living room."

She took a deep breath. "So he lived here?"

Again he hesitated. "He lived in Dallas; however, he was seeing a woman who lived here."

That day, he had no idea of the role that Abby was meant to fill in his life. But even then he knew that whatever impact she was to bring to his life, he'd never be the same. It was just a feeling, one that, even now, he didn't fully understand and could never explain.

He felt as if he were carrying hundred-pound weights on his shoulders, and like wrecking balls were tethered to his ankles. Jordan waged an internal battle with himself, believing he'd have her with him again in a matter of hours. His reputation would be shot, and his bank account a hundred million dollars lighter, but if it was the only way for him to get her back, then she was worth every sleepless night, every penny. Best-case scenario? He'd see her again, alive, and before the sun rose on another day. Period. That's the only thing that mattered.

Twenty minutes passed. Jordan called Wells again, to no avail. The bastard wasn't answering. Jordan's rage was reflected in his message.

"Get off your ass and call me!" he demanded.

Minutes were ticking by faster than he wanted. The last thing he needed to see show up in his in-box was that contract, but just like that it appeared. The sender's e-mail address was a jumble of numbers, letters, and symbols from some cryptic site. *Trans-coastal Natural Gas Pipeline Contract* was the title in the subject line of the e-mail. Reluctantly, Jordan opened the e-mail and read the instructions.

Signature required at the end of the contract and on the twelve addendums. Return no later than one hour after receipt. The note ended with account information for where his accountant needed to transfer funds. Jordan then clicked open the first contract document, and without even reading, found the signature block at the end of the document and entered his electronic signature. It sickened him to do it, but he continued signing these documents, feeling a step closer to her each time he did. He'd finally signed the final document and began the tedious process of reattaching them all to the reply e-mail. Before he could hit the Send button, his phone rang. It was Wells.

"Tell me you have her," he said anxiously.

"Not yet."

Jordan pounded his fist hard on the desk and bolted to his feet. He placed his finger on the mouse to send the damn contracts.

"But I'm sitting here looking at the people who I believe do."

Jordan held his breath for a moment and carefully sat back down. "What the fuck is going on, man? Tell me where you are."

"In a town called Richardson. It's the next exit off the highway, just past the exit to Blink. Exit 122B, about ten minutes from where you are. I'm sitting in the parking lot of a Whataburger just off the highway. You can't miss it."

"What makes you think these people have her?" he dared to ask.

"I suggest you hang up and get over here.

I'll wait, if I can."

Adrenaline flooded his veins and instinct kicked in. Before he realized it, Jordan hurried from the house, climbed into his truck, and peeled out of Abby's driveway. It wasn't until he was a mile away from the house that he realized he'd forgotten to send that damn contract. Jordan was fucking losing it! "Shit!"

It wasn't like him to forget a thing like that. Should he turn around and go back to the house to send it? He had less than an hour to get it back to those people. But what if Wells found her? He didn't have time. Jordan couldn't go back. If Wells was wrong about this —

Jordan tried swallowing the baseball-size lump in his throat as he drove. A dark and foreboding feeling washed over him. Jordan felt sick to his stomach. He had fucked up.

LESSONS FROM THE
ANCIENT ROOTS

Call it a miracle. Call it luck. Call it God. Hell, call it Shou Shou. Sometimes, things had a way of working themselves out. The trick was never to force a situation. Plato had been patient. That patience was driving Gatewood's ass up the wall, and understandably so, but from where Plato sat, being patient had finally paid off. Whereas Gatewood had counted five days to find Abby, Plato looked at it differently. He'd had 120 hours to find her. A hundred and twenty hours somehow made the whole situation feel a lot less urgent.

Crown Distributors was his only real lead to finding Abby Rhodes. And so Plato had come back to this place, parked, waited, and watched for a sign from on high, any kind of sign, really. He'd gotten it. That happy couple he'd seen this morning at breakfast, the blond woman and the brotha. Here they were again. Not a coincidence. Not by a long shot. She came out of the building, sat in his car for a few minutes, and then left. He started up his engine as soon as she did, and drove off. So did Plato. With a song in his heart and a chest full of hope, he started whistling a tune he liked. Who sang it? Old song, from the eighties. Paul Simon's *"You Can Call Me Al."* Good song.

Yesterday Plato had gotten the break he needed, or at least the beginning of one. He'd accidentally stumbled across Blondie and boyfriend, the couple who, for some inane reason, had caught and held his interest at breakfast the other day. Plato had gone to scope out Crown Distributors because he didn't have shit else as a lead to finding Abby, so why not? And there they were. Bonnie and Clyde. She'd come out of the building and climbed into his car parked in the lot.

He'd followed the boyfriend after he'd left and the woman had gone back inside, but he'd lost him at the railroad tracks. Which was an embarrassment to Plato and a sure sign that living in the lap of luxury with the lovely Marlowe Brown was making him careless and taking away his edge. But that was another conversation that he needed to have with himself at another time.

"I need you to run some plates for me,"

he told Wonder Boy over the phone.

It didn't take long for Plato to get a text from that little genius he had come to depend on so much. He texted Plato a name, James Washington, and the dude's address, a dump of a house in Clark City, just outside Blink. Plato had been shadowing Washington since late yesterday. Today the old boy had led him to this burger joint, where he joined another dude. Blondie showed up a while later. Whatever they were discussing looked serious. He started to play out a scenario in his mind on how the three of them could be involved in this.

Little Abby had put up quite a fight the night she'd been taken. It wouldn't be hard to surmise that maybe the men had taken her. The woman could've been there too, though. He quickly dismissed worrying over the details and called Gatewood.

Fifteen minutes after the woman showed up, toothpick boy, or whatever the hell it was he was chewing on, got up to leave. The other two stayed behind. Shit. A Plato clone would've come in real handy right about now. Plan of action? Follow the dude? Or stay behind with the other two?

"I'm here," Gatewood said when Plato answered the phone. "Where are you?"

Ah, yes! The cavalry.

"Black sedan, back of the parking lot in the southwest corner. I'm pulling out now."

"Where the hell are you going?"

Plato saw a light-blue-and-silver pickup truck headed in his direction and soon caught a glimpse of Gatewood's scowling face looking right at him.

"I'm going after contestant number one," he said with a nod. "Contestants two and three are inside. Black dude in a gold hoodie with a blonde sitting next to him."

Gatewood positioned his truck to pull into the parking spot backward while Plato went after Washington.

He followed Washington and a few minutes later ended up on the highway, headed south. Was he leading him to Abby? Plato could only cross his toes and hope for the best. His phone rang and it was Marlowe, with Shou yelling frantically in the background.

"Tell him to keep them peaches away from me! Tell me I can't eat 'em. They'll kill me if I do!"

"I had to call," Marlowe said, exasperated. "What the hell do you know about peaches?"

"I can't talk right now, baby. I'm in the middle of something."

"Curse him if he try to bring me them

damn peaches!" Shou shouted. "I'll turn him blind! Make him forget his own name and yours too, Marlowe. You tell him!"

"Auntie! Stop it. He doesn't know anything about any peaches."

"Marlowe, I've got to go," he said sternly.

Plato didn't have time for this. He hung up before Marlowe could say another word about her crazy-ass aunt and them damn peaches. He'd catch hell for it later, but he didn't have to catch it now.

"Shit!" Washington had been four cars ahead of him, but he turned off the road and Plato had missed the exit fucking around with Marlowe and Shou. "Gotdammit!" he cursed, slamming the heel of his hand against the steering wheel.

Plato spotted a sign telling him that the next exit was a mile up the road. He cut across two lanes to get onto the opposite side and skidded his car around, heading in the other direction. By the time Plato made it to the exit, the other car was nowhere in sight. When he came to a crossroad, he pulled his car over and stopped.

"Where did that motha fucka go?" he muttered to himself.

Straight? Left? He shook his head in disbelief. This was not happening and not now. Not when he was so damn close to finding her. Plato could feel it in his gut. This was one of those flip-a-coin moments. He had a fifty-fifty chance of getting it wrong. The same odds of getting it right, though. He pulled back into the street and turned left. Small, wooden homes, some perched on top of cinder blocks and almost all of them appeared to be abandoned, lined the street and made him feel like he'd been transported back sixty years. The only signs of life were laundry hanging out on the line to dry and an old woman sitting on her front porch in a rocking chair smoking a pipe, nodding as he drove past her house.

Plato had been driving for nearly ten minutes on that road when he started to believe he'd made a mistake. He'd taken the wrong turn, ended up on the wrong road, and Abby Rhodes might very well be dead because of it. When he reached a dead end, Plato turned off the engine. He opened the door and stepped out of his car and walked over to a sign with an arrow on it pointing left. It was hard to see, and if you didn't know to look for it, you'd surely miss it. But it was another road with a path worn into it by the tracks of tires. Over time, it had become overgrown, but someone had been on it recently, indicated by the weeds that had been pressed down into the dirt.

He looked back at that sign and swallowed hard.

"No, no, no, no," he whispered in disbelief. "That's fuckin' impossible."

Plato's big ass shuddered.

MISS PEACHES' SOUTHERN HOME COOKING. Was this what had Shou so up in arms? In smaller letters underneath it, it said HOME OF THE BEST PEACH COBBLER IN TEXAS.

Right Down to the Bone

"Since when have you been so excited about taking a life, man?"

James wasn't excited about murder, but hell! They'd come too far with this shit. The moment James agreed to kidnap that woman he started mentally preparing himself for this moment. People who do shit like this, who plan it, who pay for it — they have to know that you don't half-ass cross the line. And ultimately, DJ's naïve ass was even more useless than Naomi.

James drove angry, because the shit was real now. He was pissed that, just like he suspected from the beginning, doing this would fall on him, because neither one of their dumb asses had the balls to do it. But it came down to prison or the money. James had done more time in prison than he cared to think about, and he wasn't going back. The mothafuckin' cops would have to kill his ass before he set foot in the joint again.

He was about to get his hands on more money than he'd ever seen in his life, and she was the only thing standing in his way. So, yes! James would pull the mothafuckin' trigger on all this mess and keep it moving.

Nobody would find her back here in these sticks, and if they ever did, it'd be too late and James would be long gone. His first thought was to burn the place down, but fire makes smoke and smoke brings the fire department. He could just leave her there in that room. Nobody ever went that far back into them woods anymore, but he couldn't risk her smart little ass finding a way to get out.

James pulled up to that old run-down building, turned off the engine, and took a deep breath. What he was about to do, what he had to do, was something he'd never be able to take back.

Beating on people was one thing, but actually taking somebody out was another thing altogether. It dawned on him in that moment that the only weapons he had were his hands. Since the moment they'd plucked her out of her bed, James could barely keep his hands off of her. Now, the thought made him sick to his stomach.

It seemed to take him forever to get out of the car and go inside that old restaurant.

James stood at the door for several moments before finally unlocking it and stepping inside and letting it close behind him. He didn't need his mask anymore.

She stood up and backed into the corner of the room, staring at him with those pretty eyes of hers.

"Please — don't," she begged, shaking her head and trembling.

Did she know? Looking at her, he could tell. She knew

"Do you remember me now?" he asked, shrugging.

He had no idea why it even mattered if she remembered him, but it did.

Abby slowly shook her head. "I . . . I don't."

Of course she didn't. A woman like her would never give a man like him a second glance.

"You helped me to unload some lumber once," he reminded her taking a step toward her. "I thought you was so fine. And your little ass was strong, too. You could carry almost as much as I could."

He waited for recognition to spark in her eyes, but it never did. James would strangle her. He would choke life right out of her, because he wanted to stare into her pretty face when she died.

"I got no choice, Abby," he said, rushing over to her.

"Nooo!" she yelled, but his hands were around her neck, squeezing, cutting her cries short.

She fought him. He'd have been disappointed if she hadn't. Abby punched and kicked and scratched as he slowly lowered her to the floor on her back. He squeezed, harder, the longer he held on. James pressed his fingers deep into the muscles of her neck as his hands cramped like a vise, fueled by adrenaline, and fear of getting locked up again, and his desperate need to get as far away from this place, from her, as possible.

Abby gagged, gasped, her eyes bulging and locking on to his. James cried, releasing unexpected and powerful emotions surging through him, turning him into a man he never really knew he was capable of being. He felt like he had left his body and stood across the room, watching this scene unfold in front of him in disbelief, excitement, and fear.

Abby's arms fell limp against the floor and he could almost see the light of life leaving her eyes. His heart beat so hard and fast in his chest that it scared him. *Stop!* James wanted to, but couldn't. Too much was wrong about this, but the longer he held on, the more right he felt. If he could do this, then he could do anything. He was a fuckin' beast! James was a gotdamn gangsta!

"Fuck!" he suddenly yelled out in agony. Piercing hot and sharp pain shot through his head — his face! "What the ffffff —"

James rolled off of her, raised his hand to his face, and felt — "Oh shit! Oh shit! Shit!" he gasped. What the fuck had she stuck him with? What the fuck was in his eye?

In a jerk reaction, and without thinking, he pulled on it. "Aaaaaaaaaah!" he yelled.

He couldn't take it out. Not without taking the eyeball out of the socket. James rolled on the floor, kicking the wall, crying out. What the fuck had she done to him? He had no idea how long he'd writhed around on that floor before he realized that Abby was gone. James managed to open his other eye and saw that the door was wide open.

"No," he muttered, stumbling to his feet, pushing through the pain searing through his head. Fuck no! "Bitch!" he yelled, shuffling toward the door.

Don't Care Where
They Kick

The car parked outside was his.

Was the door open? Could the keys be inside?

Abby glanced inside quickly. *Run, Abby! Just run!*

She could hear him screaming as she ran out to the road and hesitated.

"Which way?" she asked, breathless, looking back and forth in both directions.

It didn't matter. Abby turned left and started to run again, hard gravel digging into the tender soles of her feet.

"Bitch!" She heard him call out her name.

She wasn't fast — Abby couldn't run fast enough.

In the distance up ahead, she saw a car coming toward her.

"No," she murmured, stopping. Coming toward her.

They'd caught her before, but no. No, not this time. Abby turned abruptly and cut into grass as tall as she was, leading into the woods. She ducked down and waited for the car to pass.

"Where the fuck you think you gonna go? Ain't no gotdamn where to go out here!" he called out again.

She put her hand over her mouth and held her breath. He was too close. The sounds of footsteps. Moving away from her? Coming toward her? She didn't know.

Be still, she commanded herself, squeezing her eyes shut for a moment and willing her body steady.

Abby couldn't risk the road. She had to find another way. Quietly, she began to back up through the grass to the grove of trees behind her and then started to run. She stumbled. Her lungs burned. Her legs were so weak. Jesus! Help her! Abby started running up a hill and somehow managed to get to the top and collapsed. *Get up, Abby! Get the hell up!*

Out of breath, Abby struggled to get to her feet, but as soon as she did, they were out from under her again.

"James!"

A man called out from a distance.

"James!" a woman yelled.

"The fuck you think you going?" The man chasing her growled.

Glancing over her shoulder, she saw him, her weapon still lodged in his eye.

"Noooo!" she screamed, clawing at the ground as he pulled her back toward him. "Let me fucking go!"

He crawled up the length of her, flipped her over onto her back, grabbed her head, and slammed it hard into the ground. "What the fuck did you do to me?"

Abby tried to scream.

"Shut up!" he demanded, hitting her hard across the face with his fist. "Shut the fuck up!"

Dazed, she felt his hands around her throat again, choking her. Abby clawed at his hands, and then, without thinking, shoved the heel of her hand hard against the piece of plastic stuck in his eye

He reared back, screaming and clutching his head, and then fell off of her.

Abby rolled over onto her stomach, crawled back up to the top of the hill, pushed herself up to standing, and started to run, but fell and ended up tumbling down the other side.

The sound of his heavy groaning and breathing behind her warned her that he was close again. Abby's throat burned. She couldn't catch her breath. Her legs felt like lead weights.

Again, she tripped, then rolled, and didn't manage to get to her feet again until she made it to the bottom of the hill. For some reason she turned to look over her shoulder to see how close he was and then, suddenly, she ran right into a brick wall, hitting it so hard that it knocked her back onto the ground.

Abby started kicking and sliding back away from him. It was the other one! He'd found her.

"Stop," he said, reaching for her.

Abby cried out, "Oh, God! No!"

Get up, Abby! Run!

"It's all right," he said. "It's me, Abby!"

She looked up at him. *Jordan?*

He squatted in front of her and held out his hand. "It's all right."

LOOKING FOR MY SOUL

"I found her," Wells told Jordan over the phone as Jordan followed the man and woman leaving the restaurant.

"I'm following the other two," Jordan told him.

"They may lead you here."

"Where's here?"

Jordan listened carefully to the directions Wells gave him. Sure enough, the couple driving the car ahead of him followed those same directions almost as if they were listening, too.

He couldn't let them know he was on to them. Jordan backed off in his pursuit, passed the turn they took onto a dirt road, and eventually doubled back and turned down that same road, forcing himself to drive slowly and not give in to the desperate need to find her before they got to her.

His phone rang again, and again it was Wells. "I see you. Pull over."

"Where'd they go?" he asked angrily, bitterly. "I don't see them."

"Pull over. Get out of the truck."

Reluctantly, Jordan did as he was told.

"Come east."

Jordan looked east and saw Wells standing in a heavily wooded area staring back at him as he put away his phone.

"They might see my truck," he told Wells as the two met up.

Wells turned and started walking. "They won't make it back this far."

"Ain't no gotdamn where to go out —"

Jordan and Wells stopped at the sound of a man's voice. Wells turned slowly to Jordan and smiled. "We've got company."

It took everything in Jordan to stay put. She was close. He didn't have to see her to know it, because he felt it. In this moment, the two men hurried toward the voice.

"James!" They stopped and heard first a man, then a woman call out that name.

Wells started to move in their direction. Jordan followed. Wells pulled out his gun. Jordan pulled out his. Jordan didn't give a shit about the man and woman chasing down James out here in these woods. All he wanted was Abby. Jesus! Where was she? Please! Don't let him be too late.

All of a sudden, Wells stopped, raised his

weapon, and locked on the man and the woman Jordan had followed from the restaurant.

"Oh, God!" the woman exclaimed, staring wide-eyed and stunned at the two of them, before dropping to her knees and collapsing into tears.

"In my own mind," Wells coolly responded, "perhaps."

The man with her looked as if he'd shit himself and slowly raised his hands in surrender.

"Get your girlfriend up and let's go find your little buddy, James," Wells told them, motioning for them to keep moving.

"Where's Abby?" Jordan lunged at the man, grabbed him by the front of his hoodie, and damn near lifted him off the ground.

"We don't know," he shot back in fear.

"But you're gonna take us to her," Wells chimed in, standing behind Jordan. "Right, son?"

Reluctantly, Jordan let him go, grabbed that woman by the arm, and forced her to stand. They hadn't walked much farther before he saw her, Abby, stumbling and falling down a hill, running from the motha fucka behind her. The world around Jordan disappeared, and she was all that existed.

She was alive. Abby managed to get to her feet, looked behind her, and when she turned to run, she bumped into him and then she fell, kicking and swinging at him like he was the enemy.

"It's me," he said, reaching for her. "It's all right," Jordan said as if he were in a trance. Jordan half expected to wake up in his bed, ready to tick off another day of having to try to live without her. He squatted and held out his hand to her. "It's all right."

She looked at him and he knew that he had found her and that this wasn't a dream.

That bastard trying to stop his momentum on the way down that hill after Abby caught Jordan's attention. Without thinking, Jordan stepped over Abby and made contact with that motha fucker when he landed, with a hard right to his jaw. It didn't take a genius to put all these pieces together. The bastard had something sticking out of his eye. She'd been running — from him. The only things real in this situation were Abby, this man, Jordan, and the gun he held in his hand.

That sonofabitch lay writhing on the ground — spitting out blood — cursing and crying out, but Jordan couldn't hear him. Pleading. Begging for what? Mercy? Life? Jordan turned slowly to Abby, standing behind him, trembling. She had been so brave. She had saved her own life. Abby, his love. His salvation, standing there, resurrecting him.

She peeled her eyes off of the pile of shit squirming at his feet, and locked gazes with Jordan. The connection was electric.

"Did he do that to you?" he asked her.

Blood was smeared across her nose and cheek. A gash split her lower lip. He'd warned them about what would happen if they'd hurt her. She looked at the man on the ground.

"I didn . . . I didn't touch her, man! Look! Look at her! She ran, but I didn't —"

The man, James, stared pitifully at her, realizing that she held the power over his life in this moment.

Jordan turned back to her. "Did he touch you, Abby?"

Abby looked back at Jordan and nodded.

"Nah! Don't — You know I didn't," he pleaded to her. "You know — I just — damn, you know I —"

James raised himself up to kneeling in front of Jordan. Jordan pressed the barrel of the gun against his forehead. Some trespasses could cost you every damn thing. And this one would cost James's life.

The chorus of voices coming from the people behind him got lost in a vacuum.

416

"Don't," the man behind him cried out. "Please don't, man."

The woman wailed. The sounds of birds chirping, of the wind rustling through the leaves, even the sound of the river nearby, all disappeared in that moment. The man in front of Jordan stared up at him with that one good eye and for half a second seemed to come to terms with his fate before Jordan pulled the trigger.

There is something absolute about the sound a gun makes when it's fired. Jordan had never killed a man before. Not personally. Until now, he'd never had a reason to.

Jordan turned slowly, walked past the other two, now on their knees staring shocked and openmouthed at the carnage at the bottom of the hill named James, and shoved his weapon in the back of his jeans as he looked to Wells.

"You got this?" he asked, wearily.

Wells nodded. "I'll take care of it."

Jordan walked over to Abby, still trembling and reaching for him; he gathered her in his arms, and carried her away.

Jordan needed to get her home. To his home, to their home in Dallas. Neither of them said a word to the other. He held her until she cried herself asleep in the seat beside him, and Jordan drove the nearly three hours feeling like he was under the influence of some drug. Exhaustion had set in.

When they arrived at the penthouse, he carried her inside and up the stairs to the shower. Jordan turned on the heads and adjusted the water until it was suitable. Then, fully clothed, he led her into the enclosure, let the warm water wash over them both, pressed her back against the wall, and leaned over her, resting his head against his arm against the wall above her head. All he wanted to do was close his eyes, hold her close, and sleep.

"Take . . . take these off," he said, gently at first, carefully tugging on her shirt.

That filthy bastard had touched her, and Jordan needed to wash any residue of that sonofabitch off of her. Jordan wanted him gone, every bone and muscle of him, everywhere he'd put his hands on her. James. James had soiled her, dirtied her.

"Take it off, Abby," he said, pulling more forcefully, and then lifting her shirt up by the hem and pulling it over her head.

That fucking pig had put his gotdamned hands on her! "Take it off!"

"Jordan."

"Take — take it — take it off!"

Something snapped in him. Madness rose to the surface and consumed him. He pulled down her shorts and kicked them aside. Jordan reached for the soap. Fuck! What the hell had he done to her? *Don't think about it. Don't think about it. Don't!*

All that mattered was erasing every second of this disgusting ordeal and washing it away. Erasing days like they never happened. Like she was never taken. Like she was never separated from him.

"Jordan. Stop!"

Abby's pleas came from some faraway place. "Jordan, it's okay," she said, breathless. "It's okay, Jordan." Abby cried and wrapped her arms around him. "I'm here. It's okay, baby, It's okay, now."

His hand throbbed. Jordan didn't even remember pounding his fist into the shower wall. He didn't realize that he was crying too until he felt her soft hand on the side of his face, her kisses on his cheek and lips. Abby was his weakness. And she was probably the only one he'd ever had.

"You found me, Jordan." She whispered again and again, "It's over."

He had no idea how long they stayed in that shower. Both of them bathed and dried off, then climbed into bed. He didn't even know what time it was, but it didn't matter.

419

His phone had been ringing incessantly until he finally turned it off. Jordan lay in bed next to her, and the two of them stared into each other's eyes. She stayed awake as long as she could before finally drifting off to sleep, but he watched her a little while longer, afraid that if he closed his eyes, she'd disappear. Eventually, though, sleep took hold of him, too.

Abby feverishly rolled a piece of plastic from the water bottle into what looked kind of like a straw. One end was pointed, like a spear almost, and sharp. She couldn't make a tool to open that door, but she could fashion a weapon. Next, she wrapped it tightly with bands of plastic she'd braided together from the plastic sandwich bag, making it even rigid, almost as solid as a knife. If he was going to kill her, then that bastard was going to have to work for it.

She looked up at the sound of the key turning in the door. It was him. She knew it was him. Abby crouched low in the corner, pressing herself into it as far as she could, trying to make herself small and invisible. Abby hid the weapon beneath the blanket as he pushed open the door. She held her breath and tried to stifle her cries.

Stop it, Abby! You fight this bastard. Fight him as if your life depends on it — because it does.

He saw her. Abby pressed her lips together to stifle a scream. Every muscle in her body flexed, thick and ready to spring from that corner in her defense against him. He knelt down in front of her. Abby suddenly began to shake so hard that her teeth clicked. A scream caught in the back of her throat. *Kill him before he kills you. Don't let him! Don't!*

He reached for her, and in a reflex, she slapped his hand away. Abby blinked through her tears.

"It's all right, baby."

Baby? Whose baby did he think she was?

"Wake up, Abby."

What? What was he saying to her?

"It's Jordan, sugah." He reached for her. Abby blinked again.

She shook her head. He was lying, trying to trick her.

"Abby. Wake up, baby. It's Jordan."

Jordan was gone. Jordan wasn't here. She wanted him here. She needed him. Abby blinked and shook her head. Jordan — he wasn't — Jordan was — The longer she stared at the man kneeling in front of her, the more his features changed.

"Jordan?" she questioned, not willing to

421

believe her own mind, her own eyes.

"Yes, sweetheart," he said, holding out his hand to her. "It's me, baby."

Was it? Jordan. Abby blinked and looked quickly around the room. "Home," she whispered.

"That's right, Abby. I'm right here."

Abby dared to squeeze her eyes shut for a second, no more than that. When she opened them again, she stared back into his eyes.

She was dreaming. Abby was on the floor, backed up against the wall next to the bed. How else could he be here? How could she be here? She stared at his extended hand, at Jordan's hand. Abby wanted it to be real. More than anything she wanted all of this to be real.

"Jordan?" She sobbed, tentatively reaching out to touch him.

"It's me, Abby. You're safe now."

Even if it was just a dream, it was the best dream she'd ever had in her life, and Abby prayed that she'd never wake up from it. She took hold of his hand, and he pulled her onto his lap. She wrapped her arms around him and held on with everything in her.

He held her tight, and he felt real. He smelled real. "Yes, baby," he murmured in her ear. "It's me, and you're safe."

Abby nodded, "I am. I'm home."

Please enter where You already abide.
— Marianne Williamson

As Cool as I Remain

"I've got a feeling about you," Marlowe said, coming out onto the porch where Plato was sitting.

He took a sip of his coffee. "What'd I tell you about eavesdropping on me with all that mind-reading shit?"

She sighed and sat down next to him on the steps. "I'm not psychic, but if I was, there'd be nothing shitty about it."

Marlowe leaned into him, kissed the side of his face, and rested her head on his shoulder. It was late, nearly eleven.

"How come I get the feeling that you're thinking about leaving me?" she asked softly.

Like hell if she wasn't psychic. "Your crystal ball tell you that?"

"I don't need a crystal ball when all I have to do is to read you. You think I don't feel you trying to pull away from me?" Marlowe wrapped her arm around his. "Wrestling with yourself trying not to give in to old

427

habits of taking off and never looking back. Is it really so bad being with me?"

He sighed long and deep. "Nah, you're the problem, sweetheart," he said, finally looking into her eyes. "Most of the time being here with you feels too damn good and I'm a born pessimist. Nothing this good can last forever."

Marlowe paused and gave what he said some thought. "No, I suppose nothing good ever can," she said remorsefully. "But then bad don't have to last forever, either. Right? Why you gotta be so full of secrets?"

"You knew I was full of secrets when you met me, baby, when you fell in love with me."

"And you made me promises that I expect for you to keep."

He most certainly had done that. Love made men temporarily insane. He told her what she needed to hear and at the time he hoped like hell that he could live up to those promises. But all the best intentions in the world couldn't change who he was at the core.

"I am not a good guy, Marlowe," he reminded her. "You fell in love with the villain, baby, not the hero. Thought you knew that."

Hours ago, Plato had slayed some folks,

erased them like mistakes and hidden them so good that they'd probably never be found again. And then he came home, kissed her on the cheek, showered, ate a late dinner, and now sat outside on the porch, sipping a cup of decaf as if nothing had happened.

Marlowe sat up, put her hand underneath his chin, and turned his face to hers.

"You might be somebody's villain, but you're not mine. You are the man I love and will always love, unless you leave me and break my heart. Then I swear I'll hate you for it."

The thought of her hating him broke his heart right then and there. But see, that's what kept him here with her. Love like hers was too addictive to just walk away from, but sometimes those walls of his transgressions started to close in on him and it got hard to breathe.

There was a time when Plato would finish a job and then forget about it. It wasn't smart to let his sins weigh him down. So what was this he'd been feeling since he and Gatewood had found Ms. Rhodes? Why was he carrying this burden now?

Gatewood had taken out the man trying to kill his woman, and rightly so. The sick bastard got off pretty easy if you asked Plato. Shit. If he'd come at Marlowe like that, and Plato had found him, his ass would be strung up between two trees, and skinned alive until his black ass begged for death. Gatewood had blessed him with that bullet. It was an easy kill. Justified. Plato took care of the other dude and the woman.

"Please, man," the other brotha cried. He cried like a baby, hands held up in surrender, spit and snot running down his chin. "I did it for my family. My old lady and my babies. We needed that money. I didn't know they wanted us to kill her. They said hold her. Keep her safe and then we'll tell you when to let her go."

"Who's they, son?" Plato asked, squatting in front of him, his pistol held loosely in his hands.

The woman curled up in a ball on the ground, trembling and moaning as if she was in pain, and Plato hadn't even touched her.

The young brotha shrugged and shook his head. "I . . . I never saw her. She never told me her name."

"How'd she find you?"

"I don't know, man. She just called me one day. Knew where I worked and about my family. She knew I needed money."

There was no doubt in Plato's mind that the dude was telling the truth.

"Please, man. Please just let me go home. I

430

won't say nothing. I can't. If I do, then I go to prison. My family needs me."

If he knew who'd hired him, he'd have told Plato. But not knowing was not going to save the brotha's life. Plato fired the gun and it was over for him. Just like that. The young dude never even saw it coming. That's what mercy looked like.

Loose ends, even those who meant no harm, the repentant kind, weren't given passes in Plato's line of work. It was all about absolutes and putting that period at the end of a sentence. The young man's family would somehow have to learn to manage without him.

The woman lay completely still and silent, stifling her cries after knowing that her friend had died. Did she hope Plato would forget that she was here? Plato stood up, walked over to her, and knelt down in front of her. Of course she wouldn't know shit, either.

"He's going to keep the boys," she said in a whimper, finally pushing up to kneeling, fixing wide eyes at nothing in particular into the woods.

He'd believed her to be a white woman, but being this close to her, he saw she looked biracial or something. Hazel eyes flashed at him, red-rimmed eyes. She had freckles.

"I don't know what made me think that I

could do this," she said sorrowfully, sniffing and dragging her forearm across her nose. "I got a bad habit of trusting the wrong people when what I should be doing is listening to my gut and trusting myself."

She looked at Plato and waited as if she needed him to affirm her revelation.

"I never should've married Thomas. Looking back — what is that they say about hindsight?" Somehow, someway, she managed to attempt a smile. "I wanted to save my babies," she sobbed. "To keep them from being like him. They see what he does to me, and I can tell that they're starting to think that it's okay. I never wanted them to believe that it was okay to hurt people. But then I go and do this. Makes me wonder if I'm any better than he is." She shrugged. "I'd always hoped that if something happened to me, my boys would go to my parents. I just didn't want him to have them."

He didn't know Thomas, but from the way she spoke about him, the man was a motha fucka. "What's your name?" Plato asked, embarking into forbidden territory.

He never cared about their names, until now. Until her.

"Naomi Simpson."

Plato fired again and the world was void one Naomi Simpson.

"I spoke to Shou, earlier," Marlowe told him, bringing him back to the moment.

Just hearing that old woman's name made his skin crawl. Without realizing it, she had given him clues. He was more afraid of her now than ever.

"She wanted me to thank you for no longer tormenting her with those peaches. Are you going to tell me what peaches had to do with whatever it was you were working on?"

He looked at her.

"Don't call me psychic. Women have intuition. That's all this is."

"I don't know nothing about that old woman and peaches," he eventually responded.

Marlowe shrugged. "Fine. Don't tell me, then. I'm going to bed," she said, standing up and untying her robe as she turned to go back inside, giving him a tasty view of all of her. "You coming?"

Plato bounded to his feet like a kid and followed Marlowe inside.

THE BETTER MAN

Jordan and Abby had slept off and on for the last two days. It was Sunday evening when Abby told him that she was hungry. Abby nibbled on cheese, bread, and fruit and sipped hot tea. Since he'd found her, Jordan held on to her, being sure to keep her close to him. They hadn't spoken much. Both quietly processed the last week in their own ways.

It was cool out, but they sat outside on the terrace anyway and watched the sunset. Neither one of them would ever be the same. This ordeal had the power to tear them apart or to make them grow stronger, together. The way she clung to him, Jordan had hopes that it would be the latter.

He loved her literally to death — his or someone else's. The fear of losing Abby had definitely taken its toll and pushed Jordan to limits he'd never imagined he'd ever have to face. This woman was literally everything

to him. She was the only thing that mattered, more than Gatewood Industries,
more than money, more than his reputation
or name.

There were people out there who knew
that now. People who would no doubt not
hesitate to come for her again, holding her
out in front of him like bait, and Jordan
couldn't let that happen. Abby was far too
precious to him, and if nothing else had
come of this, he hoped that she understood
that now.

"You need to see a doctor, Abby." He
eventually said what he'd been thinking
since he'd found her. "We need to be sure
that you're all right. That the baby's all
right. Phyl can make the appointment."

She reluctantly raised her head from his
shoulder. He fought back feelings of rage
every time he looked at the bruises on her
face. What had they done to her? He didn't
know and he wasn't sure that he wanted to
know. But Abby was still pregnant and she
needed to be seen as soon as possible.

Abby nodded slowly. "That's fine," she
said softly.

He raised her hand to his lips and kissed
it. Five days was too long for those people
to have held her. Whoever was behind this
had nearly destroyed him. Addison was high

on that list, but Jordan knew that he hadn't done this alone. He had deleted all of the documents they'd demanded he sign and send back. Jordan wondered if they knew that Abby was with him now, or if they were just pissing in the wind, hoping to see those contracts show up in their in-box.

Of all the things he wanted to ask her, one weighed most heavily on him, and he finally worked up the courage to bring it up. "Did you think I wasn't coming?"

Abby nestled more securely in his arms. "They wanted money," she softly explained. "I knew that. I knew you'd be worried when you hadn't heard from me."

"But did you ever think for one moment that I wasn't looking for you?"

Abby reluctantly nodded. "For one moment, I did think that."

How could she possibly believe that he wouldn't flip the world on its ear to find her?

Abby sat up and looked at him. "I thought I was never going to see you again." She paused. "But I knew you loved me. I never doubted that. I couldn't wait, though." Abby swallowed. "I had to try to get out on my own."

He smiled. "I wouldn't have expected anything less from you."

Jordan was so proud of her. Seeing the condition of the man chasing her, Jordan had drawn some conclusions of his own of how she'd escaped. But the details could wait.

"They told me that I had to wait five days," he explained. "I was to sign a contract that I'd get at the end of the week. But I didn't wait a week to start looking for you, Abby. As soon as I knew — as soon as I knew, baby, I —"

Abby pressed her head to his chest and wrapped her arms around him.

"Nothing was going to keep me from you, sweetheart," he said, choking back tears of his own. "Nothing ever will."

"I'm so sorry that I didn't listen to you," she sobbed. "I should've listened to you, Jordan, and I shouldn't have gone back to the house."

Jordan just shook his head. "None of that matters, Abby. You're here now, sugah. That's everything."

An hour later, Abby drifted back off to sleep. Jordan carried her upstairs to bed and covered her with a blanket before going back downstairs to finish up some business, beginning with a call to his accountant telling him to leave his money right where it was. The transaction fell through was all he said. His next call was to an associate of his at the state capital. He had no idea who the woman had been on the phone responsible for Abby's kidnapping, but he'd be damned if he let Addison's ass off the hook.

Jordan worked from home on Monday and Tuesday, and then on Wednesday left the office early to take Abby to her doctor's appointment.

It took some convincing, particularly from Abby, for the doctor to get past her assumptions of Abby's face to finally stand down.

"It's a long story," Abby said calmly, squeezing closer to Jordan. "And he didn't do it."

"The only thing I'm going to scold you about is your weight," Abby's doctor, Amanda Stewart, told her.

She came highly recommended as the best OB/GYN in the city, and Jordan would settle for nothing less for the mother of his child and his heir. Abby laughed at him the first time he said that to her, but as silly as it may have sounded, it was true.

"Eat, lady," Amanda said, squeezing a clear gel onto Abby's abdomen. "You're too skinny."

Abby and Jordan exchanged glances when she wasn't looking. He hadn't said as much to Abby, but she knew. No one could know about the ordeal the two of them had been through the previous week. Not even her family. It would raise too many questions, lead to investigations, and the truth of the matter was, Jordan had killed a man. He'd never believe that he wasn't justified in doing so, though. Jordan wanted whoever had done this to pay for the pain and suffering they'd caused him and his family. And he wanted to be the one to dole out that justice. His kind. His way. And he wasn't finished.

The stress of what she'd been through had them both worried about this baby. Jordan stood next to her and held her hand. Abby bit down on her bottom lip as the image came up on the screen next to her. The doctor brought images up on the screen, and clicked that thing she rolled across Abby's stomach a few times.

"What are you doing?" Abby asked anxiously.

"Just measuring your uterus, sweetie." She smiled. "Making sure it's what we think it should be."

"Is it?" Jordan asked.

"Well . . ." Dr. Stewart responded apprehensively.

Again, he and Abby glanced at each other.

"Oh, there's the little peanut," the doctor said.

Jordan was amused by the reference. Abby's nickname was Peanut and she hated it. Abby looked at him and rolled her eyes.

There on the screen was his kid in glorious 4-D, looking pretty much like, well, a peanut.

She paused and then said, "Oh, boy."

"What?" Abby asked, worried.

Her tone unsettled both of them. They didn't need this. Abby didn't need this. Dread crept in, but Jordan could not let her sense it in him. All that time alone with that bastard, of course the stress had taken its toll. Abby had literally fought to save her own life, and at some point he could only conclude that it had been too much.

"Well, Abby." She stared intensely at Abby, who was already starting to tear up. "Well. It looks like there are two nuts in this pack." She smiled at both of them. "You're measuring a little big for nine weeks, Abby, but that's because you're having twins. See. Two amniotic fluid sacs."

"Twins?" Abby asked, stunned.

Twins? That's the last thing he thought she was going to say. "They're good?" Jordan asked.

"Two sturdy-looking fraternal twins," the

doctor reiterated. "With two very strong little beating hearts."

Pride filled his chest like helium and Jordan couldn't help himself. "Yes!" he blurted out, unexpectedly and certainly uncharacteristically, pumping a strong fist in the air.

His ass had knocked out a set! A good — what was the word she'd used? "Sturdy." Hell, yeah! He had sired two sturdy kids at fifty!

Jordan didn't realize that he was practically dancing until he spun around and saw Abby glaring at him like he'd lost his mind. He laughed, walked over to her, leaned down, and kissed her.

"Twins, baby." He grinned. "We did the damn thing."

"You're happy about this?" Abby asked, appalled.

He was taken aback by her response. "You aren't?"

Abby's eyes widened. "Jordan, I don't know the first thing about taking care of one baby," she explained. "Now there are two? How am I going to take care of two babies?" she asked in her exaggerated Texas drawl.

It was the first time in days that he'd caught a glimpse of the real Abby, and he was so happy as hell to see her.

"Oh, we've got this, sugah," he assured her, gazing deeply into her eyes. "You shouldn't even question it after what we've been through." He kissed her.

She swallowed and took several deep breaths to calm herself. "Twins," she said, looking back at the doctor. "You're sure that's not just a shadow or something?"

The doctor smiled. "Positive."

He laughed. "Two new Gatewoods."

Abby stared at him in disbelief. "We've got this?" she whispered with a cautious smile.

"All day long, baby girl."

SELF-INFLICTED PAIN

Bianca sat in her office with the door closed, talking to her brother on the phone.

"DJ Washington has been reported missing by his wife," Bianca nervously explained.

Weeks had passed, and it was as if that whole episode of kidnapping, blackmail, and murder had all played out in some cheesy pulp fiction novel she'd read.

"I don't know who DJ Washington is, Bianca," Brandon calmly said. "And I don't want to know."

Bianca immediately knew that Brandon was trying to distance himself from this whole fiasco. He was a fuckin' coward. She'd learned about DJ going missing on the news a few nights ago.

"Another man and woman, James Washington and Naomi Simpson, have also been reported missing," she continued.

Gatewood never returned the signed contracts. DJ never sent proof that he'd taken care of Abby Rhodes, and she'd never wired him any money. For nearly a month, Bianca's imagination had been running wild, playing out all sorts of scenarios and half expecting the police to come knocking down her door.

"For now," Brandon began, "Congress has put the pipeline initiative on hold."

"Why? That doesn't make sense. Gatewood's money wasn't needed to move forward with the project, Brandon. There were plenty of investors and more than enough money to begin development."

"It's the money. It's the politics," he said. "Treaties still bear weight, Bianca. And protesters, these days, are quite noisy."

He was wrong, or he was lying. There was more behind halting this project than a damn treaty.

"We've been dealing with treaties and protesters since the beginning, Brandon," she argued. "Is it Addison? Does he have something to do with them halting this thing?"

Brandon paused and audibly inhaled. "Do you think she's safe with him now?"

Bianca had been waiting for the news, but Abby Rhodes's name hadn't surfaced in any network or newspaper as being missing or dead.

She swallowed before daring to beg the question. "How could he have found her?"

Brandon surprised her and laughed. "I was going to ask you that. If it's true that he has, then how do you think he did it?"

His accusatory tone came through loud and clear.

"Now what would make you think I'd know the answer to that?"

"Maybe you underestimated him and the love that he has for her."

Brandon's adoration for Gatewood's girlfriend was painfully clear and nauseating. But it made her question her brother's loyalty.

"Who were you rooting for in all of this, Brandon? Or should I guess?"

He laughed. "I thought the crush I had on her was obvious."

Was that all it was? A crush? Bianca suddenly wasn't sure of what to make of her brother's comments. "Why don't you tell me how he found her?" she asked, suspecting that Brandon knew that answer better than anyone.

Had he betrayed her and their father?

"We'll talk again soon, Sister," he said calmly. "I have a visitor." Brandon hung up and Bianca knew that her brother had done something terrible.

Someone knocked on the door to her office. "Yes?" Bianca responded.

A tall, impeccably dressed redhead walked into her office, followed by two security guards.

"Ms. DuPaul?" She smiled.

"What's going on here?" Bianca stood up and asked.

"My name is Phyl Mays. I'm Mr. Gatewood's assistant."

Bianca froze.

"I understand that before coming to work here you were recently employed at a company called Crown Distributors. Is that correct?"

Bianca didn't respond. Looking at this woman, she knew that there was no reason to.

Before accepting the position of Director of Human Resources here at Gatewood Industries, she'd been Vice President of Human Services at Crown.

The woman's expression hardened. "He's asked me to have you escorted from the premises. Please. Take only your personal belongings."

He knew? How the hell could he know? Bianca had used her ex-husband's last name when she worked at Crown. And then it dawned on her. Brandon.

Brandon stood in front of his expansive office window recalling the magical moment when he, Bianca, and their father, Lars, suspected that something was wrong. It was after four in the afternoon and the contracts had not shown up in the return e-mail they'd expected from him by three. That squeamish expression on his sister's face was telling. But the one on his father's face was priceless.

"I nearly missed it," Jordan Gatewood said, standing behind him. "I came so close to deleting those e-mails."

Brandon sighed and turned to face the glorious Mr. Gatewood standing on the other side of his desk.

"She's all right?" Brandon asked with sincerity.

Gatewood nodded slowly. "She will be."

Brandon's knees felt weak all of a sudden and he sat down before he did something silly, like topple over. Jordan eventually sat down too, which made Brandon feel more at ease.

"Why'd you do it?" Gatewood asked. "He's your father."

Brandon nodded. "It took every bit of my

courage to do what I did," he admitted. "But I would've never forgiven myself if anything had happened to her and no one paid the price for it. Even him. Even me."

Brandon hadn't told Gatewood where to find Abby because honestly, he didn't know where they had been keeping her. But he did know that what they had done to her was wrong.

"I knew that I liked her the moment I met her." He smiled.

Gatewood looked confused. He had no idea that Brandon and Abby had spoken that night at the Governor's Ball.

"It's rare in our social circles to meet genuine people," he continued. "I'll be honest, Jordan," he cautiously continued, "she is better than you or me. Does she even know what kind of man you truly are?"

Brandon expected him to get angry, but he seemed to consider Brandon's question. Rumors followed Gatewood, rumors fueled, no doubt, by facts. He and Lars Degan weren't so different deep down.

"I like to think she makes me a better man than I have been," he eventually admitted. "And I'll do whatever I need to do to make sure that she never knows more than she needs to."

"May I ask how you found out about

Bianca's involvement?"

Brandon never gave Gatewood any indication that anyone was involved in this except for his father. But Bianca had become a victim of her own circumstance, and he was truly sorry for that.

"My assistant found the connection between Crown and Gatewood Industries," he explained. "It happened to be your sister. I didn't connect her right away, of course."

"She has her mother's last name," Brandon clarified.

"She used another name," was all that Jordan offered.

"What will happen to my sister?" he asked with regret.

He loved Bianca. Brandon hoped she knew that.

Gatewood sat there for a moment. All of a sudden, Brandon regretted asking the question. Jordan Gatewood, the one his father had created, semed to awaken from his slumber as he stood up and abruptly left.

On his way home from the office, he decided to stop by unannounced. "I brought you your favorite ice cream, Dad," Brandon said, handing the package to the housekeeper.

Deep lines darkened on his father's face.

Sullen eyes sank into half-moon circles. Even his hair seemed to become dull and brittle right before Brandon's eyes. It was as if the light of his revenge had been blotted out and he recognized that he had once again been bested by that sonofabitch Gatewood.

Lars Degan's familiar shoulder slump had returned. His father looked every single one of his years, with a few more thrown in for good measure. Brandon hadn't seen him for several weeks. He'd called a few times and was told by his housekeeper that he was sleeping or not accepting calls.

Lars sat motionless, staring at the news on the television, with the remote in his hand and the volume turned off. Brandon knew what he was looking for. His father was looking for signs that Jordan Gatewood was no longer the cock of the roost that he'd been since Lars had been fired by him so many years ago.

Senator Sam Addison had made the evening news again. Brandon's father immediately turned up the volume.

"Some of Senator Addison's business dealings have come to the attention of the oversight committee, which has launched an investigation into the connection the senator appears to have with one of the pipeline's investors, Variant Alternative Fuel Resources," a dark-haired reporter explained. "If there is indeed a connection, it could pose a serious conflict of interest that could cost Addison his seat in the Senate, depending on how critical the committee deems the infraction to be."

Brandon had betrayed his father, but he was certain that the old man had no idea how. Brandon had been tasked with the final review of the contracts before ensuring that they were e-mailed to Gatewood. He'd made one addition before approving them for disposition and he'd made it at the last possible moment, giving no one else time to catch it. Gatewood would've surely missed it had he not read through the contract, but Brandon had placed it there, right on the face of the document, as a footnote.

"I'm your Frankenstein monster."

Even if they'd killed Abby, taken Jordan's money, and ruined his reputation, unless his memory had failed him, when he saw that line, Brandon had hoped he'd remember when he had said it and to who.

"Do you think that Gatewood even remembers why you hate him so much?" Brandon asked the very old man sitting across from him.

Jordan was coming for Lars Degan. Brandon didn't know when or how, but he knew that his father would be humiliated once more, unless of course, God mercifully took him first.

"Some things you can't recover, Dad. Not even your dignity. You are nothing to Gatewood, except some petrified relic who'd tried once and failed to take advantage of his weaknesses."

This time, his father blinked glassy eyes briefly in his direction.

"Is this how you want to go to your grave? A black kicked your ass, your lily white ass. Not once but twice." Brandon laughed.

"Get the hell out of my house," Lars demanded.

Brandon stood up to leave. "Enjoy the ice cream."

I'M HOLDING ON

Nearly two months had passed since Abby had been kidnapped. She was going to start therapy when they got back home. She'd learned that there were just some things she couldn't fix on her own and that was fine. Jordan had been amazing and patient and loving. He'd insisted on the two of them getting away for a while and Abby didn't argue. Anyplace with an ocean and beaches was fine by her.

They'd been on the island for two days when Abby had begged him to pack up his office and move the two of them here.

"Our babies can be born here," she explained. "You can work from the beach. We never need to wear shoes. It'll be perfect."

He just laughed. But he didn't say no.

So who, in their right mind, steps away from the lap of luxury and beauty in Saint Lucia to take a business meeting? Jordan

Gatewood, that's who. And he didn't think anything of it.

"I'll be back in a few hours, sugah," he told her, kissing her on the cheek before leaving.

Abby glowered at him and shook her head. "You ought to be ashamed of yourself," she told him before he left. "How come you can't just tell them people you're on vacation?"

He left without saying another word.

An hour later a knock came at the door. Abby jumped at the sound of it. Her heart raced and a wave of unexpected fear washed over her. She was alone and she hadn't been expecting anyone, not room service or housekeeping. Whoever was at the door knocked again.

She was being paranoid and she knew it. But the panic attacks showed up over unexpected things.

She hesitantly walked over to the door. "Who is it?" she cautiously asked.

But it wasn't like a kidnapper was really going to answer her and say something like, *It's me. I'm here to snatch you and hold you for ransom.*

"It's your daddy, Peanut."

Her dad? She hesitated before opening the door. "Daddy?"

"It's me."

Abby cautiously opened the door and as soon as she did, her whole face lit up. "Walter? Walter Rhodes?" she asked in disbelief.

"You got another daddy that I should know about, Peanut?" he asked, incredulous.

Abby stared stunned at the man. "What are you doing here?"

He laughed, walked in, and gathered her up in a warm embrace. "It's good to see you, too."

Her father was in Saint Lucia? Abby had to pause and collect her thoughts on that. "No, seriously, Daddy," she said, pulling away, "what are you doing here?"

He cradled her face in his hands, and looked her in the eyes. "I am here to give you away," he said tearfully. "Your groom is waiting, sweetheart."

Her groom?

"Hey, girl," Skye said, sweeping into the room, followed by two of Skye's cousins, Jordan's assistant, Phyl, and someone else, carrying a dress and some flowers. Skye hugged a stunned Abby and giggled. "Surprise!"

Phyl brushed past everyone. "Okay. Okay. We've got to get this party started. Dad, I'm going to need you to go find a bar, have a drink, and wait for my call to come get her."

He saluted and left.

Phyl stood and assessed Abby. "Cute sundress, but not for a wedding."

"Wh . . . wha . . . what?"

"Told you she'd be speechless," Skye said, shrugging.

"We did the best we could on size," Phyl explained.

"Got a little lycra in this," Skye added. "Can't go wrong with lycra. Especially in your condition."

Her mind was reeling and trying to put all of this together. What in the hell was happening? What had Jordan done?

Those women buzzed around her like bees, doing her hair, makeup, stripping her naked, pouring her into a real pretty dress. Abby was seriously dizzy from all the activity, and absolutely speechless for the first time in her life

He wasn't at a meeting. And her family was here. And — this was happening.

It was as if she blinked and all of a sudden Abby found herself standing behind two tall, dark wooden doors. Abby's legs wouldn't stop shaking. Hell, all of her was shaking. She did her best though to compose herself and steady herself, with one arm looped with her father's, and the other holding a pretty bouquet.

"You okay, baby?" he leaned close and asked her.

She didn't know if she was okay. She was in shock. But that didn't mean she wasn't okay. Then again, it didn't mean she wasn't. Abby was about to get married. First a kidnapping, then twins, and now a wedding. Good Lord. Could she just stop and catch her breath for a minute?

"I need to just . . . process," she said nervously.

"I understand," he said, placing a comforting hand on top of hers. "Take your time."

Walter meant that. He'd wait all day and night if that's what she needed him to do.

"I'm scared, Daddy," Abby finally admitted.

She loved Jordan, but he had a tendency to be overwhelming. Abby had been through so very much lately. Most days, she wasn't even sure if she would ever come back to herself again. And now this?

"You don't have to do this if you don't want to, Peanut."

She looked at him with tears in her eyes and knew that he was right. Abby didn't have go through with this. She didn't have to marry the man she loved more than she ever thought it was possible to love anyone. She could walk away and leave Jordan Gatewood to his own devices and get back to her life the way it had always been, well, except for having to raise two babies now.

She could do it, alone if she had to. But life without Jordan wasn't an option. Not anymore.

"I want to, Daddy."

Deep mahogany doors swung open, and Abby nearly fell over at the sight of the white silk carpet spread across the lanai and out onto sand, leading to waters as vast and as blue as the sky. She took a pensive step with her father, and everyone she loved, her brothers, her aunts, and friends, all from Blink, stood up and smiled back at her. He had done this — for her? He'd bought the people she loved to Saint Lucia for their wedding?

"I think I'm gonna fall," she whispered to her father.

"Nah, I got you, baby," he assured her.

Roberta Flack's "The First Time Ever I Saw Your Face" wafted through the warm sea breeze. Oh Lord! Could he possibly really be that much of a cornball?

Abby's tearful gaze followed the path to the end of that pathway and there he was, standing waiting for her, with that same expression on his face that she felt she had on hers, like, *Is this really happening?*

Yes, it was. And it should. Nothing in her life had ever felt more right than this moment here.

Finally, she and her father stopped next to Jordan. That preacher said something, but she didn't really hear him. Her father kissed her cheek, and placed her hand in Jordan's.

With tears in her eyes, Abby looked up at him and asked, "Did you choose that music?"

He laughed. "Phyl did." Jordan shrugged. "But I kind of like it."

"Naomi left you," some motha fucka said over the phone. "But I know where to find her." He hung up before Thomas could confront his ass and cuss him out, and then he texted Thomas an address.

Of course he knew that she'd been fucking around. Neighbors had seen some black bastard showing up at Thomas's house talking to Naomi when he wasn't home. All he could think was that she'd run off with the sonofabitch, leaving him to raise their boys.

He immediately dialed the number that the asshole had called from. "Where's my wife, mother fucker!"

He left the boys sleeping while he took off to bring their mother home, if she was lucky, in one piece.

Thomas squeezed the steering wheel so tight that his hands ached. Naomi had done some stupid shit, but this took stupid to a whole new level. He hated whipping her ass. Despite what she might think, he loved her. Jesus! He loved her more than he loved his own life. But she needed to know that she couldn't just do anything. Thomas had rules. Simple rules that weren't hard to follow. How come she couldn't see that? How come she had to make it so hard all the damn time?

Thomas got to the end of the dirt road and stopped.

"Shit," he said out loud, looking around. He'd literally come to the end of the fucking road. He looked down at the directions that bastard had given him.

"Turn left at the sign," he read, glancing up and seeing a sight in front of him.

MISS PEACHES' SOUTHERN HOME COOKING HOME OF THE BEST PEACH COBBLER IN TEXAS

Thomas peered left and saw what looked like a road that had been carved out over time by car tires. He put the car in reverse and then made a sharp left turn onto that road. He was going to double up on that ass whupping when he found her, just for dragging him all the way out here in the middle of the fucking nowhere.

Plato didn't owe Naomi Simpson a damn thing. But he'd paid up anyway. Now her children could go and live with Grandma.

ABOUT THE AUTHOR

J.D. Mason is the author of *Seducing Abby Rhodes; The Real Mrs. Price; Crazy, Sexy, Revenge; Drop Dead, Gorgeous; Beautiful, Dirty, Rich; Somebody Pick Up My Pieces; Take Your Pleasure Where You Find It; That Devil's No Friend Of Mine; You Gotta Sin To Get Saved; This Fire Down In My Soul; Don't Want No Sugar; And On The Eighth Day She Rested;* and *One Day I Saw A Black King.* She lives in Denver, Colorado with her two children.

The employees of Thorndike Press hope you have enjoyed this Large Print book. All our Thorndike, Wheeler, and Kennebec Large Print titles are designed for easy reading, and all our books are made to last. Other Thorndike Press Large Print books are available at your library, through selected bookstores, or directly from us.

For information about titles, please call:
(800) 223-1244

or visit our website at:
gale.com/thorndike

To share your comments, please write:
Publisher
Thorndike Press
10 Water St., Suite 310
Waterville, ME 04901